ALL ABOUT
ROMANCE

DANIEL TAWSE

ALL ABOUT ROMANCE

HODDER

First published in Great Britain in 2023 by Hodder & Stoughton

1 3 5 7 9 10 8 6 4 2

A CIP catalogue record for this book
is available from the British Library.

ISBN 978 1 444 97132 3

Typeset in Caslon by Avon DataSet Ltd, Alcester, Warwickshire

Printed and bound in Great Britain by Clays Ltd, Elcograf S.p.A.

The paper and board used in this book
are made from wood from responsible sources.

Hodder Children's Books
An imprint of
Hachette Children's Group
Part of Hodder & Stoughton Limited
Carmelite House
50 Victoria Embankment
London EC4Y 0DZ

An Hachette UK Company
www.hachette.co.uk

www.hachettechildrens.co.uk

For Mam

ONE

It starts with a postcard.

'International Klein Blue, by Yves Klein,' I read aloud, taking it from my locker and turning it over in my hands.

I thought postcards were supposed to be of picturesque seaside towns with images of clapped-out donkeys or over-ambitious sandcastles and brightly coloured beach huts. This one is just a plain blue square, hardly inspiring.

On the back there's a note, hurriedly scribbled in red ink.

Main hall, lunchtime – (Big Red)

This is probably some sort of queer joke at my expense. Yves Klein is no doubt a huge homo. I suppose I should be appreciative that the troglodytes of St Anselm's high school are raising the bar for my final year, homophobic locker notes of the past were scribbled on the back of detention slips, or bus tickets. A postcard like this is a treat.

'And so it begins,' I sigh, opening my bag and shoving it inside.

I take a deep breath and pull my shoulders all the way back, as if readying myself for battle, because being queer on the first day of term at St Anselm's is the equivalent of

1

being Taylor Swift at a Kanye West concert.

I'm going to use the word *unwelcome*.

I make my way out into the yard, barging my way through entitled Year 8s and petrified Year 7s like the superior Year 11 student that I am. I make a sharp turn past languages, keeping my head held high as I hurry towards the sanctuary of the art block. Once I'm there, once I'm out of sight of the masses, I know I'll be safe.

As I turn the corner, I stop in my tracks. The art block looks different this year. What was once a forgotten corner of the school, a perfect sanctuary for outcasts, is now noisy and vibrant thanks to the addition of a brand-new face.

Wait.

I should make it clear that this isn't a real face, just a painting. Someone has painted the art block wall. Although, describing it as 'just a painting' sort of diminishes it, sort of makes it sound like graffiti, like something hastily sprayed under a railway bridge or etched on the back of a toilet door. It isn't; there are no expletives or political messages or stick-man images of ejaculating penises anywhere. I don't smell a pissy alleyway just by looking at it. This painting is so much grander than that. Bubble text in bold colours surrounds a face with two sides – one green, the other red. I'm a little impressed. It's good.

The new addition to our yard means this end of the school is suddenly *the* place to be, the urban hangout for the pretty kids whose mams buy them the latest Nike Airs and North Face puffas, and let them box dye their hair. There's even music playing.

Sam Fender.

I think.

I step back into the shadows, pressing my back firmly against the wall. The pretty kids are here, which is utterly terrifying and sort of thrilling at the same time. Being this close means for a secret moment I can taste what it's like to be one of them.

It tastes like Wrigley's Juicy Fruit gum.

When the studio door opens, Mr Sharpe, art department, appears, looking all kinds of flustered. Mrs Duncan, head teacher, follows close behind, instantly recognisable by her terrible wardrobe choices. I've never seen her at this end of the school. She is the antithesis of art. Creative energy fizzles and dies in her presence.

'You're saying you have no idea who did it?' she says.

Today, her suit is the colour of dog vomit. Seriously. If someone stopped me on the street and offered me a suitcase full of cash to find an ill-fitted trouser suit in this shade of pinkish brown, I would leave not a penny richer. Beneath the dog-vomit suit flutters a purple, frilly, chiffon blouse. She looks like something out of *Monsters, Inc.* ('Kids these days. They just don't get scared like they used to.')

'No idea,' says Mr Sharpe.

I can never tell if he's a young person who looks really old, or an old person who looks really young. He's got heavy smoker written all over him.

'Don't you have any video footage?' Mrs Duncan asks.

'There are no cameras in the department.'

They stop in front of the painting. Her hands are firmly planted on her hips. I've seen this stance many times. She's annoyed. The art studio's makeover clearly wasn't planned.

Does this mean a student did this?

'It's really quite something,' says Mr Sharpe, looking at it. 'Almost Picasso-esque – don't you agree?'

'I hardly think that's the point. We do not deface school property at St Anselm's. I want the culprit found.'

'There's no way—'

'It will be one of your students, Colin!'

He takes a long, heavy breath, and I can hear his lungs rattling in his chest like a bag of popcorn in the microwave. He really needs to kick the habit. 'The piece is signed.' He draws her attention to the bottom right-hand corner.

She screws up her face, leaning forward to read, '"Big Red". Who is Big Red?'

'I have no idea.'

It takes a second for the name to register in my head.

Big Red.

Hang on a minute.

That was the name on the postcard that had been wedged into my locker.

I open my bag to find it resting on top of my make-up bag, staring right at me.

Main hall, lunchtime – Big Red

I take a step closer to look at the name on the wall. It's written in the exact same way as on the postcard. The stalk of the 'd' arches over and under anticlockwise, encasing the name in a circle. I hadn't noticed this, the artist's signature, before now. I hadn't thought a homophobic locker note required an artist's signature. But now I do. Or, actually, now I don't – because I don't think this postcard *is* a homophobic locker note, not if it's from the same person who painted this wall. The face looking back at me is nothing short of a masterpiece, way above the talents of St Anselm's regular homophobes.

'Is everything OK, Roman?' asks Mr Sharpe.

I'm suddenly aware of how close I'm standing to them, to it. 'Totally fine, sir.'

Mrs Duncan's crinkly eyes thin at the sight of me. '*Ryan* Albright.'

The crowd of pretty kids laughs, and I shrivel up like a prune. I hate that she calls me Ryan. It literally gives me goosebumps. She could change my whole high school experience by acknowledging my real gender. I don't care about official documents and exam papers and library cards. If she called me by my chosen name, Roman Bright, it would send a message to the rest that I am just as valued as them; that non-binary queer people are valued at her school; that non-binary is a real gender, not just something I've made up like the time in Year 8 when I pretended to have gout to get out of PE (we were studying the Tudors in history at the time). But I think she suspects it's something I've done to get attention. The thing is, attention isn't something I have in short supply these days.

She points at the wall. And she doesn't even have to say it. I know exactly what she's thinking. Herein lies the main problem to being the most conspicuous person in school: everything is automatically your fault.

'This has nothing to do with me, miss.' I shove the postcard

5

back into my bag because, actually, this does have something to do with me. Only, I'm not quite sure what.

'This isn't Roman's hand,' says Mr Sharpe.

Thank God for him – caring, human, Mr Sharpe. He may stink of cigarettes, but he's the only member of staff who actually gives a crap about me. He even calls me by my chosen – my *real* – name, which is something everybody else seems to have trouble with. I can't hold his addictions against him.

'And I don't have any students called Big Red,' adds Mr Sharpe.

'Please be sensible, Colin,' says Mrs Duncan. 'Someone is obviously hiding behind a pseudonym.'

For some reason this causes the crowd to laugh again.

(Pseudonym. I guess it's a funny word.)

'Haven't you all got classes to get to?' she says, turning towards them. 'Away with you. *Away!* Just because it's first day of term doesn't mean it's too early to start issuing detentions.'

I bury my chin in my chest and turn my back, hoping to melt away with the rest of them.

But then . . .

'Not you, Ryan,' she says. 'You're coming with me.'

Bugger.

Mrs Duncan's office. I hate it in here, mainly because of the anatomy diagram she has on the wall beside her desk. I'm still traumatised by the sex education class she gave in Year 9, where she held it against herself to point out where everything was.

Meaning, I now know with unnecessary precision where her cervix is.

Nobody needs to know where their head teacher's cervix is.

Next to the anatomy, there's a crucifix. They were both used simultaneously because heaven forbid anyone discuss the anatomy without a crucifix present. St Anselm's is very much *that* kind of school. We indulge in all of the punishments of Catholicism, but none of the rewards.

Actually, after four years here, I'm starting to wonder if there *are* any rewards.

'It wasn't me,' I say, before she can accuse me.

She nods her head to acknowledge I've spoken, but doesn't confirm or deny whether she believes me. 'Please, take a seat,' she says, triangular nostrils flaring. Her voice is all sticky behind her nose, like she has a permanent cold. 'I would like to have a chat with you before classes begin. This is the beginning of a new year – a fresh page, if you like, where all past misadventures are forgiven.'

But never forgotten, I think.

'I would like you to assure me, here and now, that we won't have a repeat of last term. School is for learning – and to do that you have to be here.'

I feel like she's staring into me, looking under my skin at my most vulnerable parts, my rubbery tubes and pounding heart. Surely she knows that last term was the worst time of my life. Surely she knows I didn't plan to take all that time off.

'Yes, Mrs Duncan.' *Of course, Mrs Duncan. And how does it feel to have a heart the size of a maggot's testicle, Mrs Duncan?*

'Good.'

7

I smirk, and she looks at me like I'm worse than dirt.

'Is something funny?'

'No, Mrs Duncan.'

She stands, brushing the creases out of her suit, making tiny flicking movements as if she's swatting an invisible fly. Her fingers are long and bony, like Twiglets. I hate Twiglets because I hate Marmite.

And I hate her fingers, because I hate her.

'That will be all, Mr Albright.'

I pick up my bag and walk towards the door, but before I reach it she takes in a sharp breath and says, 'And please, wash that ridiculous make-up off your face. This is a high school, not *La Cage aux Folles*.'

I leave without responding. There's no point even trying to have the last word with her. As I walk along the corridor away from her office, I take out the postcard once again, twisting it between my fingers. Front to back. Front to back. Yves Klein. Big Red. Blue square. Red circle. Yves Klein. Big Red.

Am I supposed to know what this means?

TWO

There's someone sitting at my table in English class. How annoying. I always sit alone.

'Hi,' he says. I can barely see his face under the mountain of hair. 'The teacher told me to sit here next to Ryan Albright.'

I slide my sunglasses to the end of my nose. 'It's Roman,' I say. 'Roman Bright. Google me.'

'Beau Greene.'

I recognise the name. He joined our school last year, summer term, which is weird because a) who starts a new school halfway through GCSEs – and b) who starts a new school in summer term? I never had to sit next to him in English class last year. I never had to sit next to anybody, which is the way I like it. I can't understand why he's here now.

'Pleasure, I'm sure,' I lie.

He looks half asleep, with bloodshot, dark-ringed eyes, and hair that may as well have been left out overnight in the rain. I'm going to throw caution to the wind here and assume he's already on drugs. He seems very much *that* kind of boy – you know, the kind who wears a hoodie instead of a coat, and spends lunchtime sniffing the gas in his lighter, or vaping down the side of the art block, *blah blah blah*.

(For the record, I'm anti-drugs. This is because I have an

9

addictive personality, which is something I discovered last Christmas when I ate my entire body weight in lebkuchen – you know, those sugary/cinnamony German biscuits? If I took drugs, Lord knows what would ensue. I'd probably get a crippling addiction, and it would take me years of therapy and rehab – in that well-known celebrity facility, The Priory, of course – to get over. I'm doing my future self a favour by steering clear.)

(Beau Greene's future self hates him.)

(Actually, it looks like Beau Greene's present self hates him.)

He stretches out a hand, all sweaty palm and dirty fingernails, pointing it at me. 'Is it real?' he says, his face flushing as if he's containing a fit of laughter.

'Excuse me?'

'The coat.'

'She's a cape,' I say, pulling my shoulder up to my chin. 'Not a coat. Her name is *Marlene*, if you must know, after Marlene Dietrich.'

He snorts. 'Um . . . OK?'

I take a seat, shuffling the chair so it's at the furthest edge of the table. You could literally fit another chair in between us, because I don't want to be anywhere near someone who doesn't appreciate a vintage genuine rabbit-fur cape, named after a screen legend goddess, when they see one.

There's a fresh workbook on the desk, flat and clean. It's peach. I write *ROMAN BRIGHT* in the box on the front in capital letters with my new multi-coloured pen, and draw wings around it. Drawing wings is my thing. I'm sure Orla, the school psychiatrist, would say this represents my need to fly far away from here.

And she'd partly be right.

Although, there is another reason why I always draw wings . . .

'You could see that from outer space,' says Beau Greene, smirking like he's just said something really smart.

I don't respond. I think it's important I set some sort of boundary right now. He needs to know that just because we're sitting together, that doesn't mean we are in any way friends.

Underneath my name I write: *Year 11*.

Writing it down like this makes it so much more real. I'm back. I'm here, in the place where everything happened. It's sort of a big deal.

I feel my anxiety rush through me, and suddenly it's like I'm on the kamikaze slide at Wet N Wild, and I'm plummeting eighty feet towards the water.

'You've got really neat handwriting,' says Beau Greene.

So the silent treatment clearly isn't working. It's time to bring out the big guns. 'What?' I say, giving him my death stare.

'My handwriting hasn't changed that much since primary school.'

He holds up his hand where he's scribbled something in blue ink.

He's got that right. I know six-year-olds who can do better. *Don't do drugs, kids. Don't do drugs.*

'Good for you,' I say, my eyes boring holes into his very soul. With this I think he gets the message, because he turns his attention away from me out of the window to a bunch of Year 7s who are about to start the trauma that is high school physical education.

'Ah, Ryan,' says Ms Mead, plodding towards us. One eye is looking at me. The other (the glass one) is on the Year 7s outside. 'I trust you've had a restful summer.'

'I usually work alone,' I say, ignoring her faux well wishes, because I really don't need a Beau Greene in my life right now. 'I'm happy to work alone.'

'You're in Year 11 now, Ryan. This year I'd like to encourage more critical debate from you. And you're hardly going to do that on your own. Lucky you have the lovely Beau Greene to work with – this will be his permanent English class . . . something to do with numbers . . .'

She trails off and walks away.

'Sorry,' says Beau Greene, the corners of his mouth turned up, which tells me he isn't sorry at all, not one bit.

'Don't be,' I say. And I mean it. I don't need his crappy, half-arsed apology.

Not one bit.

The door smacks open, and the white noise of a busy corridor on the first day of term fills the room like trumpets.

Send in the clowns.

First come Carl Oswald and Liam Jones, arseholes of the century. I tense up as their laughter finds my ears like a familiar song: a mean schoolyard rhyme, or 'Dude (Looks Like a Lady)' by Aerosmith. I hate that one. Next is Tyler 'Spudz' Hudson, the biggest arsehole of them all. As far as bullies go, he's pretty terrifying: well over six foot and built like a brick shithouse. He's the type of kid who'd beat your face until it resembled an omelette, and then carry on with the rest of his day like nothing had happened. I think it's highly likely he's a sociopath. Last time I saw him he was emptying a bottle of Coke over my head in front of the entire dinner hall. I remember it like it was yesterday. I remember the laughing faces of students and staff. I remember the feeling of wet, sticky fluid tangling my hair into knots. I remember the pain and humiliation. It twists in my chest and I grip my hands into fists.

'Look at the state of that,' he says, bringing me back to the present. 'Why are you wearing your mam's coat, Brighty?'

'Because I was going to wear *your* mam's, but I don't wear polyester,' I shoot back.

'Do you want to be a woman?'

'Do you want to be a human?'

I'm trying to show him I'm stronger now. This isn't last term. I'm not the same person I was then – I won't be humiliated again.

'Could you get any gayer?'

'Oh, I hope so . . .'

Unable to think of a retort because he's a complete and utter zygote, he just scoffs and turns to take his seat.

He really is a gargantuan arsehole. Professor arsehole. Knight Commander of the British Empire arsehole.

More of them come in, hooting like hyenas: Charlene Franklin, with her plain face and swishy ponytail; Jonny Dale and Norman Stokes, tech geeks, could easily pass for Year 7s; perfect Wynter Brown, and her harem of broken dolls – Gemma Crow, Sheryl Higgin, and Natalie Elliott –

13

each one looking more like her now than they did before summer. (I didn't think this was physically possible.)

They all assemble like Shakespearean actors, readying to take part in the play that is my life.

(What would the title be – *King Queer; As You Don't Like It; All's Well That Never Seems to End Well*?)

In they come, bringing with them a bucketload of all the crappy school stuff I'd almost forgotten, metaphorically dumping it over my head like some brown, sticky soft drink (which shall remain nameless).

I knew the first day back was going to be hard, but why does this suddenly feel unbearable?

I turn away to place Marlene over the back of my chair. As I do I notice the hairs on my arms are raised. I swipe my hand over my bumpy skin, but it doesn't flatten. There's electricity pumping through me, like I've been plugged in to the wall.

And looking back over my shoulder, turning in slow motion, I understand why. I'm having a supernatural experience, like a ghost has just entered the room – a really hot ghost with golden hair and dreamy eyes and a smile you could get lost in. I swear I can hear music, like he has his own rhythm, and it's dulling the noise of the classroom, making it unimportant. Only he is important: JJ Dixon, aka the male lead, aka the closest thing I ever came, and probably will ever come, to a romcom sort of romance.

My hand automatically reaches to the underside of the table to the heart shape I etched there with my biro last term, the initials R and JJ inside.

And I know exactly what the Shakespearean title of my life should be – *Roman and JJ*, the tale of two star-crossed lovers (directed by Baz Luhrmann).

I smile.

He sees.

His hair is cut, his coat is new, his shoes are shiny; he's all preened and perfect for the first day back, and the butterflies in my stomach grow feathers and bones, they grow into a flock of swallows, bending and diving as one as they migrate south of my trouser belt for the winter.

Be still, my beating testes.

He presses his lips together, but I don't know if it's a smile or not. And I really need to know if it's a smile or not. Like – *really*.

'Quieten down now, *Year Eleven*,' says Ms Mead, stressing the Year 11 part.

The class cheers, like the lights have gone down and they're ready for the film to start. But I'm still staring at the back of JJ Dixon's blonde head, wondering if that was a smile or a snub.

And how can I be losing my mind over him already?

THREE

For obvious reasons, I haven't been in the dinner hall for a while. Having the whole school laugh at you for having a bottle of Coke poured over your head, like your life is some sort of comedic play (what would the title be – *Much Ado About Arseholes?*), doesn't exactly make a person want to return to the scene of the crime.

It smells the same: like plastic-wrapped tuna fish, and sour milk, with a hint of feet (because the dinner hall doubles up as a gymnasium on Tuesdays and Thursdays). It makes me shudder. I cling to the wall, edging my way around endless tables of chattering faces. I can still hear names like 'half-gadge' and 'fag', echoing across the domed ceiling. I can make out the sound of laughter through the rustling of crisp packets. I can smell the sticky, wet Coke on my skin. I can see the hall staff, the ones who should have protected me, smirking as if it was all harmless fun, because boys will be boys, and someone like me needs toughening up anyway.

God.

That day.

I've never felt more terrified, never felt more alone. I honestly thought nothing could pull me out of the dark hole I fell into after that. I spent like a month in bed.

I hurry to the corner table and to my best friends, Solange Burrell and Adam Chung – the reason I did, eventually, get out of bed. These are my people. My tribe. Without these two, I definitely wouldn't have come back this year.

In her own words, Solange is St Anselm's only biracial, bilingual, bisexual queer icon. She's all big eyes and cool braids, and today she's totally rocking a deep aubergine lip. I can't help but smile when I see her. I feel like I haven't seen her in forever. She spent the summer with her dad in the Loire Valley, France.

Adam is my gay sister, the yang to my yin. He's sparky and ruthless, and nobody in the world can make me laugh like him. We connected in a PE class in Year 8, where we were supposed to be playing football, but instead decided it was a much better use of our time to learn the latest TikTok dance. (I think I actually scored a goal that day. I was shimmying my arse to the right and the ball whacked right off it, into the net. Apparently it was an own goal, though, which meant I had to run home from school extra fast that afternoon.) Today Adam's wearing a leather jacket and some serious black eyeliner (gorge!), and his dark hair is slicked back in a quiff. Year 11 looks really good on him, on both of them.

As I approach the table, I decide only my strongest opener will do to get their undivided attention.

'Little Latin boy in drag,' I begin, 'why are you crying?'

This line is from one of my favourite films of all time, *To Wong Foo, Thanks for Everything! Julie Newmar*, where three drag queens cross America in a vintage Cadillac. I've lost count of how many times we've watched it at sleepovers. It's so totally us. (I always take the role of the super-feminine, and super-fabulous, Miss Vida Boheme, played by the late, great Patrick Swayze. Obviously. Solange is Miss Noxeema Jackson, and Adam is Miss Chi-Chi Rodriguez.)

Solange jumps up from the table and throws her arms around me. 'Roman!'

She still smells like holidays, like sunshine and coconut-scented sun cream.

'How was France?' I ask.

'Divine,' she says. 'I met someone.'

'What, like *met someone* met someone?'

'Her name is Noelle.'

'And is she a teenage dirtbag, baby?' I ask.

'Well, she has a tongue piercing,' she says, raising her eyebrows.

'It's been a summer of spring awakenings by all accounts,' says Adam. 'I was just getting all the dirty details.'

I pull out a chair. 'Well, don't let me stop you, please carry on . . .'

She takes a seat and tells us all about the gorgeous Parisian girl she met one day at some food festival in the village square, and all the gorgeous French dates they went on over the summer.

And as she talks about sunset kisses and nights spent under the stars, I'm reminded of the summer I was supposed to have: a summer of gorgeous dates and sunset kisses and nights spent under the stars, a summer that was taken from me in this very room.

'OK – I need a visual,' says Adam, interrupting my thoughts.

Solange pulls out her phone and brings up a picture of herself with a very pretty French girl.

'She's hot,' I say.

'Totally,' says Adam.

'I know, right?' Solange says. 'She's from Paris, but her parents were renting a house in Dad's village for the summer.'

'How romantic,' I say.

'We're gonna try the long-distance thing,' she says. 'I'm going out to see Dad again at Christmas, so hopefully we can catch up then. Paris is only a couple of hours away by train.'

'*Mazel tov*,' says Adam. 'Meanwhile, I spent the summer eating my feelings.'

'Oh, stop,' I say. 'We had some fun days out.'

'Yeah, once I finally managed to get you out of your bedroom,' he says.

I roll my eyes at this as if this comment totally doesn't bother me at all. But it does. I'm still a little tetchy around this subject.

And I think Solange must realise this because right away she places her hand on top of mine and says, 'Is it weird being back?'

'A bit,' I say. 'It didn't help that Duncan gave me a piece of her mind this morning. She felt the need to remind me that *school is for learning*, and to do that I *actually have to be here*.'

'She's a dragon,' says Solange.

'Yeah – how about make your school a little more accommodating to queer kids so we might actually want to be here in the first place?' says Adam.

'I know, right?' I say. 'I'm OK though. Mostly. I saw JJ first lesson. I think he actually smiled at me?'

'It was probably gas,' says Adam.

'I hope you didn't smile back,' says Solange.

'No,' I say. 'I was more confused than anything, I think.'

'Good,' she says. 'After what he did to you, that boy does not deserve your smiles.'

I nod in agreement, though I can't stop myself from thinking about how good he looked. I know I shouldn't. Solange is right. He doesn't deserve anything from me after what he did. It's just that he's so damn beautiful it hurts. I swear, when they were handing out neck muscles this guy must have been right at the front of the queue. He's so totally my type: masculine, handsome, tall, muscular. I honestly never thought a guy like him would pay any attention to someone as alternative as me. But he did. He paid all the attention. Some days he paid so much attention I couldn't think properly. Last term was a hotbed of messages, and secret glances, and smiles across the classroom, until one night, a couple of weeks before school broke up for the summer holidays, we shared a totally trouser-movingly beautiful kiss on Longsands beach. It really was the stuff Hollywood movies are made of, and I was so sure I'd found the kind of romance I'd dreamt about since the first time I watched a happily-ever-after Disney film.

But, alas, it wasn't to be.

The week after, someone at school found out about us and spread the rumour that I forced myself on him, because that's what queer kids do, isn't it – force themselves on to poor, unsuspecting straight kids? In the space of a few days, our romance quickly turned into a tragedy. It was in this very room, in front of the entire school, where JJ Dixon made it so . . .

'Mate, he was proper begging me,' JJ says. He's surrounded by his teammates, his friends. I don't think he knows I'm standing right behind him. 'I was so wasted.'

'Mate, he shouldn't be allowed to get away with it,' says one of them.

'That's pure abuse,' says another.

'I know,' says JJ.

'What's abuse?' I say.

He turns to see me; he looks so different, so vacant.

'You, coming on to JJ like that,' says one of his friends. 'It's just wrong.'

'I didn't come on to anyone,' I say. 'He kissed me.'

They all laugh.

But JJ's face doesn't move at all.

'Tell them, JJ,' I say. 'Tell them what's been going on.'

But he doesn't say a thing, even though he knows that his words could save me.

He just leaves me to drown . . .

And then Tyler Hudson comes up behind me and empties a bottle of Coke over my head and it feels like I'm literally *drowning.*

Maybe he thought he was doing a public service drenching the queer kid, like he was punishing me on JJ's behalf. Or more

21

likely, he was just being an arsehole. Either way, I ran from the hall that lunchtime and didn't come back for the rest of the school year. I literally stayed in my bedroom until Adam Chung dragged me out four weeks later. It's all a bit of a blur now, but I feel like I lost something that day, like part of me died.

And I haven't spoken to JJ since.

'I hear the summer was pretty hot here,' says Solange.

'It was hell,' says Adam. 'That heatwave was like tropical heat.'

'Sounds amazing,' says Solange.

'It would have been if we didn't live in really well insulated, carpeted houses with no air conditioning,' he says. 'But we do, so it was hell on wheels. I didn't sleep for months.'

'It was crazy hot,' I say.

'Thanks, global warming,' says Adam.

'Yeah – thanks, humanity, for killing the planet,' says Solange, sticking two sarcastic thumbs up.

The laughter that follows is short lived, because moments later Tyler Hudson comes stomping into the dinner hall, walking like he's carrying a scrotum the size of a boxing glove between his legs.

'What you doing here, Brighty?' he says, locking eyes with me.

Immediately I bury my chin into Marlene.

He plonks himself down on the table opposite us, his henchmen quickly joining him, a plate of chips and a bottle of Coke in front of him. 'Is that the gay table, then?' he says. All three of them laugh. 'Look at this bunch of *queerdos*. I better not get too close.'

'Can I get that in writing?' says Solange.

'Have you seen this one, lads – she's begging for my dick.'

'You're grotesque, Tyler,' she says. 'You know that, right?'

He laughs as he unscrews the lid from his bottle of Coke.

I swear, if that comes anywhere near me, I'm going to scream myself hoarse . . .

CRACK!

All of a sudden there's an explosion, followed by fizzing and coughing and spluttering. I close my eyes as I hear a bunch of chairs scraping across the overly polished floor, and the sound of liquid slapping off it. Then comes laughter like I haven't heard since the last time I was here.

Oh no.

This can't be happening. Not again.

But there is no sensation of sticky liquid sliding down my face, no feeling of heaviness as my uniform becomes sodden. I quietly open one eye, expecting to see a hundred faces all looking in my direction.

The laughter isn't directed at me. Instead, everyone is staring at Tyler Hudson, who is standing in the middle of the hall covered in dark, sticky Coke.

'Someone put a Mentos mint in Hudson's bottle of Coke,' a Year 10 screams. 'It's exploded in his face!'

'Oh my giggidy God!' says Adam.

'This is epic!' says Solange.

The laughter crescendoes as the rest of the hall realises what's just happened.

I stare, open-mouthed, amazed and confused, thrilled in ways I didn't know I needed to feel thrilled in. Tyler Hudson, arsehole of the century, is covered in sticky brown liquid, just like I was that day. I can't believe it. He looks like a frightened Year 7.

'Is he about to cry?' says Solange.

Omigod. His eyes and mouth are downturned. His chin is quivering. The toughest boy in school is about to crumble under the pressure of a hall full of laughter.

I begin to laugh too. I can't help it. It's so totally brilliant, because, although I ran and hid in a cleaning cupboard the day it happened to me, although I disappeared from sight for the rest of term, I *never* gave them the satisfaction of my tears.

He's quivering, and everyone is laughing. Most have their phones out, recording Tyler's downfall for Snapchat or TikTok, and I just stare, taking this wonderful moment in.

'Whoever did this, you're dead!' he shouts, his voice cracking like salt and vinegar crisps.

But we keep laughing.

He kicks his chair as he storms out, his henchmen following behind, trying to contain laughter of their own.

'What the F?' I say. 'Talk about justice!'

'That wasn't justice,' says Adam, his eyes wide and wild. 'That was *revenge*!'

FOUR

'So, how was the first day?' Mam asks, her eyebrows crinkling up her forehead like paper. I told her I was dreading it. I know she worries.

'Don't frown,' I say, ignoring her question. 'You'll get lines.'

She slaps a hand on her forehead, smoothing the skin with her fingers. 'Did you see the boy?'

'What did I just say about lines?'

'Sorry.' She tries to still her face by pressing her lips together. 'So . . . did you?'

She's talking about JJ. When I hear stories about kids having a hard time coming out to their parents, I realise how lucky I am. I didn't have a problem in that department. Mam was really supportive – sometimes too supportive. I don't always want to talk to her about my love life, or lack thereof. She doesn't know what happened with JJ, only that I sort of fancied a guy last term. I managed to convince her that my month in bed was due to symptoms of glandular fever (rather than absolute devastation) and, surprisingly, she bought it.

'That's none of your business,' I say.

My brother Mikey's wheelchair is positioned facing the TV in the living room. I sometimes wonder if it hurts him; he never looks that comfortable encased in the rigid supports.

There's a strap right across his forehead, which keeps his head up. He's always left with a red mark after it's taken off.

I walk over to him and stroke the soft skin on his pale cheek. He smiles, his blue eyes lighting up slowly.

'You OK, sweets?' I ask. He replies with a soft moan, lightly spinning in his throat. The doctor says he might talk one day, but it's unlikely. 'Of course you are.' I stroke his hair, pushing blonde curls away from his forehead. 'You need a haircut. You look wild.'

He slowly extends a hand and I catch it in mine. His soft fingertips pad against my skin like kisses. I grip him and he grips me tighter, and it's like this is all there is in the world, and all the drama from my first day back at school eases from my mind for a blissful moment.

'What are you doing later?' says Mam. 'We could watch a film if you like?'

'Can't tonight – homework.'

Of course, I'm using the term 'homework' loosely, because what I really mean is 'sitting on my bed and overthinking everything', to my mind a far more important way to spend an evening than homework.

'Already?'

'Yup. I'm in Year 11 now, Mam.'

I run up the stairs two at a time. Then I push my bedroom door open, collapsing on the bed in a pile of school uniform and vintage rabbit fur.

'Oh, *Marlene*,' I say, stroking my shoulder, 'what an epic day.'

(I would like to state here and now that I am anti-animal

cruelty, and I often say a little prayer for the rabbits who gave their lives for Marlene. But she is vintage, bought from Tynemouth Market. She's probably hundreds of years old, so the damage was already done way before I took my first breath. And she really is all kinds of fabulous. *Thank you, rabbits. Amen!*)

I reach under the bed and pull out my shoebox full of nail varnishes. Painting your nails helps to still the mind. It gives perspective (I read this on Cosmopolitan.com), and Lord knows I need some of that tonight. I also need to get rid of the summery shade I'm wearing – Quick Shag. Summer is over, after all. There's no point clinging to it by my fingernails (literally). It's time for muted autumn tones – I'm thinking Pearl Necklace.

Nail varnish isn't allowed at St Anselm's. Neither is denim, fur or leather. And statement earrings, headwear and accessories are basically the devil. According to the uniform guide, the following additional items are allowed: girls can wear a pair of gold studs in their ears, that's it, NO MAKE-UP; boys aren't allowed to wear anything. There's no mention of what you're allowed to wear if you don't fit into those neat little boxes, as if people like me don't exist. So I style it out however I like, as an act of recognition for the queer non-binary kids all around the world. I feel like it's my duty.

And yes, I get the most horrendous shit for it from the likes of Tyler Hudson. But this is who I am. If I can't be this, then I'm dead. There is no other choice.

I've pushed the gender envelope since the first time I saw Disney's *The Little Mermaid* – the story of the mermaid who traded in her fins for a prince. I was six. To me Ariel was always a non-binary magical creature, presenting femme, with a spirit that's way stronger than her physical form. I took one look at her and saw myself. I'm aware of the whole *trans icon* status she has. And I totally get it. But to me, she lost her appeal when she gained legs. I preferred non-binary Ariel.

So that's where I live. Non-binary. Gay. Queer. Most teachers run in fear when I raise the gender issue – all but Mrs Duncan, the demon head teacher from hell – so I usually get away with wearing what I like. Herein lies one advantage to being a modern-day mermaid in Tynemouth – my tiny seaside village, which sits about eight miles to the east of Newcastle, which in turn sits about three hundred miles to the north of London, where the streets are paved with magical and colourful people.

As I paint away the summer from my nails, I realise that, thanks to all the excitement of the day, I never got the chance to tell Adam and Solange about the postcard I found in my locker this morning.

I grab my bag and plonk it on the bed. Then I dive in, throwing aside new workbooks and papers until I find it again: the postcard from Big Red, St Anselm's answer to Banksy. I turn it over in my hands, from front to back, as if this will help me make more sense of it. It doesn't.

'Yves Klein,' I say.

According to Wikipedia, he was a French artist and pioneer in the development of performance art. He died young. Thirty-four, leaving behind a pregnant widow. He had artistic parents, practised judo, and was famous for his monochrome works, which, in the later part of his life, particularly focused on one single primary colour alone: blue.

I have no idea what this has to do with me.

At least I know he wasn't a huge homo.

Which means, although I've sort of already ruled this out now anyway, the postcard wasn't a homophobic attack.

Great (*waves the world's smallest imaginary pride flag*).

The message on the back can only mean one thing, though; this Big Red person was behind today's Tyler Hudson Coke attack, which is both awesome and unsettling at the same time.

I take out my phone and watch a few videos on YouTube about the Mentos-in-the-bottle-of-Coke trick. I'd never heard of it before today, but it's definitely a thing. It takes some serious planning. The mint has to be placed into the bottle really quickly. I watch a video where this guy sticks it to the bottom of the bottle lid, so when it's screwed off, it instantly drops. It takes some serious patience, not to mention you'd have to be pretty brave to even attempt it. I've seen Tyler rearrange someone's face for way less than this. I find it hard to believe there is someone at school who would be so devil-may-care.

I open WhatsApp. I have a group chat with Adam and Solange called Ballerz. Our icon is the poster for *To Wong Foo*. I need to tell my friends about everything right now. They might be able to see something that I can't.

I click in the text box and type out, then delete, the longest message in the world. Three times. As it turns out, it isn't that easy to put into words everything that's happened today: how I think the same person who painted the art block

29

is the person who sprayed Tyler Hudson; how they also left me a postcard by some French artist called Yves Klein; how maybe it really *was* about revenge for what happened last year. After many failed attempts, I decide to leave it. I think I need more information before I put the Big Red case before the Ballerz. There are too many questions hanging in the air above my head right now.

For now, this is a mystery I have to solve on my own.

FIVE

It isn't long before karma comes to bite me on the arse in the most hideous way.

As I make my way out of last class the next day, I feel a meaty hand grab the back of my hair, swinging me round so fiercely strands come away at the nape of my neck.

'Get off!' I scream, my lip catching on the corner of one of the metal coat pegs by the door. My mouth begins to fill with blood, the metallic taste of iron alive on my tongue.

'Freak,' says Tyler Hudson, smacking his thick, salty hand over my mouth and dragging me into the bathrooms.

'Get off me!'

He grips me tighter and I go limp, trying to resist with my weight, but he still pulls me along. The bathrooms in this school are full of so many bad memories. Every toilet bowl tells a story of me getting my head flushed; every mirror has seen too many of my tears. As soon as we cross the threshold, I'm anxious Ryan Albright again, hiding in the corner while the other boys laugh.

'Look at the state of that.'

'Why are you pissing over there – do you think you're a girl?'

'He thinks he's both! Half-gadge. That's what we'll call him.'

'Do you think you're better than everyone else, gayboy?'

Tyler says, pushing me against the wall.

'I don't know what you're talking about.'

He shoves me so hard my skull thumps off the cold tiles, giving me an instant, throbbing headache.

'You make me sick. If we weren't in school right now, I'd kick your head in. Do you hear me?'

'Oh, loud and clear,' I say, rolling my eyes as if this whole thing isn't terrifying.

'Do you think you're funny?'

Another shove. Another skull thump.

'I'm talking to you.'

I look into his lifeless eyes, and I'm full of anger, like some of his rage has travelled into me through his grubby hands. In this moment I want to run at him. I want to kick and bite and scratch, like some feral animal. I want him to feel exactly what I'm feeling right now. Because if I do nothing, I know tonight I'm going to lie on my bed, staring at the star-shaped fairy lights behind the headboard, thinking about how I should have fought back.

But I just stand here, still as air, and let him do whatever he wants with me.

Turns out, I'm not braver than last year.

Not at all.

'Did you think you could get me back, is that it?' he says.

It was only going to be a matter of time before he put two and two together and ended up with seventeen, and I got blamed for the Coke incident.

'It had nothing to do with me!'

'Shut up!' He punches me in the ribs, and the pain is

like concrete. 'You try anything like that again and I'll break your face.'

I double over, gripping my stomach as I watch him walk away, watch him smash the door off the wall, watch him grunt his way into the busy corridor outside.

When I know he's gone, I walk over to the sink, gripping porcelain edges with white knuckles as I examine my bloody mouth in the mirror. I turn on the tap and splash my face. The water runs red. I place my bag on the side and dig out my red lipstick. I slide it across my lips, mixing the waxy substance with my blood so no one else will ever know what's happened here.

'What a gargantuan arsehole,' I say to my reflection.

The door opens again and I snatch in a cold breath.

'Oh, sorry,' says Beau Greene, the boy from English class. 'It wasn't locked.'

'Why would it be locked?'

'I don't know . . . it wouldn't . . . it's just, I thought I'd interrupted something. I heard you talking.'

He smells of outside, of grass and salt wind, and the scent fills the space until suddenly this bathroom isn't just mine any more. I catch him smiling in the mirror, grooves folding his cheeks in half. And where his curly hair has slightly parted, the sun shines light on his amber eyes. All at once I throw my hand to my mouth. I don't want him to see.

'What is it you want, Beau Greene – are you lost? Do you have afterschool studies or something?'

'Chemistry.'

'You've literally just walked past the science labs. Go out

33

of the door, turn right.'

I turn back to the mirror. But he doesn't move. He's still staring. (As if this could get any more awkward.)

'Who did that to you?' he says.

'No one,' I say, patting my lipstick into the cut. It hurts like hell.

'Was it Tyler Hudson?'

I roll my eyes, trying my best to appear strong and unbothered, even though my heart is racing so fast I feel dizzy. 'Look, it doesn't matter, OK?' I say, rummaging through my bag for my compact and brush. I open it and stroke the coconut-scented bronzing powder over my cheeks, as if I can paint away scared and vulnerable Ryan Albright from my face.

'You should tell a teacher,' he says. 'If you don't, he'll just keep doing it.'

'Look, Beau – thanks for the advice and everything, but I really don't need you to tell me what to do.' I pick up my bag and walk towards the door. 'OK?'

Then I yank the door open so hard it bangs off the wall again, and run across the yard and out of the school gates.

SIX

When I get home I go straight to my room, very Greta Garbo in *Grand Hotel* ('I vant to be alone'). I don't even have tea, and Mam has made macaroni cheese. The house smells of creamy and crispy browned cheese, and my mouth is definitely watering as I thunder up the stairs, adrenaline rushing through me like saltwater. My heart has taken charge and it's beating to a rhythm of *run, run*, pressing against my ribs like Tyler Hudson's heavy hands. *Run, run*. This is what he leaves me with. This is where his anger goes; it transfers to me until I become feral. I become a troglodyte, just like him. I feel like he feels. I think like he thinks. It's like I have part of him with me, here in my home. I hate violence. I don't want to be anywhere near it, or know what it feels like, or have to think about it at all. *I hate it*. And I hate that he brings it into my life.

'What a gargantuan *arsehole*!' I say (again), as I cross my bedroom and dramatically collapse on to the bed.

The mattress begins to beat along to the rhythm of my heart. *Run, run*. It's as if every spring inside is a tiny heart, creaking and pinging and pumping with Tyler Hudson's anger. *Run, run*. I have a heart in my shoulders, my elbows, and my knees. It's impossible to lie still. It's impossible to do anything but think about how much I hate him, as I mull over every last detail of the bathroom attack, which, by the way, is exactly what I knew I would do. I'm so predictable. I thought being in Year 11 would make some sort of difference, but I'm no different to the person I was last term, hiding in my bedroom because I'm scared of the world beyond the door, at the mercy of a force far greater than me, as if I'm standing under a Niagara Falls of Coke, poured by the meaty hands of Tyler bloody Hudson. This is all so triggering!

And I know I have great friends. I know I have an amazing family. But, somehow, Tyler Hudson manages to make me feel so isolated. I mean, he's never raised a hand to Solange or Adam, or poured Coke over anyone else's head other than me. It's like my friends are allowed to exist because they're just the right amount of queer, but I'm too much. I'm too queer. I can't hide it as well as them. I'm too out there, too strange, too much of a freak.

I hate that he makes me feel this way. I hate that he has this power over me. It's as if he left a piece of his anger with me the day he poured Coke over my head, like a tiny fragment of glass in my heart (very 'The Snow Queen' by Hans Christian Andersen), and now I have to live with it for ever. It's like being in love – the feelings are just as strong – but the opposite. I'm in hate. I'm in hate with Tyler Hudson. And I hate that I'm in hate with Tyler Hudson, more than I actually hate Tyler Hudson. (Which I didn't think was possible until now.)

I storm over to the mirror so I can have a proper look at his handiwork. Looking at it definitely makes it feel worse.

My entire face hurts, all the way along my jaw and around my nose. *God!* How am I going to hide this?

I'm hideous.

SEVEN

I walk through the school gates the next morning resembling something from one of those really old horror movies before prosthetic make-up got good. My face looks like a hashed-up attempt at 'zombie' or 'the Creature from the Black Lagoon'. Seriously. It's hideous. My lip is still badly swollen and since the make-up alone wasn't cutting it, I've wrapped a chiffon scarf around my lower face. And the rings under my eyes are so dark, even my Mac Studio Fix concealer, which is basically concrete, wasn't enough to hide them. Only my most obnoxious pair of Mariah Carey-style sunglasses were big enough to do the job.

When I get to English class, everyone is already seated. Their staring feels so much worse than usual because today I can't even pretend I'm any sort of fabulous.

Today, I'm not fabulous.

Today, I'm a slow-moving zombie of a mess in a school uniform.

JJ Dixon is the only one not following my path through the room. He's doing this thing where he pretends I'm made of glass. As I walk in front of him, his eyes don't even twitch. It's like he can see right through me to what's behind: the whiteboard, Ms Mead, the bin, anything.

I bury my chin into my scarf and hurry to my seat, slowing down slightly at the sight of Beau Greene. From what I can see of him, he looks even worse than I do. His dry mouth hangs in between two sallow cheeks, spittle gathered at the edges of his lips. I slide in beside him, watching his motionless form out the corner of my eye. I can't even be sure he's awake, or alive for that matter. He's giving a zombie look too, but, unlike mine, his zombie is from a recent film where the prosthetics are so good they're scarily real. He's like a CGI zombie.

'Quieten down, class,' says Ms Mead, clapping her hands together. Beau doesn't flinch. 'Today we begin work on our classic text. Could someone please hand these out?' She points at a pile of books on her desk. Nobody responds. 'Oh for goodness' sake. John Jo, would you be so kind.'

He stands slowly, unwillingly. Oh God. No. This is all I need right now.

I try to look anywhere that isn't his school trousers, which are clinging tightly to his perfect arse like the skin on a tambourine. *Ay caramba*! But it's physically impossible; he has this way of completely grabbing my attention, until nothing else exists, nothing else matters.

He glides – no, floats – down the aisle, placing each book down with careless grace, and I can hear music again, I can feel him again. My head fills with the smells of woodchips, smoke, sun cream, Lynx Africa body spray and Juicy Fruit gum as a memory begins to form . . .

*

39

'Hey,' he says.

'Hi.'

We hug. He kisses my cheek. He's warm and strong and solid. Everything a boy should be. The sun has turned his hair to spun gold and kissed him across the bridge of the nose. He looks even better out of his school uniform.

'I'm glad you came,' he says.

He takes my hand in his and leads me into the old fish shack, which sits next to the beachside wall of the lido. He pushes open the door and pulls me inside, into the smell of woodchips and smoke.

And then it just happens . . .

A book lands on the desk with a *thud!*

And I'm back in the room.

I stare at it, willing myself with every inch of my being to not look up.

'Hey,' I hear him say.

And the murmuration in my stomach takes a sharp swerve to the left.

I look up. This is the closest I've been to him since last term. God, he looks good. He's like *Love Island* good-looking now.

Lord have mercy on my sperm count!

He smiles. It's definitely a smile this time, and it's amazing to have one of his smiles meant just for me again. For a moment it makes me forget all the bad stuff. With one smile, I'm back on the beach with his warm hands cupping my jaw and his lips pressing against mine. All at once an imaginary scene from *Roman and JJ*, the film about our romance, bursts into my head.

(Today it's time for the dream ballet sequence, where we dance a *pas de deux* around an empty English classroom, leaping over tables, me effortlessly falling into his arms as he throws me high. He's wearing something loose to show off his rippling pectorals. My chiffon scarf doubles up as a totally fabulous prop, billowing behind me in a soft breeze.)

Solange and Adam would kill me if they knew I was fantasising dream sequences for the film about our romance. He doesn't deserve to feature in a film about my grand love affairs, even if he is the nearest thing I've ever had to a male lead. Not after what he did.

'*Strange Case of Dr Jekyll and Mr Hyde,*' I read aloud, picking up the book in an attempt to move my thoughts on from the realms of fantasy.

'Do you know it?' he says.

'Oh, yeah,' I lie. 'It's totally a classic.'

He nods. 'That's cool.'

The chiffon in my mind billows, like sails, and my insides do the same.

'We'll be working on this text all term,' Ms Mead is saying from the front of the room. 'Your homework for tonight is to read the first three chapters.'

'Anyway . . .' says JJ, 'it's good to see you, Roman.'

I sigh, the love scene in my mind fading away at the edges, as I watch the most perfect arse ever created float back to its seat.

All too suddenly the cold hand of reality and English class and homework and Beau Greene brushes against my neck. *Damn it*. He's dribbling now. A long line of saliva is dangling

41

on to his tie. I can't help but scrunch up my nose in disgust. (I can't help but miss the good old days where the class was made up of an odd number, and I got to work alone, too.)

'Did you hear that?' I ask, nudging him.

He jumps awake. 'What?'

'The homework.'

'Um . . . yeah, read something?'

'The first three chapters.'

'Right.'

He scratches the side of his nose, and I notice his hands are shaking. He really does look awful; he's gaunt and so tired. It's probably low blood sugar. He's the type to skip breakfast.

'I have a cereal bar hidden somewhere,' I say. I pick up my bag and rummage through years' worth of crap: empty crisp packets, lipsticks, eyeliner pencil shavings. 'Here. I keep it for emergencies.'

'Um . . . what's this?'

'It's to perk you up.'

The corners of his mouth turn up to show me a pair of totally unexpected dimples. He looks better already. 'Thanks.'

'Ryan,' says Ms Mead. 'Do you have something you'd like to share with us?'

'I don't think so, miss.' *I only have one emergency oat and mixed berry cereal bar. I'm not a vending machine.*

'Perhaps you'd like to tell us what the book is about?'

'No.'

'You were talking. I can only assume it's about the book.'

(She's doing that passive-aggressive thing all teachers do. I thought she was better than this.)

'No,' I say. 'It wasn't.'

'Well, maybe you could tell us what you know about *Dr Jekyll and Mr Hyde* anyway. Stand up. Big voice, Ryan.'

I take a deep breath, pushing my chair back with my legs.

Of course the class laughs. They're all staring at my hideous eye bags, my swollen lip. This is like some medieval ritual. I feel like I'm being flogged in the village square.

I hate English class. I hate any class I don't share with Adam and Solange. I feel isolated without them, like I'm waving the (totally inclusive of all sexuality and gender expressions) rainbow pride flag all on my own.

'Well,' I begin, 'as far as I'm aware, it's a story about some guy with a split personality.'

Laughter, the kind that nightmares are made of, the kind that makes you need to check you're not completely naked, smothered in Nutella, thunders into me, big as the sky.

'That's not quite accurate,' says Ms Mead.

'It totally is, miss!' I say. Now that she's made me stand, I'm determined to see this through, to show them I'm not afraid of their laughter. 'I'm sure I've seen the film. That Dr Jekyll guy has psychotic episodes. My aunty Sheila was the same, that's how I know. She had one on a flight to Tenerife, once. She punched a stewardess. Well, she says it was a psychotic episode; Mam thinks it was down to all the Bacardi she drank, but—'

'Yes, very good, Ryan,' says Ms Mead, holding up her hand. 'Let's get back to this story, shall we? You can sit down now.'

Ridiculed and silenced. I often wonder why I bother turning up to this place. I really do.

I take a seat, sliding down the chair as far as I can.

'You're funny,' whispers Beau Greene.

'Don't you start.'

'I'm serious. They're laughing because you're funny. Nothing more.'

'They're laughing because they're arseholes,' I say, grabbing my copy of *Jekyll and Hyde*, and throwing it in my bag. 'Nothing more.'

EIGHT

'Did you punch him back?' asks Adam, as I follow him into the science lab. 'I definitely would have punched him back.'

'No, you wouldn't,' I say. 'And my split lip isn't even from being punched; I just caught it on a coat peg as he shoved me against the wall. It's totally tragic.'

'Doesn't matter. I would have punched him.'

'If I'd punched him, I would be carrying at least six of my teeth home, wrapped up in toilet paper. Anyway, I've never punched anything in my life – I can't clench my hands into fists.' I splay my fingers as I say this. 'See? It's physically impossible with these nails.'

'You could have scratched his eyes out, then.'

'Yeah. Well. I definitely thought about it.' I examine my nails as I say this, because actually, I've never thought of them as weapons before, but they totally could be. I guess I could have torn him to shreds with my autumnally toned talons. If I were a superhero, I would definitely be Catwoman (the Julie Newmar version, of course).

We make our way to our table at the back of the room. I dump my bag on top and pull out my usual stool. It's weird; technically we're in a new year now, so this is a new class and we could sit wherever we like. But everyone just slots into the exact same places as last year. I suppose this is because there are no new additions here, no Beau Greenes to screw up the system.

The classroom door slowly creaks open and in walks Professor Owen, science teacher and fossil. Everything about him, from his wiry grey whiskers to his worn-out clothes, to the way he shuffles into the room with about as much energy as a sloth who's just completed a triathlon, screams 'tired'. If I were to describe him in one word it would be *dusty*, and not in the fabulous, spotlight-dust-flecked, Dusty Springfield sense of the word, but in the prehistoric sense of the word. Big difference. When he talks about Darwin and Newton, it's done so in a way that makes me think he knew them personally.

'I just hate that Tyler gets away with it,' says Adam.

'I know,' I say, sighing.

'We shouldn't have to deal with this crap because we're queer.'

'Actually, this time it wasn't about that. Well, it sort of was, because with Tyler it always is, but it was more about what happened in the dining hall.'

'What – the Coke thing?'

'Yeah. He thought I'd done it. He thought I was getting him back.'

Adam goes quiet for a moment as he pulls his workbooks out of his bag and neatly places them on the desk in front of him. 'Don't you think that's interesting?' he asks, when his books are stacked, all lined up to the left-hand corner of the desk.

'What?'

'That he thought you would get him back,' he says. 'It means, on some weird level, he sees you as a threat.'

'It does?'

'Yeah. He wouldn't accuse you otherwise.'

'I don't know.'

'He's threatened by you, Roman. Remember that the next time you're considering whether or not to punch him in the face.'

'I think he was just looking for an excuse to kick the crap out of someone.'

'Adam Chung,' says Professor Owen, waggling a decrepit finger, 'stop talking.'

Professor Owen doesn't acknowledge me, because he never does. I don't think in his 367 years on this planet he has ever seen a non-binary person. I'm an enigma to him, and his way of dealing with me is to pretend I don't exist. He knows there's a boy in his biology class called Ryan Albright, but he has no idea which one of us he is, which suits me fine because, firstly, Ryan Albright is long gone, and secondly, it means Adam gets blamed for everything I do.

'Anyway,' I whisper to Adam, 'long story short, he got it wrong. But I think I know who did put the Mentos in Tyler's Coke.'

'You do?' says Adam, almost too quickly.

'Yeah. I've been meaning to tell you—'

'Who?'

'OK, are you going to let me talk?'

'Yes.'

'Big Red.'

He waits for a moment before he answers. I can almost see his thoughts flashing behind his confused eyes. 'Is this a joke?' he asks finally.

'No.'

'Big Red, like the giant dog?'

'No, Big Red, like the person who spray-painted the giant face on the art block – I don't suddenly think a giant fictional dog is slipping Mentos mints in Tyler Hudson's soft drinks.'

He throws his hand to his mouth to cover his laugh. 'Okaaaay.'

'I'm being serious.'

'No you're not.'

'I am! The same person who sprayed the art block sprayed Tyler Hudson. Big Red.'

'Adam Chung!' says Professor Owen, in a voice that wouldn't be out of place in the court of George III. 'Don't test my patience.'

We fall into silence, staring at our workbooks as the register is called out.

Then, when Professor Owen starts messing about with the electronic whiteboard (pining for the good old days of chalk and slate), Adam turns to me and says, 'Roman, please tell me you're joking.'

He gives me this strange look, concerned but sort of scared at the same time. And all of a sudden I'm aware of how differently Adam looks at me now. Maybe it's because we're here, back in familiar surroundings, but it's the first time I recognise the look, which I'm guessing has been a permanent fixture on his face since the day he pulled me out of my

48

bedroom all those weeks ago. He's looking at me as if I'm made of china or something, like I'm vulnerable and at any moment might smash (aka run back to my bedroom in floods of tears). Basically, he thinks I'm teetering on the edge of a psychotic break.

And now I'm not too sure that pursuing the Big Red conversation is a good idea any more.

'It was just a crazy idea,' I say. 'As in – the idea was crazy, not me,' I add quickly. 'I'm not crazy.'

'Okaaay?' he says, still looking at me like I might be. 'If you say so.'

'I do.'

'EVOLUTION,' barks Professor Owen suddenly, having gotten the electronic whiteboard working and turning around so sharply I'm sure I hear the bones in his neck crack, 'is, by definition, any cumulative change in the characteristics of organisms or populations over many generations . . .'

'Oh God,' says Adam, throwing his forehead into his hand. 'I'd forgotten about biology.'

'Yup,' I say, slowly nodding. 'We're definitely back at school.'

'I'm sooo failing this subject. I just know it.'

'Hey, I wouldn't be so sure. Look, he's talking about evolution, and, honey, we're about as evolved as it gets.'

He turns to me and snaps his fingers in my face. 'Honey! You know it.'

'Adam Chung, pay attention!' says Professor Owen.

I rest my chin on the edge of my fingernails, a smug smile on my face. 'Yeah, Adam,' I say, '*you* better pay attention, guuurl.'

NINE

Mam has taken Mikey to his Saturday morning swimming class. It's rare for the house to be this quiet. After a summer of cartoons in the living room, 90s R'n'B in the kitchen, loud phone calls in the hallway and health visitors at the door, it's nice to have a moment to myself.

Right now, I'm sitting on my bedroom window ledge, my trainers dangling over the wisteria that clings to the wall below. I dig my feet into the thickest part, where lazy blossoms hang like unanimated puppets bending away from slack strings. The sweet perfume blows up at me and I take a deep breath. Really, I should be using these silent hours to crack on with homework, but I'm doing everything I can to avoid it. Days like this weren't made for homework. The world is too beautiful. The sun is shining. The air is warm. It's like summer has reared her fabulous head for one last outing, and with her comes the need to bask. I'm no longer here; I'm lost somewhere between procrastination and dreaming. I definitely have the right setting for it, sitting here on my bedroom window ledge. *Very* Audrey Hepburn in *Breakfast at Tiffany's* ('It's a mistake you always make, Doc, trying to love a wild thing'). I should be wearing diamonds right now. Actually, I should be wearing diamonds always.

My bag sits open on the bed, yawning at me with a stomach full of papers and textbooks, a jarring reminder that I'm not Audrey Hepburn, but a Year 11 student, and the work won't magically do itself.

Sigh.

Inside, I can see the edge of *Jekyll and Hyde*. (I suppose reading fiction is a good compromise between dreaming and homework.) I take it out and open it at the title page. Instantly the smell of dust and age blows up into my face. I love that smell, the smell of old books. The school must have had this copy for ages. It's pretty tatty. I run my finger across the paper. It's coarse and yellowing. Proper old.

I turn the title page over carefully as it's already coming away from the binding, but instead of another page of black print on white paper I see something totally unexpected – but not totally unfamiliar. Something not black and white, but blue.

International Klein Blue.

The painting on this particular postcard is made up of five forms – are they insects, or maybe orchids? I'm not entirely sure what they're supposed to be, but I don't think it's important.

I quickly turn it over to read the message on the back.

Longsands beach – (Big Red)

I stare open-mouthed at the message in my hands, because I don't know how Big Red did it. How did they manage to wedge this postcard into a book in my bag without me looking? It makes me feel cold, the tiny hairs at the back of my neck standing on end. I suddenly feel really exposed sitting here on the window ledge, swiftly becoming aware of how many dark corners there are in the alleyway behind our street, every wheelie bin and parked car and net curtain a potential hiding place.

I swing my legs back into my bedroom, and duck under the window, then I slide on to the bed, still clutching the postcard in my hand so fiercely my knuckles are turning white. *Longsands beach*. This isn't the first time I've received a message containing these exact words. *Longsands beach* was one of the last WhatsApps JJ sent me, right before we shared the most romantic moment of my entire life.

The memory that forms in my head plays in real time, like I'm back there, reliving that day. I'm the Roman Bright before the bullshit, before the bottle of Coke, and the rejection, and the days spent in the darkness of my bedroom.

I leap – no, *fly* across the bed, sending schoolbooks and papers tumbling to the floor on dying wings. I find Marlene sprawled across my bedroom carpet. I pick her up and throw her over my shoulders. My keys are on the dresser. I grab them and lunge at my door, checking my reflection in the mirror on the way to the hallway.

And there I stop immediately, because I see my reflection, my shorter hair, my eye bags, my bruised lip.

All at once the me in the mirror changes shape. Shrinks. All at once my shoulders are rounded, my mouth is downturned, and I look sort of silly and small because my new hideous bruise has just dragged me back into the present, and right away I feel embarrassed because I totally should know better. This isn't last term. And Big Red isn't JJ Dixon.

I pace back into my bedroom and slump down on to the side of the bed, deflated, just a husk in a rabbit-skin cape. I feel so stupid, and sort of shocked, that my mind went to this in the first place, because it means only one thing. I guess deep down I've known it ever since our eyes met across a crowded English classroom: I'm not over JJ Dixon. There. The truth. Even though he put me through the worst weeks of my life, I still can't move on from that day, that kiss, and the feeling I get in my gut when I see him. It's physically impossible, like he has this power over me. When he walks into a room, I melt into a puddle on the floor. When he looks my way, my heart skips a beat. I can't control it. I'm hanging on for a reconciliation with the person who, according to Cosmopolitan.com, I should have cut out of my life entirely. I'm ignoring every single voice of reason that exists in my head because romance is the nemesis of logic; it overpowers everything else. *JJ* overpowers everything else. I still want him, and I know I can't have him. I never thought returning to school would make me feel this way. I thought I'd processed all of this stuff, and I really felt stronger. Now I'm not so sure I am stronger, and it's all because of the postcard in my hands.

I grip it so firmly the card begins to bend.

OK.

Now I definitely need to know who is hiding behind these stupid messages, because it seems like they know exactly how to destroy me all over again. First the postcard that directed me to the dining hall, which led to me being physically attacked, and now this one, which feels like an emotional attack. And I've come too far to be beaten by some anonymous postcards.

I'm supposed to be stronger now. I *am* stronger now. I have to be.

There's a clock on my bedside table. It's navy blue with stars around the face. I've had it since I was a kid. On some days this past summer, its ticking was the only thing keeping me out of my head. I listen to it click around a full sixty seconds before I make a move, before I grip my house keys in my hand, before I lunge at the door (ignoring the mirror this time), and storm down the stairs and out into the world.

Heading straight for Longsands beach.

TEN

I arrive at the promenade a hot and sweaty mess. Wrapping my hands around the warm metal balustrade, I look down at white sands and calm sea. Longsands beach really is the best part of living in Tynemouth. Avoiding it all summer was super hard but even Adam couldn't drag me down here. Whenever we hung out we went to King Eddy's Bay, or just sat on the grass at the far end of the high street by the old priory. I wasn't ready to come back here.

I'm still not sure if I am.

As I descend concrete steps, the memory of that day comes back so easily, so completely, just like I knew it would. It's always been here, waiting for me, etched into sea-weathered stones. Rooted in the sand like dune grass. The closer I get to the beach, the stronger it becomes. The wings in my belly are flapping like crazy. My lips begin to tingle, as if they're being pressed against another's. I can smell summer on the wind: the sweetness of Wrigley's Juicy Fruit gum and the sharpness of aftershave freshly sprayed over sun-blushed skin.

The memory that comes is fully formed.

All I can do is step right into it . . .

*

His hands cup my jaw as I lean into him, pressing myself against his body so he can feel all of me, so he knows I'm completely his.

When I open my eyes he's smiling, so close I can only see him in small pieces: rosy lips, sun-kissed skin, tiny white hairs, bright eyes, a halo of light around his face.

'That was good,' he says.

'Yeah.'

I didn't think it would ever happen. That it could feel this good. For months it'd been nothing more than shared glances and secret messages, starting from the day I got that first WhatsApp from him at the beginning of summer term. Him, *the captain of the school football team, the most beautiful guy in school. He wanted me, he'd been messaging me constantly all term. Still, I never expected this. I thought messages and shared glances were all I was going to get. But now I'm here, fulfilling my Disney-happily-ever-after fantasy, and it's so much more than I imagined it could be.*

'This is crazy,' I say.

'What?' he says.

'Just this, you . . . I never thought someone like you would choose someone like me.'

He grabs the back of my neck and we kiss again. Then he takes my hand in his and pushes it against lower places. I'd never held a boy there before. It was an evening of firsts . . .

A biting wind snatches away the memory, sending it flapping across the dunes. It's autumn again. But I can still taste last summer on my lips, sweet as Juicy Fruit gum.

I realise I'm standing at the edge of the old lido. Without

meaning to, I've arrived at the exact place where it happened, where our love scene played out in the most idyllic setting.

But it doesn't look the same.

The nearside lido wall has changed colour, just like the art block changed colour on the first day back. Where I expect to see grey blocks, covered in seaweed and swirling copper rust, I see turquoise and purple stars, and bright blue lightning bolts, and feathers, spread right across the wall in the shape of a giant pair of wings.

Wings.

Wings are my thing.

I draw wings everywhere. Anybody who knows me knows this.

I approach slowly because, now I'm here, now that I'm seeing more of Big Red's art, I'm realising I might have been wrong. Maybe the person behind this isn't trying to destroy me . . . because this art? It's not violent. It's warm and soft and welcoming.

Up close, the painting is even more detailed. There are words swirled around stars and lightning bolts, floating in and around the painting like smoke. *Love. Joy. Freedom.* They cover the old lido wall all the way to the old fish shack.

The old fish shack.

My nostrils fill with the smell of aftershave and woodchips as I feel the weight of his hand against my neck.

This is all too much! I'm trying my best to resist, but the feelings are too strong. What we shared here was so special, and now there are painted wings on the wall for added drama, and I'm lost somewhere in a summer memory again. I'm back there, feeling everything I've resisted for months. I know what we had here was real. And I know that if I still feel this way, then there's a chance that he still feels this way too . . .

And then it comes to me.

It comes to me as easily as the breeze, as easily as the sea erasing the day from the sand like a cloth on a blackboard, leaving only white foam marks behind, leaving only one thought behind:

The postcard was hidden in a book JJ Dixon handed to me.

Which means he wrote it.

Which means he wanted me to come here, to our place and this painting.

My hand automatically finds a word sprayed in bright red amongst the beautiful blue chaos of feathers and lightning bolts and stars. *Love*. And I'm suddenly able to see so clearly that this painting and my summer memory are both part of the same love story, are both part of our love story: *Roman and JJ*.

I pull the postcard out of my pocket. Yves Klein. Blue square. I have no idea if that's significant or not. Is it just another way of hiding his true identity? Last term JJ's big thing was secrecy. He didn't want anybody to know about us – so much so that when they found out, the proverbial crap hit the fan in a major way, resulting in yours truly being covered in Coke in front of the entire school. (Shivers.) Is all this – Big Red, Yves Klein, these brilliant works of graffiti – his way of secretly telling me he still wants this, wants us? Making sure we can be together without the intervention of idiots like Tyler Hudson?

Tyler Hudson. The Coke explosion. Revenge. Of course, if JJ *is* still into me, it makes sense that he would want to right the wrongs of last term. First, taking revenge on Tyler for me. He couldn't have predicted that Tyler would attack me as a result. He was just trying to make amends.

And now this. A grand romantic gesture in paint, like saying, *Look how sorry I am, I still care for you.* And that it's in the place we shared the most magical moment of my life? Sooo poetic!

My head says I might be jumping to some almighty conclusions here, and that I need to be sensible and remember my gloomy summer and listen to my best friends. But my heart says there can be no other explanation for these painted wings, the physical embodiment of romance, here in our special place. Here, where we shared an evening of so many firsts. My heart is screaming at me that it all makes sense, and that JJ Dixon has to be Big Red!

I didn't even know he was good at art. But, now I think about it, my male lead would definitely be an artiste. I'm so sure of that.

I begin to laugh and cry, my stomach bouncing like a trampoline with the feelings roiling inside of me.

This Big Red stuff has only ever been about one thing: romance.

I knew it wasn't over. I *knew* it.

I have to let him know how I feel. I have to. This game of postcards and paintings is cute and everything, but I need to make my feelings known. I need to let him know that I still care too, I'm in the game, I'm going to play along, and I'm down for whatever ride he wants to take me on.

I take out my phone and scroll to our last WhatsApp chat. Then I begin to type. And yes, I know Cosmopolitan.com told me I absolutely shouldn't do this because messaging an ex is sooo weak and pathetic. But I don't care. None of that matters now. Because our romance isn't weak and pathetic; look at everything he's done to win me back! This is Disney-scale romance. Cosmopolitan.com is wrong! Cosmopolitan.com can kiss my arse!

Roman Bright

I miss you x

ELEVEN

Big Red's latest painting has made the local news.

I'm lying on the sofa waiting for Mam to put Mikey to bed so we can crack on with our Friday night ritual of facemasks and a film, when I notice the reporter on the TV is standing on Longsands beach, interviewing local octogenarians about vandalism, and graffiti, and empty lager cans left behind at night, and how the world has changed, and how disgraceful it all is. In the background, a group of people in high-visibility jackets are scrubbing away Big Red's wings, returning the wall to sandstone and seaweed and rust.

And right away I get a twinge of sadness, because the painting was so . . . everything, and the memories it brought were even more so, and now the wings will be nothing more than a memory too. This makes me feel sort of panicked, and I half-want to run down to the beach right now and scream at every person wearing a high-visibility jacket to stop, to tell them all how important this painting is, how it needs to stay to remind me of the most romantic moment of my life.

'Oh, turn it off,' says Mam, walking into the room. In her hands she's carrying my shoebox of nail varnishes. 'I wish people would pick up after themselves on that beach. You had a great-uncle who died of sepsis after stepping on a shard of glass before penicillin was invented, you know? Poor Uncle Jimmie – gone before his time. I don't know what's wrong with people. I really don't.'

Mam always talks about poor Uncle Jimmie. She never met him.

'What do you want to watch?' I ask, grabbing the remote.

'Something girly,' she says, splaying her fingers in anticipation, because I promised I would paint her nails tonight. 'Something fabulous.'

I click the remote and immediately Prime Video shows me a screen full of too many options.

Luckily, I am a pro at selecting the perfect film for the perfect occasion. It's a particular talent of mine. Films are my thing. When it's time to escape the dramas of life for a while, I always turn to films. It's something I've done since I was really young. Because in films, real magic exists and problems can disappear in a single montage. In films, true love conquers all. In films, the worst part is never the end and when things get tough, it means something good is right around the corner. I suppose what I'm saying is: films give me hope. They basically saved me from the dark cloud that descended upon me this summer.

'I think this calls for *Grease*,' I say, stopping on one of my faves. 'Is one hour and fifty minutes of pink hair, black spandex and suspected teenage pregnancy girly enough for you?'

Mam snuggles into the corner cushions. 'One hour and fifty minutes of a young John Travolta will do me.' She sighs into her glass of white wine.

She looks happy. I like that I can do this for her. I like that I can make her happy. She's always so busy.

And I bloody love this film – the musical story of two star-crossed high school students and the hardships they face trying to be together. I have a theory about it; I think who we are in *Grease* is who we are in life. I'm obviously Rizzo. Firstly, because the neighbourhood thinks I'm trashy and no good. And secondly – she's a femme fatale. She's guarded, outwardly confident and secretly vulnerable. I think I'm that way too. I believe the world would be a better place if we all knew our *Grease* character – sort of like doing the Myers-Briggs personality test. It would probably bring about instant world peace and general well-being.

I shunt the box of nail varnishes towards her. 'Not Really a Virgin or Squirter?' I say, holding up two different shades.

'They're not the names?' she says.

'Read the bottom.'

'I don't know how I feel about you owning nail varnishes called that.'

'Oh stop – I'm nearly sixteen.'

'Is that really what they're called?'

'Yes!'

'*Jesus*. What's wrong with calling them red and peach?'

'Red and peach have already been done, babes.'

'It's moments like this when I feel like a proper old fart.'

'Well, do you feel like a Not Really a Virgin old fart, or do you feel like a Squirt—'

'The red one! And don't you let your grandma see them, for God's sake. She'll have a heart attack.'

'Good choice. Shall I do your toes too?'

'Nah, I wouldn't bother. No one is going to see them.'

I click the play button and lay her hand out on the nearest pillow.

The film begins with Sandy and Danny's summer of love, where they kiss on the beach at sunset as perfect waves crash into a perfect shore. Usually I'd mindlessly watch this bit, waiting for Rizzo's grand entrance in her Studebaker Commander, painted entirely pink ('OK, girls – let's go get 'em'). But today as I watch the opening sequence, I feel something sharp twist in my stomach, clawing right behind my belly button. A cold feeling rushes over me, and my hands begin to shake, because what used to be a scene I could watch with no emotional attachment has turned into a reminder of something real – my very own perfect beach scene.

'Careful, lover!' says Mam, because I've just painted the top part of her finger.

'Sorry!' I reach over for the cotton wool and dab it in some remover. 'It comes right off, see?'

'Is everything OK?'

'Fine.'

'You sure?'

'Yes. I'm totally fine.'

'*Roman.*'

'I'm just enjoying the film,' I say.

She gives me a hard look and I force a smile across my face. I don't want to talk to her about Big Red. For now, I want to keep it just between JJ and me. I feel like he's taking me on an adventure, and keeping the secret is all part of the fun.

'Oh, I forgot to say – *Disney on Ice* is coming back to the arena,' she says, abruptly changing the subject. 'I'm thinking of taking Mikey. Would you like me to get you a ticket? You loved it last time.'

'Yeah. Lovely,' I say, giggling to myself as memories of last term take charge of my senses.

'Did you even hear what I just said?'

'Yeah. Lovely.'

'Olivia Newton-John was nearly thirty when she filmed this. A lot of them were, actually. Imagine that – already in their thirties and playing school kids. I reckon I could pass for a teenager. Don't you?'

'Yeah. Lovely.'

'Alright!' She snatches her hand back. 'What's going on?'

'What?'

'Are you sure you're feeling OK?'

'Yes. Why wouldn't I be?'

'Well, for a start, there's no way you think I could pass for a teenager. You're always telling me off for my frown lines.'

'I would never . . .' I say, clutching my imaginary pearls.

'You're all flushed, Roman.'

'No, I'm not,' I say, pressing a hand to my cheek.

'I recognise that look. This is about the boy, isn't it? Ooh – come on, give me all the details!'

'About what?'

'Spill the beans – or "the T" as the kids say.'

I don't answer right away, because I can't. Like, literally can't. My throat feels constricted, like I've just swallowed sand. 'No. It's just this film. It's one of my favourites.'

She screws up her face, and I know she was totally expecting something juicy out of me, because she usually gets something juicy out of me. Usually I love spilling the sweetened tea with Mam; it's one of my favourite pastimes. But I'm not ready to explain this yet. Because telling her about Big Red would mean going through everything that happened last year too. And then she'd be biased against JJ before she even meets him. But I know she isn't buying whatever lie I'm trying to sell her. She's my mam. You can't lie to your mam; it's physically impossible, like snogging your elbow.

'*Roman?*'

I look away: at the fireplace, out of the window, at the table lamp, at anything that isn't her eyes, because if I want my happily ever after, then I'm going to have to be a little more selective about the things I tell her from now on.

'It's nothing,' I say. 'Now, give me your other hand before I tell you what the other colours in the shoebox are called.'

TWELVE

Solange Burrell is the best artist in our year. No matter how long I spend, and how much detail I pour into my final pieces, hers are always better. She has this ease about her, this grace in the way she paints that I swear even da Vinci would be envious of. And she knows it. She's definitely taking art as an A level subject, and she's definitely going to art school afterwards, potentially in Paris now, because of beautiful Noelle, her summer love.

I rest my head against her easel as she sweeps the tiniest brush in the world across the canvas, shifting forward and back as if on a rocking chair. It's lunchtime and Solange has decided to spend it working, which on some level I sort of respect her for. (On another I think she's totally crazy.) I'm here because Adam has detention and I didn't fancy wandering the schoolyard alone. To be a lonely queer person out in the wilds of St Anselm's is to make oneself vulnerable these days.

'So, how is love's young dream?' I say.

'It's good,' she says, with a paintbrush wedged between her teeth.

I take a step to her side to take a look at her latest masterpiece.

'Impressive,' I say.

It's coming together already, and we're only a few weeks into the term. Needless to say, I'm yet to put brush to canvas. My final piece still only exists as black and white pencil sketches . . . in my head.

Each term our coursework has a theme. This term our theme is Passions. I, of course, have chosen films. My plan is to incorporate as many screen legend goddesses as I can into my composition, with a background of sweeping red velvet curtains, black film reel and silver footlights. I've spent most of this term so far perfecting Marilyn Monroe's beauty mark, which is time well spent in my book. Although, looking at Solange's work in progress, which wouldn't be out of place in Michelangelo's Sistine Chapel, I'm starting to doubt myself.

'Anyway,' she says. 'Nobody has used the L word yet.'

'The L word?' I say, raising my eyebrows.

'You know to which word I'm referring.'

I smirk.

I do.

Love.

That's the word of the hour, the day and the week. Which, by the way, is how long it's been since I discovered that the love of my life is leaving totally romantic paintings for me around the school, and now the village. Actually, one week and one day, to be precise.

I sat through the rest of the movie with Mam that night as if in a dream, and I've pretty much remained that way ever since. On the days when school has been crap, or it's rained, or I've had a load of homework to get through, I've just thought of Big Red, and everything hasn't seemed so bad.

'It's hard,' Solange is saying. 'I didn't realise how tough the long-distance thing would be.'

'You sound deflated,' I say.

'I'm not deflated . . . just a little bit frustrated. I miss her. I want to be with her. But I can't be.'

I stick out my bottom lip because I know exactly what she's going through. 'I'm sorry.'

'It's fine,' she says. 'It's just . . . summer is over, and we're back at school, and it all feels like a hundred years ago. But Christmas still seems so far away it might as well exist in another galaxy.'

'You sound like you've got it bad.'

'I do. I don't. I'm OK. I'm just having a moment.' She dips her brush into some red paint and I notice the tips of her fingers are stained red. Her fingers are always stained with a load of different colours, because she spends every free second she gets in the art studio. 'Painting always helps. How are you, anyway? What's been going on? You've been AWOL on the Ballerz group chat.'

'Have I?' I say. 'No. Nothing. Nothing at all's been going on.'

Her eyes flick up towards me. 'Okaaay.'

'I'm fine,' I say. 'Actually, I feel great – like I'm back to my old self again.'

She tilts her head to one side. 'Hmm.'

'What?'

'I mean – that would be great . . . if it were true . . .'

'It *is* true.'

I smile, and it's a totally forced smile, and I can see she

69

can tell it's a totally forced smile, but it's really the best I've got. I'm a terrible liar.

I wish I could tell Solange everything about JJ and Big Red right now. I wish this was something we could share: being in love, being unable to see our loves because we're separated by land and sea (or, in my case, by the prejudices of St Anselm's High). But I'm not sure she'd want to hear it. I'm not sure she'd understand. After what happened last term, I know she doesn't trust JJ at all.

Also, I'm aware of how precarious the situation is. I mean, I still haven't heard back from him, and I messaged over a week ago. Which, by the way, is classic JJ. I know him well enough to know that now. Last term was an intricate dance of messages and glances, smiles across the classroom, WhatsApps at midnight, and then days of silence, the all-of-a-sudden awful days when he looked through me as if I were made of glass. It feels different this time, though, thanks to Big Red. I think JJ's changed, like he's finally becoming the person I always knew he could be, not the vacant hot-and-then-cold boy of last term. He may not have responded to my text, but the paintings and postcards are leading somewhere, and how I choose to play will mean the difference between getting everything I've ever wanted – like a trouser-movingly beautiful kiss in some idyllic film-set-like place – and screwing it all up.

And I'll be damned if I'm screwing up any chance of romance again.

Another thing to come out of this is that Big Red/JJ Dixon has unknowingly started a revolution of epic proportions.

It seems like everyone has become a secret graffiti artist. In the weeks since the face with two sides appeared on the art block wall, no less than ten other paintings have appeared around school. None of them are anywhere near as detailed or as brilliant as Big Red's but JJ has inspired a whole generation of rebels (I know for a fact there's a guy in Year 9 calling himself The Wyrm, who's leaving dragon-themed stuff all over the main building). Mrs Duncan is apoplectic, threatening all kinds of punishments to anybody she catches even looking at a can of spray paint in the wrong way. Which somehow makes all of this even more exciting, adding the kind of dramatic tension befitting of only a great romance.

Swoon!

'Well, if you've definitely moved on from all that toxic JJ stuff, then I'm happy,' Solange says, bringing me out of my reverie.

All of a sudden I freeze. It's like this statement has suddenly turned the air between us cold, because in one sentence Solange Burrell has confirmed everything I knew already: she'd never accept a JJ and me. She's not buying a ticket to see *Roman and JJ*, the film about our love. She's not munching on popcorn throughout, staring misty-eyed at the screen. She's not putting up a five-star review on Amazon. She's *out*.

And now I feel like I don't want to be here, in this art studio at lunchtime. Now I feel like I'd rather take my chances out in the wilds of the schoolyard.

'Course I have,' I say.

She goes quiet, staring intently at her painting, and biting her bottom lip at the same time.

'Just . . . be careful,' she says.

'What does that mean?'

'You know what it means.'

'No. I don't.'

'Look . . . I'm just going to say this once, and then I've said it, and then it's done.'

'Okayyyy?'

'I've noticed a few times over the past week or so that you've started looking at him again.'

'*Looking* at him?'

'Like you used to.'

This makes me clench my teeth, my hands and my arse cheeks all at the same time, because right away I realise how obvious I've been. She's absolutely right. I have been looking at him. I mean, how could I not? The boy is stunning for a start, as if painted in oils by one of the great masters. But also, I haven't been hiding my feelings as much any more, because with all of this Big Red stuff I haven't felt a need to. When he passes me in the corridor, I let myself smile; when we accidentally catch eyes across a crowded classroom, I give him my very best Audrey Hepburn 'demure'. I can't help myself; for the first time in my fifteen years and six months of living, my life looks exactly how I imagined it would all those years ago when I first watched *The Little Mermaid*. For the first time in my fifteen years and six months of living, everything looks every bit as fabulous as it does in my head. I mean, the guy is obviously still into me. And there's nothing wrong with a little harmless flirtation. *Right?*

'I'm not looking at anyone like I used to,' I say calmly.

72

'Be. Careful.' She says it again, slowly as if I'm an idiot and didn't hear her the first time.

'How am I not being careful?' I ask sharply, because I'm starting to get pissed off. 'Because sometimes I look at JJ when he's walking towards me down the corridor? We go to the same school, Solange. I'm going to see him from time to time.'

'I know, but—'

'But *what*?'

'But if you have to do it, don't make it so obvious. You're not doing yourself any favours, Roman. If the wrong person sees you—'

'The wrong person? Tyler Hudson has already tried to ruin my facial symmetry—'

'I'm not talking about Tyler Hudson—'

'Who are you talking about, then?'

Her face goes completely still, all of her usual warmth disappearing as if one of the studio spotlights over her head has suddenly gone out.

'What?' I say.

She doesn't answer, doesn't move.

'Solange – *what*?'

'Just be careful,' she says for a third time.

'Oh for God's sake,' I say.

Then I grab my bag and storm out.

THIRTEEN

'Hi, Roman,' says a sing-song voice behind me.

I turn slowly to see Wynter Brown: drop-dead gorgeous Wynter Brown, the most popular girl to ever walk the earth, Wynter Brown, her eyes beaming at me like almond-shaped light bulbs.

'Hi, Wynter.'

'Or is it *Roman Bright*?'

'Just Roman is fine.'

There's a story here. We were best friends when we were five because we lived near each other and our mams worked together. This was before Mikey, and before Mam had to stop working. It was also before her parents won the lottery. Literally. Now she lives in a giant house with its own gate and driveway, way on the other side of the village. Over the years she's gone from strength to strength, getting prettier and prettier, while I faded into the depths of the forgotten kids, getting weirder and weirder. (Until I came out as Roman Bright.) I wouldn't say she's a friend any more, but we've known each other for longer than anyone else here, so there's a kind of mutual tolerance thing going on; our parents sort of know each other, we used to play together . . . *blah, blah, blah*. This doesn't mean I'm not surprised she's approached me on a busy stairwell between classes like this.

'*Omigod*, I love the fur coat,' she says.

Her harem nods in agreement.

I've heard she buys her harem of broken dolls (this is what I call the girls that hover around her like flies around a particularly fresh turd) the latest iPhone – complete with AirPods – every Christmas, and she already has the white Range Rover of dreams parked up in her parents' garage, even though it'll be at least two years until she can legally drive it.

Also, and here's where the cliché ends, she's smart, smarter than smart; she gets the highest grades in our year in every subject, even sports. She's straight A*s and rich and gorgeous.

There's no need to compete with her. Take the gloves off. She's already won.

'She's a cape,' I say, giving Marlene a stroke.

She doesn't acknowledge this, instead she gets right into the reason she's stopped me on a busy stairwell in between classes like this. 'You're coming to the Halloween party, right?'

'. . . ?'

'My party. You *have to* come, it's going to be *insane*.'

'*Insane*,' says the harem with emphasis, as if they are one being, one voice and – I hasten to add – one brain. That brain probably belongs to Wynter.

'I *need* Roman Bright there,' she says to the faceless girl nearest to her, before flashing me a smile. It isn't a proper smile; it doesn't reach her eyes, and that's what makes me realise it isn't a proper invitation either. I haven't had a *proper* invitation from her since her seventh birthday when I dressed as a mermaid. (Obviously.) She wants me at her party looking all kinds of fabulous because she knows damn well that every queer kid worth their salt makes an effort on Halloween. I'm basically a decoration, like one of the neatly carved pumpkins that line her driveway, or the plastic skeleton she dresses up as a witch every year. (I've seen this on Snapchat.)

I don't know whether to be offended or not. I do love dressing up, and sometimes I totally want to be Naomi Campbell doing community service in couture Dolce & Gabbana, on show for the whole world to see. But also . . . sometimes I don't. Sometimes I want to be invited properly, as a friend, not a decoration. Am I asking for too much?

For a split second I seriously consider telling her to take a running jump, because my friends and I have never needed to attend this party before. But I'm no fool. I know exactly what attending Wynter's Halloween party means.

Acceptance.

And on the kind of scale that people like me can only dream of.

'I would totally love to,' I say.

'*Amazing*. Can't wait to see you there. Bye, babes.'

She's hard to hate because she's so *everything*. She's gorgeous. She's rich. She's smart. And she can have any boy she wants.

Oh, to do high school on those terms.

As I watch her swish away, leaving a cloud of vanilla-scented air in her wake, I wonder what it would be like to be fawned over and adored wherever I went. I wonder what it would be like to have the crowds part before me to make room when I leave school, rather than weaving left and right to avoid the queues for the buses; to be bought bottles of Coke during lunch, instead of having them emptied over my head; to be accepted, not rejected.

I can but dream.

So, I guess this means I'm going to Wynter's Halloween party.

Wow.

OK.

Thank God I've been planning my outfit since last year.

WhatsApp Group Chat: Ballerz

Roman Bright

hey

Solange Burrell

sup

ok so something happened

Adam Chung

you've got my attention

i'm invited to Wynter's Halloween party!!!!!!!

Adam Chung

WOW

dead. literally

Solange Burrell

are you going?

WTF? Of course I'm going!!!! It's the party of the season

...

hello?

...

anybody have anything to say?

Adam Chung
such as

something along the lines of FML that's amaze

Adam Chung
FML that's amaze

now I know you don't mean it

Adam Chung
no I don't

rude

are you going to come with?

Solange Burrell

what do you think?

come on

you could be my guests

Adam Chung

i'd rather burn myself with cigarettes

Adam Chung

she's an epic bitch why would you want to go to her party???

IT'S THE PARTY OF THE SEASON

Adam Chung

says who

LITERALLY EVERYBODY

Solange Burrell

come on Roman we never go to that

coz we're never invited

Adam Chung

whatevs

true though

Solange Burrell

SO not interested

serious?

Solange Burrell

very

and I don't think you should go either

WHAT

Solange Burrell

seriously

Adam Chung

you know why she's invited you, right?

FOURTEEN

One of the perks of being in Year 11 is we can leave the premises at lunchtime, but only to go to the Subway in the village. There's a chip shop a bit further down the high street. It's far nicer, and far less crowded. Technically Year 11s aren't allowed to go there, but it's my firm belief that rules are made to be broken.

So, that's where I'm going.

As soon as the bell rings to signal the end of class, instead of heading to the main hall and our usual Ballerz table, I bound through the empty yard as quickly as I can. I wouldn't say I'm avoiding Adam and Solange on purpose per se, but I definitely feel like there's a teensy bit of tension going on since I accepted Wynter's invite. And I avoid tension like the plague, so chips for lunch it is.

When I get to the gate, I see someone else has got there first. Beau Greene is doing tricks with his skateboard on the pavement right outside, scraping it along the kerb, making the most annoying scratchy sound.

'Hey, Roman,' he says, as I scurry past.

'Hi,' I say, not stopping.

The sound of plastic wheels on pavement rolls up beside me. 'Hey. I never got to thank you.'

'. . . ?'

'The cereal bar.'

'Oh, right. Don't mention it. It was a gift – "to you, from me, Pinky Lee".'

I speed up. So does he. 'What does that mean?'

'It's nothing, just a quote from *Grease*.'

'What's that?'

'You've never seen *Grease*?'

He shakes his head.

'What – *never*?'

'Nope. Should I have seen it?'

'Who we are in *Grease* is who we are in life,' I say, flicking my head towards him. 'You're giving me serious Patty Simcox vibes right now.'

He looks at me like I'm speaking Russian, and I don't care to explain myself further, so I carry on walking as if he isn't beside me. But he is. He's right there, not taking the hint at all. And the silence is so awkward I could die.

'You going to Subway?' he says.

'No.'

'How's your lip?'

'Fine.'

'Did you go to a teacher in the end?'

'No.'

'Why not?'

'Because.'

'I think you should.'

'Look,' I say, giving him my death stare, 'it's really none of your business.'

The skateboard stops with a sudden clicking sound. And I carry on walking, chin poking high into the air because I'm sooo Rizzo right now.

But I only take a few steps before I do something strange, something totally un-Rizzo-ish, something I would never normally do.

I stop too.

I turn to see him, standing behind me. His curls have parted and I'm able to see the disappointment drawn across his not-too-displeasing face. And straight away I feel bad for being rude to him when, really, he was only being nice.

'Sorry,' I say. 'I didn't mean to sound . . . rude.'

He leans on the front of his skateboard and pushes off the pavement towards me. 'You didn't sound rude,' he says. '*Grease*. I'll definitely watch that one.'

'You should.'

I cross the road to the quieter side, the sound of wheels following close behind.

'So, if you're not going to Subway, where are you going?'

'Chippy.'

'You're such a rebel,' he says. 'I like it. Want some company?'

I don't. But I'm trying my best to not sound like an arsehole again, so I say, 'It's a free world, Beau Greene. You can go wherever you like.'

We take our chips to the top road that runs between the school and the high street, and stop to eat at the foot of a statue of Queen Victoria. She's sitting on a throne looking down on

Beau and me like some sad, lifeless deity turned green by time. I imagine she once looked majestic, but she's been humbled thanks to the bright orange traffic cone sitting on her head, and a healthy covering of pigeon shit left over the years. (I read somewhere that Queen Victoria threw the wonderful Oscar Wilde into Reading prison for being gay. This makes me think the pigeons have the right idea.)

'I can't believe you don't like ketchup,' he says.

'Ew,' I say, scrunching up my face, 'don't even . . . if you've got any there, I'm leaving.'

'Do you really hate it that much?'

'It's the devil's condiment.'

He laughs. 'That's ridiculous.'

'It's a very real phobia, actually.'

He watches me eat, following my hand from the tray to my mouth as I pick up every chip as delicately as I can. I hate people watching me eat.

'Why are you looking at me like that?' I say.

'I'm just trying to figure you out,' he says. He shoves a fistful of chips in his mouth and starts chewing really loudly.

'Beau, hun – give up now. It's never going to happen. You barely know me.'

'Isn't that the point?'

'What?'

'Well . . .' he begins, nervously pulling at the corner of his chip paper, 'I guess I'd like to know you more. Making friends here hasn't been as easy as I'd hoped.'

He carries on eating and it's my turn to watch. I look through the curls to his amber eyes. He has this intense stare thing going on, like his eyes are searching for the truth.

'Don't you have friends at all?' I say.

He shrugs. 'Not really.'

I press my lips together, because I don't really know what to say to this. I feel bad for him. Everybody needs friends.

'I suppose I'm pretty alternative,' he says. 'You can't be the new guy *and* be alternative. It's a recipe for disaster.'

'You're really honest,' I say. 'Too honest – kids at St Anselm's can sniff out vulnerability like a shark can sniff out blood.'

'I'm just . . . trying.' He shrugs.

'Trying?'

'To make friends.'

He smiles. And it's a warm smile, a kind smile, a smile aimed directly at me.

It's weird, but I feel like I'm seeing him for the very first time. Like all at once he's no longer Beau Greene from English class, the druggy, the waster, but some new person, a person who, like me, is on the outside looking for a way in. I know I have my queer sisters Adam and Solange, but as the only openly non-binary queer gay person in the village, I still often feel like an outsider, even amongst my friends. Sometimes they just don't get it. There comes a point when our different experiences limit our understanding of each other. I know this because if they really understood me, they'd understand what a big deal it is for me to be invited to Wynter's Halloween party. If they really understood me, they'd know how much it means for me to be included. The invitation to Wynter's party was the first time I've been invited anywhere as Roman, not Ryan. It's really, world-changingly huge, and they should recognise this. They should be at my side as I walk into Wynter's totally gorgeous house, not shunning me via WhatsApp.

I know what it's like to feel misunderstood. And I guess what Beau Greene is saying is that, as the only alternative new kid from out of town, he does too. We have a mutual understanding. There's a language between us, the language of outsiders, which sort of transcends everything else.

Which gives me a radical idea.

Beau's desperate plea to fit in might just make him the perfect plus one to accompany me to the most fabulous party of the season. I mean, it seems as if we're both in the same position here. It seems he needs this party just as much as I do.

And really, the only thing more tragic than not being invited to Wynter's party is being invited but turning up alone. This would put me in the company of the pity invites like family friends, relatives, neighbours, etc. (basically someone who doesn't attend St Anselm's, and therefore doesn't know how much of a big a deal Wynter actually is). Or, it makes me one of the losers who are only there so the popular kids have something to point and laugh at. I don't want to fall into either category, especially the latter.

'What are you going as for Halloween?' I say.

'What?' he says, clearly surprised at the sudden change in topic.

'Halloween. You. Costume?'

'I'm not going as anything. I'm not going anywhere that requires me to dress up.'

'That's incorrect on both accounts. You're coming to a party with me, and you're dressing up. Though,' I hasten to add, 'this won't be a joint costume vibe.'

'What party?'

'Wynter Brown's. She's rich. She always throws a blowout Halloween party at her parents' house. It's the event of the season, arguably as important as prom. Everyone will be there. Everyone will be drunk. And someone will definitely lose their virginity. So, what are you coming as?'

His mouth hangs open, guttural noises flipping and popping in his throat before he speaks again. 'I . . . I can't. I can't dress up.'

'Don't be ridiculous.'

'I'll probably have to stay at home with my sister, anyway.'

'Get a babysitter. It's like three weeks away; there's plenty of time. Didn't you hear what I said? It's the event *of the season*. Everyone who's anyone will be there.'

'Sounds like something out of *Bridgerton*,' he says, nervously biting his thumbnail.

I don't respond to this; I'm too busy thinking, my ideas taking flight on wings made of Billie Eilish wigs and Wednesday Addams dresses (the Tim Burton version, of course) and . . . 'Maleficent!' I say. 'You could come as Maleficent. *Omigod*. That would be stunning. I could make the horns out of papier mâché. We have loads of old newspapers in the house. Grandma gives them to Mam when she's finished with them—'

'I'm not dressing up as a girl,' he says quietly, like he's suddenly self-conscious.

'Who said Maleficent is a girl?' I say.

'Um, Angelina Jolie?'

'Maleficent is a magical creature; their gender shouldn't be assumed.'

'I'm still not going.'

'Beau, hun, this is going to get really boring *really* quickly. You're coming to the party if I have to skin you alive and wear *you* as a costume.' I look him up and down, seeing if any other ideas come to me. 'You could go generic and be someone from *Stranger Things*?' I say unenthusiastically.

'I don't want to be generic.'

'Well, at least that's something. Let's see, what about Pugsley Addams?'

'No.'

'You're right, what are we, twelve? *I've got it!* The Joker. The Joaquin Phoenix version, obviously.'

'Remind me of what that looks like again.'

I take out my phone and scroll through Google for the creepiest picture I can find. 'It's been done to death,' I say, holding it up. 'But I don't think I'm going to get much more out of you.'

'It's a cool film,' he says. 'And Joaquin Phoenix is a cool guy. I suppose I could do that.'

'Perfect! This'll wipe the smug looks off their faces.'

'Um. Off whose faces?'

'Doesn't matter,' I say, standing. I scrunch up my chip wrapper and throw it in the nearest bin. 'OK. Now where am I going to find a red blazer?'

FIFTEEN

Ms Mead is wearing a headband with a mini pumpkin on it. I think it's super cute (and sort of surprising) that she's made an effort. I didn't have her down as the type who got into Halloween. But, looking at her now, with her dark eyeliner and amethyst choker, I can see the faded remnants of a punk rocker. She's even gone to the trouble of decorating the classroom with orange and black streamers, and there's a cauldron full of Celebrations chocolates sitting on her desk. Though the empty wrappers clenched in her hand tell me she's the only one who's eaten any of them so far.

The class is excitable today, and for very good reason. It takes three hard bangs of Ms Mead's stapler against her cauldron to gain any sort of composure from us.

'Before we begin, I have a message from the head of the upper school,' she says, attempting to raise her voice, but sounding like she has a biscuit caught in her throat. The class groans as one, like a giant Halloween monster, rolling on to its belly. She reads: 'As St Anselm's students, I expect you all to adhere to the school's very high standards when celebrating in the local area over this All Saints' weekend. Please act accordingly. Any student found to be demonstrating disruptive behaviour will face severe consequences.

Northumbria Police have a very close relationship with our school. I have provided the officers on duty in the area this evening with a list of your names. You are being watched.'

I don't know why Mrs Duncan has to be such a killjoy. St Anselm's used to go crazy for Halloween. Every year we had a non-uniform day, basically an opportunity for girls in the upper school to dress like sex workers – which I loved. It was like *The Rocky Horror Picture Show* ('Do you think I made a mistake splitting his brain between the two of them?') every Halloween.

God. I used to look up to those girls so much, with their short skirts and box-dyed hair and lipstick. I remember thinking, *When I get into Year 11, I wish I could be just like them.*

And really, my wish came true. I don't need anybody to tell me my make-up looks fierce today. I'm all chocolate lips and smoky eyes. Very 90s *The Craft* vibes ('Light as a feather, stiff as a board . . . light as a feather, stiff as a board . . .'). There are probably some closeted queer kids in Year 7 and 8 looking up to me right now, wishing to be just like me one day. This makes me feel proud. Lord knows they certainly don't have anyone else to idolise. Apart from the odd cat-ear headband or black fluffy scrunchie, nobody in my year has made an effort at all.

When Mrs Duncan took over, she put an end to non-uniform day, and therefore any Halloween frivolity. Which is ironic, considering she's the biggest witch of them all. I suppose with her wardrobe, every day is Halloween.

(I have a theory about teachers. I think they were all made to feel small at some point in their childhood, leaving them with a need to assert authority in adulthood to make up for it. Mrs Duncan must have been made to feel microscopic.)

'Make of that what you will,' says Ms Mead. 'I have no intention of telling you how to live your lives. Personally, I can't see the appeal in partying. I'll be spending the evening watching *Interview with the Vampire* and crying into a glass of full-bodied Rioja, but the less said about that the better.'

'Am I still meeting you at the gate after school?' whispers Beau Greene, leaning into my ear.

'Yes. Why wouldn't you be?'

'I was just checking you hadn't changed your mind.'

Over the past few weeks, the thought had occurred to me. And I came very close to calling the whole thing off (something along the lines of 'I contracted hookworms in last lesson. Party's off'). But I thought better of it. The party is happening, which means I'm going, and I wouldn't be caught dead turning up alone.

'Party starts at seven p.m.,' I say. 'We'll be arriving at eight. *Obviously*. Which gives me a few hours to turn you into something spectacular.'

'The Joker,' he says, like it's really important.

'Yeah. The Joker.'

'The Joaquin Phoenix version.'

'Yes, Beau, the Joaquin Phoenix version.' I can tell he's really nervous, which is totally annoying. I don't have time to placate him. Tonight is all about me being my most fabulous self. 'Lighten up, will you? It's Halloween.'

SIXTEEN

After school, we walk along the top road into the village, Beau beside me on his skateboard. There are kids already out trick-or-treating with their parents, traipsing through the village in bin bags tied and cut in different ways (cinched at the waist means witch, frayed at the edges means monster, tied around shoulders means vampire. Who knew bin bags were so versatile?).

The pubs along the high street are decorated with caution tape, and cobwebs, and 'enter at your peril' signs written in red paint to represent blood. There are carved pumpkins and fairy lights dancing all the way down to the ruins of the old priory, which sits on a cliff at the end of the high street, overlooking the sea.

'Is it me, or is Halloween on steroids this year?' I say.

'You guys really go for it here,' he says. 'The last place I lived wasn't like this.'

'Where were you before here?'

'Oxfordshire. We were there for four years with my dad's work. We always move around.'

With this statement I realise I know very little about my new party companion/friend, Beau Greene. I guess I should show some interest.

'What does your dad do for a job?' I say.

'He works for the RAF.'

'I love a man in uniform.'

'Don't do that.'

I throw my hands up as if to say, *What?*

'Don't say that when we're talking about my dad.'

'I wasn't saying it about your dad *specifically*. I just mean in general. Chill out, Beau.'

He skates alongside me without saying a word. I've noticed awkward silences don't seem to faze him, because he slips into them quite often and seems fine with it. Meanwhile they literally make my toes curl in my trainers.

'What's your favourite Halloween film?' I say, in an attempt to cut through the atmosphere.

'I don't really have one.'

'*Everybody has one.* What did you like to watch when you were a kid?'

He takes longer than expected to think about this, as if I've just asked him some deep and meaningful question, like what's the meaning of life, or what exactly is scampi. '*Labyrinth.* David Bowie,' he says finally. 'I think he's incredible. He's a legend of our times.'

'Nice choice,' I say, before bursting into my rendition of 'You Remind Me of the Babe'.

'Amazing!' he says when I'm done, clapping his hands. 'Never mind the babe, you remind me of Bowie.'

'I do?'

'Yeah. Like, early Bowie. Ziggy Stardust, his alter ego during the early 1970s. You've got the same energy.' He takes another long pause. 'You're unique. You sort of have an alter ego too, like you used to be Ryan and now you're Roman.'

'I was always Roman,' I say assertively.

'I know. I get it. It's just, Roman is like the rock star side of you. I think it's amazing that you embraced that.'

He skates a little way ahead, leaving me alone with this comment, a comment that may be the nicest thing anyone other than Mam has ever said to me. Of course, I've always thought of myself this way. I just didn't think anybody else had.

'Do you really think so?' I call up to him.

'Yeah. Totally.'

'I wish everybody else thought like you.'

'Screw everybody else.'

He does this trick thing with his skateboard where he presses down on the back and quickly swivels, then he heads back towards me and loops around until he's at my side again.

'Are your other friends coming tonight?' he says.

'They've abandoned me,' I say.

'Seriously? They're not going to be there?'

'Nope.'

'Why?'

'Because . . . they don't like Wynter.'

He nods. 'Right.'

'And we're not really vibing at the moment anyway. They just . . . don't get me. It's fine. Whatever. Like, I get it. You do you, hun. But – I dunno, I thought they'd get how important tonight is for me.'

During the last few weeks, things have grown increasingly more awkward between the Ballerz and me. Whenever the word 'Halloween' comes up in conversation there's a deathly silence, which makes me think they're either planning to do something together tonight that they absolutely don't want me to know about, or they hate me for accepting Wynter's invite. Either way, I'm finding both Adam and Solange totally annoying right now. So I'm sort of glad I don't have to deal with them on the night when I want to sparkle the most.

'Why *is* tonight so important to you?' he asks.

Because this is the first time I've been invited anywhere as Roman, not Ryan.

Because this is the first time the pretty kids have included me.

Because being invited sort of legitimises my very existence.

Take your pick, Beau Greene.

Take.

Your.

Pick.

'It just is,' I say, shrugging.

He smiles. 'So, it's just you and me, then?'

'And everyone else from St Anselm's.'

'That's cool.'

I stop immediately, throwing my hands out dramatically, as if framing my face in a spotlight. 'Oh Beau, hun, "cool" doesn't even cut it. Tonight is going to be so much more than cool. Tonight is going to be *everything*.'

SEVENTEEN

Beau's costume (a red suit with one of my green shirts to go underneath) is hanging on the back of the wardrobe.

'*Ta-da*,' I say, presenting it. 'Perfect, isn't it? I found the suit at Tynemouth Market. You'll have to wear your own shoes, but nobody will be looking at them.'

'It smells.'

'It's vintage,' I say, wafting his comment away. Although he's totally right. The blazer still reeks of the dead person it once belonged to. 'Try it on.'

'Really?'

'Yes. I need to know it fits.'

He throws off his hoodie and unbuttons his shirt.

And for some weird reason I feel embarrassed, because, although it's just Beau Greene, there's a shirtless guy in my bedroom for the very first time.

I pass him the green shirt, and our hands accidentally touch. And there's this weird moment where he looks at me and I see something other than the curls and the moody expression. I see something other than the skater boy get-up. He looks sort of gap-year chic; he's wearing these multicolour beads around his neck with a shark tooth on them, and his abs are totally defined.

'Don't do that,' I say, as he fastens the very top button. 'It's not your school shirt. You want to look edgier.'

And I don't know why I do this, because he could absolutely do it himself, but I stand right in front of him, close enough to smell him (he smells surprisingly pleasant, like fresh bedding, dried in the sunshine) and I unbutton three of the buttons on his shirt for him, my fingers brushing against his warm neck, his defined Adam's apple.

'There,' I say. 'You look good. It's a bit oversized, but I think it all adds to the character. Now, let's get started on your make-up.'

'Make-up?'

'Clown make-up. Don't worry – you're not going to look like a drag queen. More's the pity.' I grab his shoulders and turn him to face the mirror. 'We need to get this hair out of the way first.'

I go into the bathroom and fetch some gel. Then I slather it over my fingers and run them through his curls. Using a wide-tooth comb, I slick his hair away from his face. (Very Danny Zuko.) It's amazing what a little bit of effort can do, because he looks great. Now that I can see his face properly, I'm noticing all sorts of things: how it's pretty symmetrical; how plump his lips are; how good his eyebrows are; how smooth his skin is. I pull my comb down the back of his head and notice he has a scar, hiding in between the curls, stretching horizontally across the right side behind his ear. Instinctively, I run my finger over it, and his eyes meet mine in the mirror. And for a moment I think he's going to tell me how he got it, but when he opens his mouth he says, 'What will you be wearing?'

I tilt my head to the side and look at my own reflection, giving him my strongest femme fatale pose: hands in pockets, eyebrows raised and lips firmly pouted.

'That, Beau Greene, is the question on everybody's lips tonight.'

I open the drawer of my dresser and pull out my make-up bag. Then I get started painting his face (white base, blue triangles around the eyes, giant red mouth). I can tell this is the best Halloween attempt he's ever made by the way he's looking at himself in the mirror (wide-eyed and wondering), and it's sort of giving me a kick. I'm enjoying him enjoying himself.

Once the make-up is done, I shake the can of green hairspray I bought on Mam's Amazon account, and completely cover his hair. And he's done. I must say, he looks amazing. The hair and make-up are really effective, and the vintage suit is nothing short of genius. He looks really authentic.

He lowers his chin and does this creepy smile in the mirror.

'You're really getting into character, aren't you?' I say.

Though his face is completely painted, I can tell he's blushing.

Of course, no matter how creepily he looks at himself in the mirror, none of Beau Greene's efforts are going to come close to the awe-inspiring gorgeousness of my costume. (Sorry not sorry.)

I slip off into the bathroom and zip myself into the red gown that fits my body within an inch of its life. Then I pin the crazy curly wig (which is actually two wigs – one white, one black – sewn together) to my head, and top it all off with this jewelled and feathered facemask, all so I look exactly like Emma Stone when she crashes the ball in the film *Cruella* ('I'm just getting started, daaarling').

As soon as I saw the movie about the villain character from *101 Dalmatians*, I knew she would be my Halloween inspiration. I love it when the villain gets a backstory, and we find out what made them turn so villainous. And Cruella de Vil really is the most fabulous villain of all. I've been working on this look for months. It's as if I knew Halloween was going to be important this year.

As I catch my glorious reflection in the bathroom mirror, I say a little *thank you* in my head to Wynter Brown, for giving me the chance to be this person, even if it is only for tonight. Without her, this outfit wouldn't get anywhere near the exposure it deserves.

'How do I look?' I say, twirling through the door into the bedroom.

'Are you really going like that?' asks Beau, suddenly standing.

'Excuse me?'

'I mean, you look good – very convincing. It's just . . . what will people think?'

I roll my eyes as I strut past him, because although we hardly know each other, I would have thought he'd at least know me better than this.

'Beau, hun – let's clear a few things up right now. Number one: it's Halloween. Number two: I couldn't give a shit. And, number three: everybody is expecting a certain level of *drama* from me. I'm Roman Bright. Me dragging up is as vital to this party as contraception.' With this little punchline, I waft him away from the mirror so I can strike my most

Cruella-ish pose. '*Simply faaabulous, darling.* Now, are you ready to go? Taxi will be here soon.'

'Yeah. I guess I'm ready, if you think I am?'

I pull him towards me so we're side by side in the mirror.

And we look really good together. I've turned him into the perfect party companion.

'I think we look pretty damn fabulous,' I say.

His mouth twists into a creepy smile.

Mam gives us a round of applause as we descend the staircase, pulling a party popper so a stream of rainbow glitter confetti falls over us.

'Oh, look at you two,' she says, pressing her hands against her cheeks. 'You both look fab!'

'Watch my wig,' I say, swinging around the banister and presenting myself as if I'm about to walk a red carpet.

Mikey is dressed as a pumpkin. He looks so cute wearing his little green hat. 'Look at you, my gorgeous one,' I say, stroking his cheek.

'Get together,' says Mam, 'let me have a picture to show the girls.'

'OK, but do it quickly. We're already fashionably late as it is.'

Beau and me squeeze together as the flash goes off.

'What time shall I book your taxi home?' says Mam.

'I'll message you. I don't want to put a time on it.'

'Fine. But nothing past midnight – I need to assert some sort of parental authority.'

'Why start now?' I say.

'You cheeky bugger. Does your mam let you stay out all night partying, Beau?'

'No,' he says, too quickly.

'You must think I'm terrible,' she says.

'Not at all.'

'Come on,' I say. 'Enough chatting – I have an entrance to make.'

EIGHTEEN

The house looks like something out of a Halloween film. The driveway is decorated with about a hundred pumpkins, and there's a staircase leading up to the open double doors that's covered in hanging cobwebs and cauldrons and all the other expected Halloween paraphernalia. There are people everywhere: in the front garden, sitting on the steps, hanging out of windows, dodging through the inflatable ghosts that are swaying in the wind; it looks like the entire school has turned up.

OK, Roman, I say to myself. *Shoulders back – tits first. Larger than life is just the right size.*

Wynter is standing at the top of the steps, as if she's been awaiting my arrival.

'Shut up!' she squeals.

She's wearing black leggings and a red top, and the most stunning ginger wig I've ever seen, styled in a 1940s wave (she can't have styled this herself). She has these creepy white contact lenses in too, and a circular mirror has been stitched into her top at the front and back, as if to resemble a hole.

'Oh my GOD!' I scream. 'Goldie Hawn in *Death Becomes Her*. I'm dead. Like, done. "Madeline, I need to speak to Madeline at once!"' I quote.

She even appreciates a classic Halloween film.

Could she be any more perfect?

'Let me have a look at you, you crazy bitch,' she says.

I give her and her harem a twirl. (They've all at least attempted to match her in the glamour stakes, but failed miserably; I see a sexy kitten, a fairy and a generic witch. *Yawn.*)

'Cruella,' she says. 'So imaginative. OK, so – drinks are in the kitchen. My mam made punch; it's super strong.'

'Amazing.'

'I'll be making my official entrance in about ten minutes. Make sure you're there.' (Of course she's making another entrance. She's so extra.) She grabs me by the shoulders and pushes me into the house. 'EVERYBODY – look who's here!'

The house smells of sugar and vomit. I strut through the crowds, embodying Emma Stone's *Cruella* – the outcast, the party-crasher, the punk. I figure that if I'm going to play the token queer I might as well go all the way and give them a show.

I'm met with cheering and applause, where I'd usually be met with jeering and laughter.

God. I love Halloween.

We head for the kitchen and Beau goes straight for the punch bowl, which is full of something bright green.

'What's in it?' I say.

'I can't be sure,' he says, sniffing it. 'It smells like the taste you get in your mouth when you drink orange juice right after you've brushed your teeth.'

'That'll be the alcohol,' I say. 'Pace yourself, Beau Greene – I'm not holding your hair back while you spew.'

The kitchen is full of costumes: Rhaenyra Targaryen (with inflatable dragon), Pennywise the clown, Barney the dinosaur (I wonder who's inside?), numerous random cast members from *Stranger Things* (of course) and zombies with blood and scars on their faces, all jumping up and down like lunatics. It's like these aren't St Anselm's students at all. Halloween has changed them, and for one night they're not judgemental. For one night they're free and open, and willing to accept me.

'I want to dance,' I announce.

'I don't dance,' says Beau.

'Don't be ridiculous.'

I strut on to the makeshift dance floor in the middle of the kitchen and throw my hands in the air. Then I start vogue-ing like my life depends on it, throwing my arms in every direction as if I'm on the TV show *Pose*, walking in a ball in New York City, not in a kitchen in Tynemouth village. I'm lost in my own fabulous world of parties and glitter and magical people. And it's truly wonderful and freeing and exactly how I thought it could be. Out of the corner of my eye, I see Beau's face crack into a smile. He starts to mimic me, doing this weird flailing thing with his arms. Before I know it, we're throwing some serious shade, trying to out-vogue each other. I didn't realise Beau was so limber. At one point he backbends all the way to the kitchen floor. I stand over him, framing my face with my hands (very Willi Ninja), and he tries to jump back up, but ends up falling back into Rhaenyra Targaryen, who spills her drink over Pennywise the clown. I laugh so hard my head throbs. I think it's funnier because Beau is so mortified.

'That was the funniest thing I've ever seen!' I shout above the music.

'It wasn't that funny,' he says.

But his words echo as if from somewhere else, another place, another time. I'm no longer there. And that's because someone special has walked into the room, and the world has stopped and there are only two of us left standing.

That's right – JJ Dixon has arrived.

From the moment I was invited, I knew he would be here. From the moment I was invited, all I wanted was for him to see me like this. I wanted him to notice me. I wanted him to look at me like he did on the beach, and then confirm what I already know. I want him to whisper in my ear that he is Big Red, and that our romance is alive and well because it never died, not really.

He's dressed as Superman. I have to talk to him. I have to. I know he's already noticed me, because everybody's noticed me. I'm Roman Bright – the most talked-about kid in school, dressed as punk Cruella. You'd have to be blindfolded not to notice me.

The music changes to 'Bad Guy' by Billie Eilish, and the world starts moving again. The kitchen goes mental. His mates start bouncing around him, doing weird dances to make him laugh.

Is there anybody in this room who doesn't want his attention?

He stands in the middle of them, tall and so damn handsome it hurts. If I can just get in his eyeline, if I can just get his undivided attention, then maybe I can convince him that we should go somewhere and talk. There has to be a quiet corner or a bathroom we could escape to. I'm guessing there are about seven in this house.

In a moment of pure adrenaline, I jump on the kitchen table and start lip-syncing for my life. And it's all eyes on me. His friends break apart and move towards the table to watch, and I can see he's watching me now too. It's working. It's really working.

I beckon him over and he shakes his head.

Come on, I mouth.

He shakes his head again. (This boy takes 'hard to get' to another level.)

The crowd is jumping, arms in the air, and the attention moves from me to loads of other places, loads of smaller groups dancing with each other. I need to get it back.

I throw my arms out either side as a signal that I'm going to go.

'TIMBER!'

Then I let myself fall.

The kitchen goes mental as I crowd-surf over heads towards him. And he sees me, and he's cheering, and everybody is screaming, as warm hands carry me right to him. I'm a bloody genius. It's like *Dirty Dancing* ('I carried a watermelon'), and I'm Baby and he's Johnny, and we were meant to be together from the beginning. He's looking into my eyes, and I'm looking into his, like there's no one else here, and I'm just about to reach him. I'm just about to make contact when . . .

Something happens. Something terrible and heartbreaking and wrong. Wynter appears – gorgeous, beautiful, cisgender Wynter. She holds out her hand and he takes it. She tilts her face up so she's looking up into his dreamy blue eyes, slotting into the space I should be as if she was meant to be there all along.

The arms holding me up thin out and I'm placed on the floor where the party carries on around me, but after being carried so high, I feel low, so low. All I can hear is my heart in my ears, beating so loudly the music disappears.

Why is she dancing with him? She doesn't like him. At no point in the years I've known her have I ever got the impression she likes him. And he's never mentioned her. There are no rumours at school about them. She's not the person for him. I am. I am the person for him. I am so obviously the person for him. *What is she doing?*

It gets worse. He cradles her face, his strong hands holding her perfect jawbone. She leans back, and it's like I'm watching a car crash, and I can't look away from the chaos, no matter how tragic and awful it is.

He tilts his head towards her, and with one final glance towards me, he kisses her.

I take in every detail: every fluid movement; every tender touch, here in her fabulous kitchen in her fabulous house full of fabulous people who love her so fabulously much.

I hear a smash, and I can't be sure if it's something glass or if it's my heart, shattering into a thousand irreparable pieces, because now Wynter Brown really does have it all.

Now she has him.

NINETEEN

'WHAT THE HELL WERE YOU THINKING?' screams Wynter.

She even looks pretty when she's annoyed. The end of her perfect little nose is glowing pink.

We're standing on the steps outside. I don't know how we got here. The last thing I remember is the kitchen, the kiss. The *only* thing I remember is the kitchen, the kiss. All other thoughts have left my mind because all other thoughts are insignificant in comparison to the moment you hear your heart breaking into a thousand irreparable pieces.

'The vase you smashed was a one-off!' she says.

And you think I have more than one heart?

'You threw a broom at me!'

'My hand slipped,' I say.

'Bullshit! I knew it was a mistake inviting someone like you.'

I don't have anything to say to this, because she's absolutely right. It *was* a mistake inviting someone like me to her perfect party at her perfect house with her perfect friends. It's always a mistake inviting someone like me anywhere. I'm so perfectly imperfect it's laughable.

'What did you say?' says Beau Greene.

'Excuse me?' says Wynter.

'You can't speak to people like that – who do you think you are?'

She rolls her eyes. 'Tell your boyfriend to shut up, *Ryan*.'

'You need to be careful, Wynter,' he says. 'Before you start playing your little games, you should know who you're up against.'

The harem squeezes in tighter, like bees protecting their queen.

'What's that supposed to mean?' she says.

He doesn't answer, just stares, the corner of his mouth curled up. For a moment it feels like I'm looking at the real Joker, like the Beau Greene under the make-up has disappeared and he actually is a creepy character from a Halloween film.

'It doesn't matter,' I say, grabbing his arm. 'Let's get out of here.'

TWENTY

The streets are packed with groups of kids clinging to orange pumpkin buckets and Sainsbury's shopping bags, which already look heavy with treats. Parents stand on street corners making small talk, while their little monsters run from door to door, frothing at the mouth with excitement. Older sisters walk in twos and threes, arms folded, talking about how *over* Halloween they are.

The pubs that line the high street are full of people now. Noise and coloured lights spill out on to the pavement every time a door opens, accompanied by the smell of perfume and alcohol.

And I don't know how the rest of the world can be so alive, when my world has just ended.

JJ kissing Wynter, the perfect embodiment of beauty and femininity, is too exquisite a pain for me to bear. In one kiss she's stolen everything from me. As if she doesn't have enough already.

'I hate her.' It comes out too easily.

'Ignore her,' says Beau.

'She's just so effing perfect.'

'She's not that perfect.'

'She is! She has it all. There's no competing with someone

like that. The world was designed for her.'

'You don't need her or her stupid party.'

'That's the thing – I do! Without her party I'm nobody. Without her party I don't matter.' My words are too visible in the cold night, swirling into the light of a street lamp, hanging in front of us as if the harsh truths I'm speaking are made of something heavier than just hot air.

'I thought you knew about JJ and Wynter. I thought everybody knew.'

'Knew what?'

His eyes begin to dart around me, as if they're following an invisible moth flying around my head. 'It doesn't matter.'

'What did you think I knew?'

'Nothing. It's nothing.'

'Beau – tell me!'

'That . . . they've been dating . . . since last term.'

No.

No, no, no.

'You're lying. I would know. I would've noticed. He would've told me.'

They can't have been dating since last term. They can't have been. There's just no way. Last term he was mine. He was definitely mine.

'Told you?' he says. 'But I thought you guys hated each other. After what happened at the end of the school year . . .'

His voice trails away but an echo rings off the back of his words, followed by a silence so huge I feel like I'm going to fall into it.

So even him, even Beau Greene – the new guy, the most

inconspicuous person at school – has an opinion on what happened last term. Even though I didn't know him then. Even *he* thinks he knows the ins and outs of JJ and me. It's as if I'm not even a person with feelings; my life is fodder for the St Anselm's rumour mill and nothing more.

I didn't think I could feel any worse.

But here I am, feeling worse.

Out of these feelings springs a memory from last term, from the night I spent with JJ. It's a memory I don't want to see right now, a memory I hoped I was done with . . .

He changes. In the blink of an eye he goes from really wanting me, to looking at me like I disgust him. And it's so jarring and strange that I begin to feel really self-conscious.

'Is everything OK?' I ask.

'Yeah,' he says, buttoning up his shorts. 'Totally.'

His face looks different; the light has left his eyes, the flush has gone from his cheeks, he's looking through me like I'm made of glass, as if what's going on behind me on the beach outside of the fish shack is way more important.

'JJ?' I say.

'I should get going,' he says. 'I said I'd meet the lads down on King Eddy's Bay.'

'I could come with you?'

'No. No, don't do that.' He lunges at the door and pulls it open. 'See you, then.'

'When?' I ask.

'Dunno?' he says, shrugging.

Then he's gone, hurrying across the sand, leaving me alone with all these weird, confusing feelings because I have literally no idea what's just happened between us . . .

'You don't know what happened last term,' I say, suddenly snapping out of the memory.

'I know you had feelings for him,' says Beau Greene. 'I know they gave you a hard time for it.'

He says it so easily, shrugging his shoulders as if it isn't important.

Of course that's what he's heard. Of course the word in the yard, or the main hall at break times, is it was all me. *I* had feelings for him. It was one-sided. The queer kid had unrequited feelings for the straight kid, and ended up with a bottle of Coke over their head for being so weird, and pathetic, and wrong. *That's what happened, isn't it?* I mean, why spoil a good story with the truth?

I turn my back on him and head up my street alone, because I don't have the energy to defend myself right now. I don't have the energy for anything that's happened tonight. I feel like I'm back there, standing alone in the fish shack, filled to breaking with all of these heavy, dark, confusing thoughts.

'Is that you, Roman?' Mam shouts, as I storm through the front door. I don't answer her, just carry on along the hallway, Beau Greene walking somewhere behind me because he needs to collect his things from my room.

'Why are you back so soon?' she says, appearing from behind the living room door.

'Because Wynter Brown is an epic bitch,' I say, lifting my gown so I can climb the stairs.

'Oh, lover – what happened?'

I could answer her question. I could make up a story about how fine and unbothered I am, like I usually do, because it's what she needs to hear. But there's no room inside me for lies. I can't pretend tonight, not even for her.

'I'm going upstairs,' I say.

'Don't do that,' she says. 'Stay down here with me. We can talk about it.'

'I don't want to talk about it, OK?' I say.

And I know I sound totally harsh right now, but I really just need to be in my bedroom and away from the pitying look in her eyes.

'Are you OK, Beau?' I hear her ask, as I stomp up to the landing. 'Can I get you anything?'

'I'm OK,' he says. 'I think I'll get my stuff and go.'

The first thing I see in my bedroom is my school bag, sitting open by the bed. I dive straight in, without the intervention of reason, rummaging until my hands find the Yves Klein postcards somewhere near the bottom.

'Here,' I say, handing them to Beau as he walks in behind me. 'Read them.'

'What are they?' he says.

'Just read them.'

He takes them from me, reading one, and then the other. 'Who is Big Red?'

'JJ Dixon.'

'*What?*'

'You might think you know everything, Beau, but you don't. Nobody does.'

'These are from JJ Dixon?' He sounds confused.

'I know what you're thinking,' I say. 'Why would someone as perfect as him like someone like me? But he's the one who started this whole thing. *He* suggested we meet up that night. *He* kissed me, not the other way round. *He* wanted me.'

I catch myself in the mirror when I say this, wearing Cruella, the Halloween equivalent of a ballgown, and I suddenly realise why I was so desperate to wear her tonight. She looks so much like a prom dress. And I so wanted to be his prom queen tonight, but my own version of a prom queen, my own queer, Halloween, non-prom version of a prom queen.

'I can't believe he's done this to me again,' I say.

'I had no idea,' says Beau. And I know he's looking at me with the same pitying eyes he looked at me with in the bathroom that day, and I can't look back.

'Why would you?' I say. 'I never told anyone.'

'But you should have! You should have gone to a teacher, or something.'

'It would have been an absolute waste of my time – who is going to believe the queer kid over the captain of the football team?'

'I would choose you over JJ any day,' he says, shrugging his shoulders so easily, as if anybody else would do the same. (I know they wouldn't.)

He walks over to the dressing table to change out of his costume, taking one final glance at his Joker make-up in the mirror before pulling off the suit and folding it neatly over the back of the chair. Then he quickly pulls on his school trousers and hoodie. On the dresser there's a packet of baby wipes. He takes one out and begins to wipe away the make-up.

'That guy is bad news,' he says to his reflection. 'I can't believe he let that happen to you last term, if all along it was him . . . and then tonight – kissing Wynter right in front of you? What a dick.'

'He's not a dick,' I say. As soon as it comes out of my mouth I feel sort of pathetic, because I shouldn't be defending him right now. His name should taste like dirt in my mouth.

'Well, it's a pretty dick-ish move.'

'Can we just talk about something else?' I say, though all I really want to happen now is for Beau to leave so I can be alone with my thoughts.

We fall into one of Beau Greene's famous awkward silences, which feels so much worse right now because the inside of my head is so loud.

'Or not,' I say, holding my hands up in defeat. 'Let's just hash out my life dramas until I'm a quivering mess on the floor.'

'You want to talk about my life dramas instead?' he says.

'Yes. No. I don't know. I want to talk about anything other than what's just happened.'

More silence, longer this time. It makes the hairs on my arms stand on end.

He takes a deep breath, 'My dad is the only drama I have, really.'

'Your dad?'

'Yeah.'

'Because he works away?'

'Sort of. It's complicated . . . do you really want to hear about this?'

'I need the distraction,' I say, nodding.

He hesitates, takes a breath, scratches his fingers through his still-green curls, holding his hand at the back of his head. Then he says, 'We had an argument before moving here. He said some things – did some things – and I don't know if I can forget them. And now he's thousands of miles away so we can't sort it out. There. That's my drama.'

'What things?'

'He went through my phone and found some messages he didn't like, and we had a bad row.'

'You rowed over messages?' Despite myself, I'm a little intrigued now.

'We rowed over messages, over him going through my phone, over what a disappointment of a son I am to him. We rowed over pretty much everything, really. I guess we're not "vibing" at the moment.'

He smiles at me when he says this, but I sort of miss it because my attention is suddenly drawn elsewhere, because my phone is lighting up on the bed next to me.

And I truly cannot believe what I'm seeing.

JJ Dixon

hey Cruella

It's all I can do to stare at the screen, because I don't know what else to do. I mean, he's got to be kidding. He's humiliated

118

me in front of the entire school (again), and now he thinks it's OK to message, like this is all some super fun Halloween party game. (What would the game be – Pin the Tail on the Pariah? Bobbing for Homos? Or how about just whacking the Roman-shaped piñata until they're nothing but an empty shell?)

'Roman?' says Beau. 'Are you OK?'

I don't answer him. Instead, I pick up my phone and begin to write, furiously, my fingers moving quicker than I thought possible.

Roman Bright

are you joking?

JJ Dixon

joking?

why don't you go and kiss Wynter Brown

you seemed to be enjoying that

you sound pissed off

i am

cos I kissed her?

you came with that new boy fair's fair

i know you've been seeing her since last term

who told you?

does it matter?

i'm not seeing her

you're lying!!!

why don't you believe me?

why should I?

because you remember last term

you remember that night

you still like me

And it's as if the wind leaves my sails. I want to stay mad at him. I want it more than anything. I should be doing exactly what Cosmopolitan.com told me to do, deleting his number and deleting him from my life. But I'm not, because he's right. He's speaking directly to the most powerful part of me, the part that still believes in romance, that still believes he's my happily ever after: my heart. It's like he has a direct line to it, and it wants more than anything to listen.

I feel betrayed. Not by him, or Wynter, but by myself. My heart has betrayed me, whispering things like, *At least he's messaged you* and *What about Big Red?* and *This, whatever it is, has to be better than nothing at all!* in a familiar, comforting voice, like I'm supposed to trust it.

'Is it JJ Dixon?' says Beau.

'He's just messaged,' I say.

'You're joking? That guy is such a player.'

He *is* such a player. It's so obvious. He's such a player. Tonight proves it. So, what in gay hell am I doing?

'If it weren't for this Big Red stuff I'd delete his number,' I say. 'I'd delete him from my life. Done.' I nod as I say it because I need it to be true. I need to believe I haven't lost my mind, or that I'm some kind of masochist who enjoys being treated like absolute shit.

'And the reason you won't is because he sent you postcards?' says Beau, scrunching up his face like fish and chip paper.

'He painted the murals too. You must have seen them around school.'

'He did those?'

'The better ones he did, yeah. We've got this secret thing going on.'

'Have you talked to him about it? Is JJ even any good at art?'

'No I bloody haven't! I'm not supposed to know. That's the secret part.'

There's a beat of silence. 'Do you realise how weird that sounds?' Beau asks.

To anyone else it might sound weird. But it doesn't to me because I know how JJ operates. 'I just don't know why he kissed her,' I say.

'He kissed her because he's a dick,' says Beau.

Heart: He did it to protect his secret.

Heart: He did it because he was jealous.

Heart: He did it because he's still so madly in love with you he can't bear to see you with another guy, even if it is Beau Greene. Why else would he message you right away?

'I was just about to tell you about Dad when he interrupted me,' he says.

'Sorry,' I say, 'what were you saying?'

'Doesn't matter,' he says, picking up his schoolbag.

'I'm listening,' I say, though I'm definitely not. Not really.

'Look – it doesn't matter. Let's just go back to plotting our revenge on JJ Dixon.'

I roll my eyes. 'Oh, don't joke.'

He throws up his hood, and though the make-up has been wiped away, for a moment I think I can see the Joker again.

'I wasn't,' he says.

*

At some point he leaves.

At some point I climb out of Cruella and stuff her in the wardrobe.

At some point I climb into bed and pull the covers over my head.

I lie there, not sleeping, the kiss replaying over and over in my head. I really don't know how I'm going to come back from this. I really don't know how I'm going to mend a second time.

TWENTY-ONE

Mam always says when you find yourself getting stuck you should retrace your steps and unpick the thread until you arrive at the point where it all went wrong.

So I'm standing outside the art block, looking up at the face sprayed on the uniform grooves of a brick wall.

The weekend was a blur. I guess I just retreated into my bedroom. I returned to darkness with nothing but the clock on my bedside table for company. And it was really bloody horrible to go back to that place, to be that person again, as if I haven't progressed at all since the summer. It was really bloody horrible.

'It's quite something, isn't it?' says Mr Sharpe, appearing from somewhere behind me (in a cloud of smoke, quite literally). 'There was talk of painting over it, but I fought my corner and – miraculously – won. This department has needed some TLC for a while now.'

I can't remember the art block without it now. I feel like it's always been here, screaming for my attention in this quiet corner of the school.

'The same person painted the old lido on Longsands beach,' I say.

'Is that so?'

'Big Red.' I brush my hand over the name. 'They painted wings.'

'They?'

'I didn't do it,' I say, because I can feel him watching me, as if a confession is imminent. 'If that's what you think, I'm afraid you're mistaken, sir. In fact, I don't even have any idea of what it's supposed to mean. I wish I did.'

'Mean? I don't know if it necessarily has to mean anything.'

I shake my head, because I don't agree. Mr Sharpe is always harping on about 'the inspiration': the artist's motivation, or the idea behind the work. This painting definitely means something. It was Big Red's first gesture, JJ's first declaration of I-don't-know-what. Up until Friday evening I was pretty sure it had something to do with him and me. An acknowledgement that he showed one face to me, and another to the world. An apology for being two-faced. Now I'm not so sure. Now, instead of a face with two sides, I'm realising this could be two faces kissing; it could be Wynter and JJ. I could have been mistaken all along.

'What do *you* see?' I ask. 'When you look at it – what do you see?'

'Come on, Roman, we're about to start.'

'Please.'

He sighs a smoky breath and takes a few steps back. 'I see conflict. I see a struggle between light and dark.'

Of course he does. It's a face with two sides. 'But what does that even mean?'

He looks at me, kind, caring Mr Sharpe, his bushy eyebrows knitting together. And the weight of my problem grows even heavier, making it hard to move, hard to breathe. I'm not really asking him about the painting. The painting is secondary to what's really going on. I'm asking for help. I'm asking him to rescue me, because I think I'm drowning again.

'Roman, is everything OK?'

'I'm fine . . .'

My chest feels tight, as if I'm suddenly breathing through smoke.

'Are you sure?'

I throw my shoulders back, and with all the strength I can muster, I scrape out a lie from somewhere at the bottom of a very dirty barrel. 'I'm completely fine, OK? Why wouldn't I be?'

'You seem a little preoccupied.'

'Busy people are always preoccupied, sir. And I'm practically rushed off my feet.'

'You can talk to me,' he says, ignoring my little act. 'It doesn't have to go any further if you don't want it to.'

I swallow, hard, ensuring any feelings are sent safely back down where they belong.

'Class is about to start, isn't it?' I say, turning towards the door.

And then I walk into the building.

As soon as I walk in I see Solange, set up in her usual corner. I throw her whatever kind of smile I can muster, and she returns it with this weird look, as if to say, *We need to talk*. I slide into my chair and nod, although I really can't think of anything worse than one of Solange's lectures about how I shouldn't have gone to Wynter's party right now.

I think it would tip me over the edge.

The studio is full of whispers today. You can usually hear a pin drop as we all chip away at our respective masterpieces. But today the dust hangs heavy with gossip, rumours repeated from easel to easel as the whole of Year 11 waxes lyrical about Wynter's absolutely iconic party. (I imagine her Olympic gold medal/OBE/Nobel Prize for Being So Everything is in the post.)

Of course, I hear JJ's name a lot. Wynter and him are the talk of the school thanks to a series of social media posts showing them kissing on Halloween night, meaning they're now officially official.

And I'm officially at my lowest ebb.

I should have taken the day off. Today should have been filled with endless bowls of cereal, and pyjamas, and *Loose Women*, instead of this utterly thunderous bullshit.

I'm way too fragile to listen to this.

Headphones in for the rest of class, I think.

After the bell rings, I don't wait for Solange; I make a brisk exit and head straight for my locker. But I don't quite make it there. Wynter Brown is standing blocking the hallway, her harem huddled round her in a thicket of whispers. She looks upset, like she's been crying. I wonder why. I mean, what the hell has she got to cry about? She's just hosted the party to end all parties – which no one can stop talking about – and bagged herself the hottest guy who ever walked the earth. If I had her life, I would kiss the ground every morning. I would leave offerings to the gods of luck and love. I certainly wouldn't be crying like some ungrateful brat.

I drop my head to hurry past, but before I can, she stops me.

'I'm surprised you're able to show your face,' she hisses.

Usually I'd let words like these roll off my back, but today my venomous hatred for her won't allow it.

'What?' I say, as sharply as I can.

'After what you did.'

I can't believe she's still going on about her stupid vase. 'What happened, happened,' I say with a shrug.

The harem gasp as one; I have who-knows-how-many sets of overly lined eyes staring at me, spidery lashes clinging to the edges. 'He doesn't even feel bad about it,' one of them whispers.

I take a deep breath, because I'm getting annoyed. Why should I feel bad for breaking her stupid vase when she broke my stupid heart? 'Sorry.' It comes out more like a grunt than a word.

'It's too little too late,' Wynter says haughtily. 'I know you've always been jealous of me, but doing this just to hurt me is so wrong.'

(*Blimey*. She must have really loved that vase.)

'Oh yeah? What are you going to do, Wynter – report me to the vase-smashing police? It was a bloody accident . . . well, sort of . . . but that's not the point—'

'Vase?' she says, her pretty face pressing into a question mark. 'You think this is about the vase?'

'Yeah. What else?'

'This is about JJ.'

His name in her mouth is enough to make me want to

projectile vomit all over her perfectly laundered uniform. How dare she say it so easily, like she owns him, like she got there first. He was mine before he was hers. She should be asking for my permission, or something, shouldn't she? I mean, just because they're TikTok official now doesn't mean she can sweep me to the side like, like . . . well, like shards of broken vase.

'I don't want to talk about that.'

'But you're not going to deny it.'

'Deny what?' I am well and truly confused now.

She takes a step towards me, her usually beautiful eyes thinning into reptilian slits, not a good look on anyone.

'I'm going to make sure everybody knows it was you. I'm going to make sure everybody knows how obsessed you are with my boyfriend. I'm going to make sure everybody knows exactly why you did it, *Ryan*.'

And with that, she and her harem trounce off, leaving me alone, and more at a loss than ever.

TWENTY-TWO

'He's been attacked,' says Adam. 'How can you not know? It's all over school.'

'Headphones. Wait. Attacked? Like, *attack* attacked?'

'It happened on Friday,' says Solange. 'I tried to tell you in art.'

'Shit. Is he OK?'

It's already dark. We're sitting on the green at the end of the high street. Two people in high visibility jackets are clearing up the mess left over from Halloween, throwing lager cans and glass beer bottles into industrial-sized bin bags. I only wish chucking a few things into a bag could clear up my own Halloween mess.

'But the party was on Friday,' I say.

'It happened when he was walking home,' says Solange.

'No way,' I say.

'Yes way,' says Adam. 'His face is a mess, apparently.'

It only takes a second for the light bulb to go off above my head.

When it does it's more of an explosion.

'Oh my GOD!' I say, throwing my hands to my face. Now I understand why Wynter was being such a cow. Now I understand completely. 'She blames me.'

'Who does?' says Adam.

'I threw a broom and smashed a vase, and now she thinks my jealous rage made me attack him too.'

'*Who does?*'

'Who do you think? His perfect new girlfriend.'

I hate even saying the word. *Girlfriend*. He shouldn't have a girlfriend. It sounds so wrong, because I've already thought of what my official title would be when I take my rightful place at his side. *Theyfriend*. (I know. Iconic.)

'Wynter thinks you attacked JJ?' says Solange.

There it is – their names, spoken together like they're one thing now, one beautiful unit of love brought even closer together by this dramatic incident as the plot thickens. He's the wounded white knight. She's the virtuous ingénue. And I, once again the villain of the piece, am about to be burnt at the stake for witchcraft.

Olivia Newton-John, take the wheel!

'She threw me out of her party.'

'She's such a twat,' says Adam.

'We told you not to go,' says Solange.

I begin to pace, biting the skin off the end of my thumb. 'This is bad.'

'It's not that bad,' says Solange. 'Look, if you didn't do it, what does it matter? This is no different to any of the other lies she spreads. The truth always comes out eventually.'

'This is different!' I say. 'I'm going to look like some lecherous creep who can't let him go. This is going to ruin everything! *Omigod.*' I throw my hand to my mouth. 'Have I just been cancelled? I have, haven't I? Wynter's cancelled me. *Shit*. I'm Chrissy effing Teigen.'

'You're not Chrissy Teigen.'

'I totally am! They're going to chase me out of the village with pitchforks.'

'Where would you get a pitchfork from around here?' asks Adam mildly.

All of a sudden my fear is no longer a memory; it's real, it's happening right now. I'm a target again, just like I was last term. And right away I feel like I have to get out of here; I feel like I have to get back to my bedroom where I know I'll be safe and nobody can pour any soft drinks over my head.

'Where are you going?' asks Solange as I stand up.

'Home!' I say, stomping to the edge of the green.

'Hiding will only make things worse, Roman,' says Adam. 'We've been through this.'

'Why is everything always my fault?' I shout. 'Why is it always me?'

'It's not!' says Adam.

'Stop, Roman,' calls Solange, but I continue to walk away.

'If I get drenched in Coke, it's my fault. If someone paints a mural on the art block wall, it's my fault. And if someone gets attacked on Halloween night . . . you guessed it . . . IT'S MY BLOODY FAULT!'

With this, I begin to run, without looking back, as if I'm running for my life.

TWENTY-THREE

By first break the next day, the whole school knows that I attacked JJ in a jealous rage because I'm still completely – and pathetically – obsessed with him. So begins Wynter Brown's reign of terror. And who's going to argue with the prettiest/richest/smartest girl in school? Nobody. That's who. Arguing is futile. Denial is hopeless. As far as everyone else is concerned, I'm guilty as charged. I hear their whispers everywhere I go. They hang in the air like cobwebs. Some say I broke his jaw/ribs/wrist. Some say I scratched his eyes out and now he's blind.

And some (Tyler Hudson) say the most horrendous things, accusing me of all kinds of assault as if all queer people are sexual predators waiting to catch unsuspecting straight folk down dark alleys on Halloween night. (I mean – WTF?)

Essentially, I'm treated like Frankenstein's monster.

It leaves me no choice but to do the one thing I promised myself I wouldn't do this year. It leaves me no choice but to do the one thing Mrs Duncan made me promise I wouldn't do at the beginning of term. It leaves me no choice but to miss days, and skip lessons.

It leaves me no choice but to hide.

I avoid the yard and main hall at lunchtimes. I avoid busy corridors in between classes. And I avoid Adam and Solange, my friends, because even they don't know what this feels like. They've never been made to feel like *this* much of an outsider. Never. They've both been accepted into various groups over the years: Solange is in art club, and clearly adored by the artsy kids, whether she buys into it or not. And Adam is so obviously hilarious that wherever he goes people warm to him. There's power in being funny; the laughter is never aimed directly at him. I don't have this. I've never had this.

It's just me, alone, again.

TWENTY-FOUR

There comes a knock on the cubicle door, and I nearly jump out of my furs.

'It's only me,' says Beau.

'You almost gave me a heart attack.'

'Can I come in?'

I slide the lock across to let the door fall open slightly, stopping it with my hand.

'Why are you wearing sunglasses inside?' he asks.

'Because I'm in mourning for my soul.'

'You know, you're only letting them win by hiding.'

'I'm not letting them do anything. They *have* won. That's why I'm hiding.'

'They've only won if you say it's over.'

'Well, I do. It's over. There. I said it.'

'I don't think that's true,' he says, his hand diving into his pocket and pulling out a scruffy-looking pink envelope with my name on it. 'Here.'

I raise my eyebrows as if to say, *What's this?*

'It's an invitation,' he says. 'To a party.' He smiles, and a shallow laugh escapes through his nostrils. 'But try not to throw any brooms this time.'

'Way too soon,' I say, snatching the envelope from him.

I dig my finger under one corner and tear it open. Inside there's a folded piece of paper with a rainbow unicorn on it. 'Cindy Greene is turning seven,' I read aloud.

'It's my sister's birthday party. It's just a little afternoon thing at home. Mum told me I have to be there, because Dad isn't going to be. Again. She said I could bring a friend. That's where you come in. I thought it would cheer you up.'

'You thought wrong.'

'It'll be fun,' he says, shaking his hands like he's about to break out into a song and dance.

I go to push the door shut again, because I don't want to talk any more; I'd like to continue wallowing in the art block bathroom alone.

'Roman – you're coming to the party,' he says, stopping the door from closing with a hand, 'even if I have to skin you alive and wear you as a costume.'

'Very funny.'

'I went to Wynter's for you . . .'

'And look how well that turned out.'

'. . . so you're coming to my sister's for me,' he finishes, ignoring me.

'I'm not.'

'It's on Saturday. It'll only be a few hours. Mum would like to meet you.'

Surprised that he's mentioned me to his mam, I relax my hold on the door, but with Beau still pushing against it from the other side, it flies open and bangs off the partition wall with an almighty *SMACK!*

'Bloody hell!' I say.

'You're so jumpy today.'

'And wouldn't you be if the entire school wanted you hung, drawn and quartered?'

'You're being dramatic. I heard some Year Nine kid defend you earlier, by the vending machines.'

I slide my sunglasses to the end of my nose. 'You did?'

'Yeah. Someone was calling you a rapist, and this Year Nine kid said you didn't rape JJ, only made him go blind, or something . . . ?'

The sunglasses get firmly wedged back up. 'Is that supposed to make me feel better?' I say, grabbing the door again. 'Screw them all! Screw you for telling me – and screw your stupid party!'

He slips into the cubicle before I can shut him out.

'Get out!'

'Look – I'm just trying to show you that it doesn't have to be this way. You don't have to let them get to you this much.'

'That's easier said than done.'

'Come to the party. I sprayed my hair green for you; you can at least do this.'

'*I* sprayed your hair green. If anybody owes anybody anything, it's—'

'Please, Roman.'

'Why me? I'm only going to sit in the corner and make everybody else feel as miserable as I am. I'll be a terrible party guest.'

'Look, you don't have to be anyone other than yourself. I just want my family to meet you.' He smiles really broadly, clenching his teeth so he looks like that toothy-smile emoji.

There's something different about him today. He doesn't look as tired, doesn't look as hidden. Either he's happier, or we've swapped and I'm the tired, miserable, looks-like-I'm-on-drugs one now. It's probably the second.

'Did you cut your hair?'

'No.' He shrugs his shoulders – they go up and down so easily, so lightly, when they usually look like they're carrying the weight of the world on them.

'Why do you want your family to meet me anyway?'

'Because . . . you're my friend.' He gives me the cheesiest grin ever, which makes what's left of my fragile glass heart twinge a little.

'Oh for God's sake,' I say. 'Fine! But stop being all like that – it's freaking me out.'

'So . . . that's a yes?' he asks hopefully.

'It's a pencilled yes – very faintly drawn, barely visible on the page.'

'I'll take that,' he says.

Then he quickly walks out before I have time to change my mind.

WhatsApp Group Chat: Ballerz

Solange Burrell

how you feeling Roman?

Roman Bright

two words

Chrissy

Teigen

Adam Chung

you wish, sis

Solange Burrell

it will blow over by the end of the week

Adam Chung

i don't know you know

thanks

not you Adam

Adam Chung

rude

Solange Burrell

what are you doing Saturday night?

nothing

Solange Burrell

old skool Ballerz sleepover?

???!!!

Adam Chung

YES!

really?

Solange Burrell

yes

you can even pick the film

Adam Chung

god

ok

Adam Chung

no Bette Midler though

TWENTY-FIVE

Saturday morning.

I roll out of bed and creep over to my bedroom mirror, deflating into a heavy sigh as I see myself.

'Olivia Newton-John, give me strength.'

How am I supposed to pull a party look together when I'm feeling so completely off my A game? I'm not even confident in my ability to brush my own teeth right now, never mind get dressed.

I dive, hands first, into the wardrobe, hoping the queer gods will guide me towards something effortlessly fabulous. They owe me right now after completely abandoning me on Halloween night.

The first fabric to brush against my hands is silk, ruched and gathered in all the right places, with a tulle underskirt for volume.

'Cruella,' I whisper.

I grip her tightly and pull her towards me.

The Halloween I had planned for this dress was exceptional. I was going to be the talk of the school, but for all the right reasons. I was going to show JJ exactly who I was, channel my inner Emma Stone, surprise him with how beautiful and feminine I could be. This dress was going to be the moment everything changed. This dress was going to be me at my most powerful.

'How did I get it so wrong?' I say, rubbing blood-red silk between my thumb and forefinger.

I really wish I knew the answer to this.

How depressing that she's been buried in here without so much as a few kind words, never mind a funeral. I didn't make her for this; I didn't spend all those hours getting her as close to the dress in the film as possible for her to die amongst the mothballs. It makes me so sad.

I pull her out and hang her on the wardrobe door. I don't think she's appropriate for a seventh birthday party; she's far too wild, but her time isn't over. Not yet. She can hang here, in the light, until I know what to do with her.

'You'll get your moment,' I whisper, giving her a final flourish with my hand.

I reach for my faux fur headband – the one that I added the totally epic jewelled brooch to – and put it on, making sure the brooch sits just off-centre.

OK.

This is definitely a start. And, might I add, quite a fabulous one. (Why just be extra, when you can be *the most?*)

I tilt my head from left to right, taking all of me in, the jewelled headband sparkling in the light.

Oh, who the hell am I kidding?

I can always pull a look together.

TWENTY-SIX

Beau is already waiting for me on the doorstep under a pink and white balloon arch with *Happy Birthday Cindy* written on it in gold letters. As I approach the house, I can hear music and chatter and screaming kids.

'You came!' he says. He's wearing an Olaf hat. 'I'm so glad.'

'I said I would, didn't I?'

'Come in; I was just about to light the candle on the cake.'

Candles. Cake. Joy. Noise.

I'm already yearning for a standard Saturday of bed and cereal (because that's what weekends are for, right?).

But before I can run towards the priory cliffs and jump into the sea, Beau grabs my wrist and pulls me into the sweet-smelling madness of a house full of sugar-fuelled seven-year-olds on a Saturday afternoon.

Lord, have mercy on my eardrums.

Straight away, before I even have time to check my make-up in the hallway mirror, I'm dragged into the front room, where about twenty kids are dancing to some song from *Moana*. Around them, perched on the arms of three very plush-looking sofas, are the children's parents, poised and proud, watching their little darlings wreak havoc on the soft furnishings.

'This is my friend Roman,' Beau shouts above the noise,

which is totally unlike him. I've never heard him raise his voice.

Not that it makes any difference; not one of the kids stops what they're doing or pays the tiniest bit of attention. They think *Moana* is far more interesting than me. (Oh how little they know.)

However, one of the adults jumps up off the sofa and smiles her way towards me, dimples appearing in her cheeks. And I know this has to be Beau's mum. She looks just like him.

'It's so lovely to finally meet you,' she says, pulling me in for a hug (which actually feels really nice – she smells like lavender). 'Beau has told me so much about you.'

I turn to face him. 'Oh, he has?'

'He didn't say anything about bejewelled headbands, though,' she says.

'You like?' I say, fanning my hands around my face.

'You look gorgeous.'

I could say the same thing to her. She's wearing a houndstooth-patterned jumpsuit, tailored to perfection, and patent leather loafers. OK. So, *gorgeous* doesn't even come close.

'I haven't said that much about them,' says Beau. 'You make it sound like I talk about Roman all the time.'

She raises an eyebrow. 'OK. OK. I'll stop with the clichés. But it is lovely to finally meet you, Roman. I'd say grab a seat, but we're all pretty packed in here.'

'I was just about to do the cake,' says Beau.

'Good thinking,' she says. 'The sooner we get that part out of the way, the sooner we can all get on with our weekend. Am I the only one around here who thinks weekends should be spent wearing PJs and eating cereal?'

I audibly gasp. With this statement she's just secured her spot in the cool mam hall of fame for all eternity.

'Cake,' says Beau.

I follow him along the hallway into the kitchen. 'OK, so she's fabulous,' I say. 'Why didn't you tell me your mam was so . . . everything?'

'Um, because she's my mum?'

'Fair point.'

'Come and look at this,' he says, beckoning me over to a white box, which is sitting on the bench.

I peer inside and see the cake I only wish I had at my seventh birthday (and every other birthday thereafter). It's the stuff dreams are made of: pink and sparkly and fabulous, with sugar roses nestled between glittery stars and snowflakes, all swirling around an enchanted castle centrepiece. Stunning. My eyes become dry from staring. I'm like a moth to a flame when it comes to inanimate items of sheer femininity. Always have been. 'Wow. Don't tell me your mam made this? I may have to ask her to adopt me.'

'It's pretty special, right? One of the bakeries in the village made it. Gayle's, I think?'

'A bespoke birthday cake from Gayle's? Bougie.'

'It's not that bougie.'

'It's pretty damn bougie – the only bespoke birthday cake *I've* ever had was made by my grandma. Let's just say it didn't look like this.'

He opens a drawer and pulls out a box of matches. 'Are you in fine voice today?' he says, shaking out a rhythm with the box as if it's a percussion instrument. He starts singing

'Happy Birthday' in a Spanish accent as he shakes his way around the kitchen. And it's so silly, especially in the Olaf hat, but also sort of cute at the same time.

I place my hand on my throat and make a few siren sounds. 'I'm always in fine voice.'

'Good. Then you can start the singing.'

'Oh I see – that's why I'm here, is it? I'm the entertainment.'

'No.' He puts both of his hands up. 'Definitely not – this isn't like that. You're here because you're my friend.'

My mouth twists into a smile. 'Beau, I was joking.'

'OK. Good. Do you want to light the candle?'

'What an honour,' I say.

He presents this giant wax number seven from his pocket. 'Where should I stick it?' he says, staring at the cake of dreams.

'Somewhere that won't ruin its aesthetic value.'

He hovers the candle over one of the castle turrets, which is so obviously not the place to stick a candle of this size, and he's just about to plunge it down when I grab his hand.

'Not there!' I say. 'It'll fall apart. Right at the bottom, like here.' I guide his hand to the perfect position on top of the portcullis, and we both fix the candle in place together.

And then something quite strange happens.

We're standing here, in the kitchen, my hand on top of his, and he turns to me with this look in his eye that can best be described as *mysterious*. (And mysterious in the Harry Styles sense of the word, like there's no way of knowing what he's actually thinking, but you know it's sort of mischievous. I'm not talking about the vacant eyes of Kylie Jenner, which I assume is a side effect of Botox. I don't think Beau has had

Botox; his face is too expressive.) The muscles in his neck begin to tense. His full lips part. His eyes widen. His hand clenches under mine. And I wait, staring back at him, because I think he's about to say something important, something that explains the look of mystery on his face.

'Roman . . .' he begins. He pauses. He takes a deep breath, his shoulders rising up, his chest puffing out. 'We should light the candle.'

'Right,' I say, and my voice sounds high and thin, because that totally wasn't what I was expecting him to say. 'The candle. Sure.'

I pick up the box of matches from the bench and take out a match. I strike it against the side and the end immediately crisps and crackles into fire. Then I hover it over the wick of the giant seven-shaped candle until it catches.

'OK,' he says, carefully picking up the cake. 'When I give you a nudge, sing.'

'Oh, don't you worry, I will.'

I follow him back along the hallway and then he bursts into the front room. Immediately I jump to his side, ready to receive my nudge so I can show these kids just how much better than Moana I truly am.

But the nudge doesn't come.

We just stand here, numerous expectant faces looking from us to the cake and back again, waiting for something to happen. I give Beau the side eye. He's completely still, eyes wide, like he's spontaneously crapped his pants and dare not move in case, well, you know. (I didn't even know stage fright in your own living room was a thing.)

Deciding to take matters into my own hands, I begin to sing. '*Happy birthday to you . . .*'

Thankfully, the rest of the room follows my lead, which snaps Beau out of his trance. He steps forward and places the cake on the coffee table, where I notice an iPad has been propped up against a pile of books. On the screen, there's a man wearing a pixelated uniform, beaming with a pixelated smile.

Cindy, Beau's little sister, steps forward to receive her bougie cake. She's wearing a full Elsa dress, blue and silver and shimmery, complete with tiny crystallised heels – very extra for a seven-year-old. She leans forward, eyes tightly closed to make her wish, and then she blows out the candle.

'Look at my cake, Daddy,' she says to the pixelated man. 'And my dress.'

'You're a princess,' he says after a slight delay.

'I am.'

'What do you say to your daddy for buying you the cake you wanted?' says Beau's mam.

'Thank you, Daddy. I love you, Daddy.'

The room *ahh*s as a collective at this tender moment.

'Don't forget to save me some, princess.'

'I won't, Daddy.'

'Oh, is he due back soon?' asks one of the other mams.

Beau's mam squints her eyes and subtly shakes her head, which tells me, and everyone else over the age of seven, that Beau's dad isn't coming back any time soon.

About a minute of cute exchanges between Cindy and pixelated Dad follows, where she tells him about her party, and all of her new friends, and all of her wonderful presents, before Beau's mam picks up the iPad and says, 'Anyway, we'd better get back, John. We've got a houseful today. Thanks for calling.'

'Happy birthday, princess!' he says.

'Say bye to your daddy, Cindy.'

'Bye, Daddy,' she says. 'I love you so much, Daddy.'

Beau's mam taps the red button, and he disappears.

The excitement of imminent cake from Gayle's bakery is enough to send the room into a frenzy once again (as if these kids needed any more sugar today). As the screams ping against my eardrums, I turn to lock eyes with Beau, who I assume is standing right behind me, only to find he isn't here.

He's disappeared.

I poke my head out into the corridor.

He isn't there either, or in the kitchen at the end of the hall.

'Hey, did you see where Beau went?' I ask his mam, who is now handing out slices of pink cake.

'Try his bedroom,' she says, as if retreating to his room is perfectly acceptable even though he has a guest. 'Upstairs. Second door on the left.'

I make my way up, and the second door on the landing is already open, so I slide in.

Being in someone else's room without invitation is like taking a look inside their head, seeing all the things they definitely would have cleared away if they knew you were coming. This one is pretty cluttered, and full of boxes with *Beau's room* written on them, stacked one on top of the other. These really should have been unpacked by now.

He's sitting on the floor, head down, curls tumbling over his face.

'Is everything OK?' I ask.

He doesn't answer. He doesn't seem to notice me.

'Beau?' I say, knocking on the wrong side of the door three times.

He looks up. 'Roman?'

'Who else? What are you doing up here?'

For a brief moment he looks confused, the whites of his eyes too white as he searches his bedroom for answers.

I edge further in and he moves further away, like a scared animal backed into a corner.

'What's wrong?'

'Nothing at all's wrong.'

'Why did you leave? We were singing "Happy Birthday".'

'I just . . . needed a minute. I felt dizzy, I think. I'm OK now, though.'

He smiles, and it's so totally forced that I'm not buying it at all. If I've learnt anything about Beau Greene, it's that he's crap at lying – even worse than me.

'Is this about your dad?' I say, taking a step closer.

'Why do you say that?'

'Just a guess.'

It's not a guess. I don't think it's a coincidence that he started acting strangely right when the pixelated man appeared on the iPad.

'I didn't know he would be calling,' he says. 'It was a shock – I mean surprise. He . . . he didn't call on my birthday.'

'Maybe he forgot?' I suggest, though I'm not sure this is

much better than choosing not to call.

'I don't think you can forget the day your first child is born.'

For once, I'm at a loss for words. My dad has never been around, so it's not like I've really known him to be able to miss him. (Facts.) But to have a dad who knows you and then one day decides to start ignoring your birthdays? That seems like a different story altogether.

'Do you want me to bring you some cake?' I ask finally.

'No. I'm OK.'

'You sure?'

'Yeah. Let's go down.'

There comes a knock on the door.

'What are you doing up here, love?' asks Beau's mam, poking her head in.

'Nothing at all,' he says. 'We're coming now.'

'I set you both some cake aside before the little people annihilated it. It really is delicious. Can you believe your dad?'

'I know,' Beau says, standing. 'So thoughtful.' He sounds robotic.

'Well, it's in the kitchen when you're ready for it,' his mam says, smiling and then removing her head from the door.

Beau begins to walk past me, but before he reaches the door, I grab his arm. 'I'm your friend, Beau,' I say. 'Even if you don't think you've got anyone else, you've got me. You know that – right?'

He presses his lips together into a hard line, as if he's trying his best to keep his face as neutral as possible, before quickly following his mam out of the room.

TWENTY-SEVEN

'Did you know Ms Mead used to be an actress?' asks Solange.

'No way!' I say. 'I don't believe you.'

'Google doesn't lie,' she says.

It's Saturday night, and the old school Ballerz movie night is in full swing. We've already changed nail colour (me: Slut Drop, Solange: Orgasm, Adam: Bondage Bitch), and used some totally bougie cloth face masks from Charlotte Tilbury. I'm feeling totally radiant. I've selected a super queer film: *But I'm a Cheerleader* ('5,6,7,8, God is good, God is straight'), however, we're not going to start it until the pizza arrives.

Which was supposed to be half an hour ago.

We're using the wait time very wisely by googling St Anselm's staff members to see if we can dig up any dirt on them.

'Ms Mead has graced the silver screen?' I ask.

'Well, according to IMDb, she was once in an episode of some TV show called *The Bill*,' says Solange.

'What's that?' I say.

'Some police drama. She played a sex worker.'

'Well I never,' I say, splaying a hand on my chest.

'Where in God's name is this pizza?' says Adam. 'We ordered it like an hour ago.'

He's standing at my bedroom window, staring at the back

alley like some fragile ingénue in an Alfred Hitchcock film.

'You do know the driver will come to the front, right?' I say.

'I'm *starved*,' he says. 'I could eat the arm off a baby through the bars of its cot.'

'Wow.'

He throws his hand to his mouth. 'Sorry. It's the hanger talking.'

'Do you think they cast her for her glass eye?' says Solange, still focused on IMDb.

'I'm not sure having a glass eye is a prerequisite to being a sex worker,' says Adam.

'Yeah, this isn't eighteenth-century Paris,' I say.

This prompts a verse of 'I Dreamed a Dream' from the musical *Les Mis*.

'*He spent a summer by my side. He filled my glass eye with endless wonder . . .*' Solange and I sing in unison.

'OK, you two have officially lost it,' says Adam, rolling his eyes.

'Oh, lighten up,' I say.

'I can't. I'm hangry.'

'Should we just start the film?' suggests Solange.

'I'm not watching a movie without chewing on a slice of Pepperoni Passion,' says Adam. 'It's unseemly.'

'There's popcorn,' I say, rattling the bucket.

'It's not satisfying my needs. I need greasy, cheesy carbs.'

'I'll check where it is,' says Solange, tapping the app on her phone.

I grab a fistful of popcorn and shove it in my mouth.

Then I pick up my phone and scroll to the last message I sent Beau Greene, this afternoon after I left the party.

Roman Bright

u ok

He hasn't responded.

There's definitely something going on there. He changed so quickly when he saw his dad, scarily quickly; one minute he was being silly in the kitchen, the next he was right back to being the weirdo from the first day of English class, which I now know totally isn't him. And I want to know why.

'What are your guys' views on Beau Greene?' I ask.

Solange scrunches up her nose. 'Who?'

'Come on – you know who he is. I sit next to him in English class.'

'I thought you didn't sit next to anybody in English class?' says Adam.

'I didn't last year,' I say. 'I do now.'

'Oh God, has a whole other person popped up without me realising?' says Solange.

'He started last year,' I say. 'Summer term, I think.'

'I don't know him.' She shrugs.

'How do *you* know him?' Adam asks me.

'I don't. Not that well,' I say. 'He just seems nice.'

'Boring.'

'Not boring – nice! And he doesn't have any other friends . . .'
I raise my eyebrows when I say this last part.

'What are you saying – that you want to make him an official Baller?' says Adam.

'We could maybe let him in,' I say.

'No way,' he says. 'We're in Year 11 now – it's way too late for newbies.'

'He's really sweet,' I say.

'Sounds like you fancy him,' he says.

'I don't.'

'Sounds like you do.'

'Look, he's just . . . a nice guy.' Adam rolls his eyes at my use of the word 'nice' again, because we don't generally use it as a compliment. If 'nice' were a colour it would be beige. 'Not like boring nice, but *sweet* nice, *kind* nice, *cute* nice.'

'Cute?' he says. '*Yak*. Who are you and what have you done with Roman Bright?'

'Oh, stop. I'm just saying – the guy needs friends and I think we should oblige.'

'It's too late in the game to oblige,' he says.

There's something about the way he's talking to me tonight, like his words are weapons and he wants to wound me. I know Adam can be acerbic at the best of times. I get it. And I know he's hungry. But that doesn't give him free rein to be a complete arse.

'All I know is he's super kind,' I say. 'I mean, he came with me to Wynter's party, while you both abandoned me.'

I swear the entire room, including the posters on the wall (*Hocus Pocus*, *Some Like It Hot*, *The Wizard of Oz*, *Calamity Jane*) stare at me with daggers behind their eyes when I say this, because yes, I've totally gone there.

156

'Don't,' says Solange, holding a hand up.

'Why are you bringing that up?' says Adam. 'I thought we all agreed – you never should have gone in the first place.'

'That girl is bad news,' agrees Solange.

'And you think she's so everything,' Adam says to me.

'She sort of is,' I mumble.

'She's a troll!' he says. 'You should hate her. She's verbally kicking your ass all over school right now. I caught her the other day telling a bunch of sixth formers that you beat JJ with a baseball bat.'

'I do hate her. That doesn't stop her from being St Anselm's next top model.'

'She's vile. It doesn't matter how pretty she is; her insides are putrid.'

'Putrid,' says Solange. 'Good word.'

'And JJ Dixon is the same,' Adam says.

'I was waiting for his name to come up,' says Solange.

'You need to move on from them both, Roman,' says Adam. 'Especially him. Big time.'

'I have moved on from him,' I say.

'Yeah, right,' he says.

'I have!'

'Every time he enters a room you get an instant wide-on.'

'I do not!'

'You totally do! Look, you're even going red now!'

'I'm going red because of the use of the term "wide-on", nothing more.'

'I can't understand why you would even still care about him,' Adam says, ignoring me. 'The guy's a total arsehole for doing what he did to you.'

'He's right,' says Solange.

'He's not an arsehole,' I say quietly.

My mind takes a photograph of the two shocked faces looking back at me. It sticks there in my head, pinned right at the top so I can't un-see the moment my best friends looked at me like I was losing the plot.

'Wow,' says Solange.

'I told you,' Adam says to her, as if they've already spoken about this stuff behind my back.

'Roman,' says Solange, 'you stayed in your room half the summer because of him.'

'It wasn't him, it was Tyler—'

'Tyler never would have swilled you if JJ hadn't denied your existence!' says Acerbic Adam. 'One word from him and he could have stopped it.'

'He's not a good guy,' says Solange, piling on. 'Yeah, he's cute AF, but that's all he is. Don't hand him the power to break you again.'

'I'm not,' I protest.

'He's just another troglodyte,' says Adam. 'You've put him on a pedestal.'

'You've been his cheerleader for way too long,' says Solange.

'Yeah. It's time to put down the pompoms, sis.'

If Halloween hadn't happened, this would be the moment I fought back. This would be the moment I pleaded JJ's case, maybe even told them about Big Red, and the Yves Klein postcards, and the totally romantic murals painted only for me. But I get the feeling that them knowing would make things ten times worse. And I'm really not in the mood for defending every decision I've ever made right now.

'Let Wynter have him,' says Solange. 'Let him play around with her like he played around with you. It's nothing less than she deserves.'

'You don't need him anyway,' says Adam. 'You have us.'

Then they both do this cheesy smile thing, and it sort of makes me cringe because I feel really annoyed. I don't need to be told who I can and can't be friends with. And I certainly don't need a lecture about JJ Dixon right now. This sleepover has suddenly gone from my 1950s pink-hair fantasy to a modern-day nightmare – from 'Look at Me, I'm Sandra Dee' to *Mean Girls* ('You can't sit with us'). And I'm not here for it. I knew I wasn't totally vibing with my friends right now – I felt that way the moment they told me they were happy for me to attend Wynter's party alone – but tonight has shown me that we're on completely different pages about pretty much everything.

This makes me think about Beau Greene again. I sort of wish he was here right now, instead of them. I wish I had someone here who understood me, and not my totally unsupportive, judgemental friends.

I don't say anything else, because anything else would lead to an argument, so all three of us pick up our phones, because that's what you're supposed to do when things get awkward; it's like an unwritten rule.

'Oh, hang on,' says Solange. 'I realised why the pizza's not here yet . . .'

'Why?' Adam and I ask in unison.

'I ordered the pizza to my house.'

'You're joking?' says Adam.

'My bad.'

'*Please* tell me you're joking.'

'Sorry.'

'You idiot!'

'Calm down, hangry – it's an easy mistake to make.'

'I need food!'

'Don't worry, I'll sort it,' she says, pressing the phone to her ear.

'In the meantime, let's just play the film,' I say. 'Or it'll be midnight by the time we finish.'

'Fine,' says Adam. 'But if it doesn't come soon, I'm eating this cushion.'

TWENTY-EIGHT

The longer JJ stays away from school, the wilder the rumours about me being a queer, back-alley-lurking villain become. And, honestly, I don't think I'm strong enough to ignore them. Because, although I know this isn't me, although I know I would never attack him – or anyone for that matter – I'm still queer, I'm still non-binary, I'm still gay, and I'm starting to feel like I've been wrong all this time, and that these things are villainous, and I should be ashamed of them. I know how totally screwed up that sounds, but I sort of can't stop myself.

In between classes on Monday afternoon, I catch a glimpse of my reflection in the outside window of the dinner hall. And I'm shocked. I don't see me at all – just a tired, basic boy with absolutely no remarkable features. *God.* What a sad day this is. I haven't even put make-up on. Me. No make-up. It's a bloody travesty.

I couldn't be any more lost right now.

I'm like the film version of *Cats* the musical. (I know. Awful.)

After lunch, I hang back in a quiet corner of the yard until the crowds disperse before I make my way to the art block bathroom. Next class is French, with Solange, but I won't be attending because, you know, *je suis triste.*

'*Mr Albright.*'

Her voice comes galloping towards me, stirring the very leaves on the ground.

I turn around to see a lime green tweed two-piece suit, trimmed with tomato-red faux fur, coming at me. She looks like a tropical plant. This is all I need right now – an altercation with a Venus flytrap.

'Mrs Duncan.'

'I must say, I'm surprised to see you,' she says. I can tell by the tone of her voice (patronising, sing-song) that this is leading somewhere, because, with her, it's always leading somewhere. Passive-aggressive should be her zodiac sign. 'After all – you've decided that Year 11 is a part-time affair now, have you not?'

The penny drops. She's referring to my attendance record, which by now looks like a game of noughts and crosses because I've been sporadically attending classes. Sporadically is the best I can do at the moment. And really, sporadically is better than not attending at all. *Right?*

'Where is it you're supposed to be now?' she says.

'French,' I say.

'And you're not there because . . . ?'

I say nothing.

'I thought as much. May I remind you that classes are not optional, Mr Albright – you don't get to pick and choose which ones you attend. I thought I made myself quite clear at the beginning of term.'

'You did.' I say it flatly, without any deference, which I can see instantly annoys her because her eyes thin as she looks at me, up and down, as if she's sizing me up (because at any moment she's going to snap shut and eat me).

'Do I strike you as the type of person who takes kindly to being ignored?'

I don't think that's possible in that outfit, is it? 'No, miss.'

I feel like such an idiot, standing here, as she looks me up and down. As if I didn't feel stupid, and guilty, and pathetic enough, she's come to make me feel worse.

'I should get to French, then,' I say, wanting to make my escape.

'Not so fast,' she says, her Twiglet-like fingers splaying out to stop me from moving past her. 'There is another matter.' She smiles, rivers of foundation and lipstick falling into every crack on her face. 'I'm not usually one to listen to rumours, Mr Albright; however, when serious accusations are made regarding the safeguarding of my students, I can't ignore them.'

'What accusations?'

Her eyebrows shoot so far up her forehead, they join her hairline.

I know this look. She's doing that thing all teachers do when they invite you to reflect on your behaviour, with the intention of making you accidentally drop yourself in it. It's an invitation to think, long and hard, about what I've done.

'Regarding Mr Dixon,' she says. 'Both of your names have come to my attention recently . . .'

'They have?'

She nods.

And I'm confused. I don't see how she could know anything about JJ and me. I've been so careful to keep quiet about the whole thing. And it's been totally challenging; every time I see Wynter Brown's smug face, I want to tell her that her boyfriend

163

leaves romantic gestures in the form of graffiti around the school/village meant only for me. But I always stop myself. I always suffer in silence for our romance, because great romance needs suffering; it feeds off it. I've been so bloody careful . . .

Wait.

Wynter.

Oh no.

No, no, no. I'm a complete idiot.

'I didn't do it,' I hear myself say. 'You can't prove that I did.'

She shakes her head. 'Mr Dixon's absence has been a shock to us all. Like I say, I'm not one for rumours, Mr Albright. I prefer to deal with the facts, not the fiction—'

'It literally has nothing to do with me. I haven't done anything wrong.'

'That remains to be seen. I'll have to hear what Mr Dixon has to say when he returns.'

Her words land in the pit of my stomach like a dead weight, and I grip the wall to stop myself from toppling over. I know blaming me for everything is her favourite pastime, but she can't be serious about this, because this is really, *really* serious. If JJ lies (like he has before), and she believes him (which she will), this could ruin my life for ever. I could be charged with assault, and sent to prison.

Olivia Newton-John!

'But I've already told you it had nothing to do with me,' I say, as calmly as I can manage.

She shrugs, and it's so careless and cold that I shiver, because that shrug shows in one easy movement just how many shits she gives about my future.

Absolutely none.

'Now, off to class with you, Mr Albright,' she says. 'I'll be checking Madame Walker's register.'

I walk away, slowly, carefully, because my mind is still trying to figure out what's just happened.

Prison.

Shit.

In the blink of a false eyelash, I've gone from *Grease* to *Orange Is the New Black*.

And I look hideous in a boiler suit.

TWENTY-NINE

I don't go to French. The last thing I need to be thinking about right now is how to ask for a one-way ticket in a foreign train station (*Je voudrais acheter un billet aller simple*). This is completely irrelevant considering I'll never be allowed out of the country again due to my impending criminal record.

I hide out in the art block until English class, which, I've decided, I will be attending. Mainly because I need to talk to Beau. I need to tell him what's happened. I need to make him promise to visit me in prison and smuggle in essential items, like moisturiser and Boy Brow by Glossier.

Having Mrs Duncan believe I would attack someone is next-level horrible. It's one thing to have rumours flying around the student body – they'll believe anything – but an adult? Someone who is supposed to be responsible and reasonable? I feel so sensitive and raw right now, like I no longer have skin. I'm all nerve endings and vulnerable parts, completely at the mercy of the troglodytes of St Anselm's. Thank God for Marlene, and all the rabbits that gave their skin so I can have something to protect me when mine feels like it's been peeled away.

When I walk into class, everything goes suddenly quiet. Keeping my eyes directed at the floor, I hurry to my table at the back, where I find Beau Greene.

'*Omigod*,' I say, collapsing into my chair. 'I'm going to prison.'

He doesn't respond.

'Did you hear what I just said?'

'What?' he says. 'Um, sorry – prison?'

'I can't believe it. This is the worst day of my life.'

'Wait. Why are you going to prison?'

'Wynter Brown – she's told Mrs Duncan that I attacked JJ, and Mrs Duncan believes her. She won't listen to me. I'm going to be charged with assault and forced to wear orange . . . with my skin tone . . . this is a disaster. My life couldn't be any worse.'

He takes a breath and sighs heavily. 'You know – it actually could. It could be so much worse.'

'I'm too pretty for prison – I'm no Jean Valjean.'

'Who?'

'The prisoner in *Les Misérables*. Hugh Jackman plays him in the film?' Beau gives no sign of recognition. 'That will be me. *24601*. I'll go to prison, then I'll escape and have to go on the run for ever!'

As I say this, Ms Mead enters the room, looking all kinds of festive in a sparkly turtleneck jumper and headband, drinking from a steaming mug that has *Espresso yourself* written on it. (I'm starting to see the thespian within.)

'Does everybody have their copy of the text with them?' she says. 'If not, there are spares on my desk.'

I don't have my copy, because I never have my copy. It lives on my bedside table now. This is partly because JJ handed it to me (yes, I know – I'm pathetic), and also partly because my school bag is only for the essentials: lip gloss, perfume, a change

167

of accessories (pearls, rings, earrings, wristbands), emergency snacks and chewing gum.

I walk to the front and swipe a book off the pile, making sure to give Wynter Brown the filthiest look as I pass. She returns this with an evil smile, sharply aimed, giving me serious *I'm determined to ruin your life* vibes.

God. Where does this bitch get off?

'Please open your books at Chapter Seven, titled "Incident at the Window",' says Ms Mead. 'Can I now draw your attention to the whiteboard?'

She clicks it on, but nobody looks forward. The entire class is (somewhat ironically) staring out of the window, thirty heads looking across the yard at the sports hall where a crowd of netball kits and football strips is quickly gathering.

'Quieten down now,' says Ms Mead. 'Or we'll work in exam-room conditions today.'

There are maybe one or two of the most studious of my classmates (Jonny Dale, Norman Stokes) who are waiting patiently to begin, but the rest of us are transfixed on the far more interesting events happening outside.

The crowd is looking up at the wall, a look of shock and excitement on their faces, which instantly makes me think of Big Red.

'Really?' says Ms Mead, giving up the ghost and taking a peek between the blinds.

Mrs Duncan has joined the throng outside, which is never good. I can see her, parting the crowd like Moses, the red trim of her suit turned to spiked teeth as a warning to anyone who would stand in her way.

'What's going on here?' Her voice echoes across the yard and in through one of the slightly open windows. 'Why aren't you all in class?'

The crowd offers a few mumbles/apologies, but I don't hear the reason they've gathered, and I sort of need to know the reason they've gathered, because I have this bad feeling in my stomach, like rocks.

Mrs Duncan disappears into the thick of it, and it's too much for me to be still. My heart won't allow it. I need to know what's going on out there.

'Ryan, what are you doing?' says Ms Mead, because I'm standing.

I walk down the aisle between the tables, my body doing all the work for me, putting one foot in front of the other without me needing to tell it to, because I'm lost somewhere in the heat of what's about to happen.

'Ryan Albright, do not leave this classroom!'

I yank the door handle towards me and step out into the echoing excitement of the yard.

As I approach, I immediately see the thing that has St Anselm's in a state of chaos once again.

It's another painting.

This time, Big Red has painted an angel. But its wings are bent and broken and it's falling down the side of the sports hall to the ground. Across the mangled feathers and exposed bones, words are written: *broken*, *wrong*, *lonely*.

This painting looks different to the others. There are no colours here, only tones: charcoal grey, chalk and ash, which makes the image seem so stark. Just looking at it leaves me with this horrible taste in my mouth, bitter and salty, like seawater. I never thought a painting could make me feel this unhappy. But as I stand here, staring at the angel's twisted face, I feel so totally dark.

Mrs Duncan walks right up to the wall, Venus flytrap suit shivering in the breeze. She leans forward, her bony finger tapping off her thin lips as she inspects the artist's signature.

'Who did this?' she says, turning around slowly, a mad look across her face because she's being made a fool of in her own school.

Of course nobody answers.

Her eyes meet mine and I look straight back. She can't possibly think this was me. She can't possibly accuse me of attacking JJ *and* being St Anselm's answer to Banksy all in one day. She knows what everybody would do to me if she did. Even she isn't that evil.

'There's CCTV everywhere in this school,' she says, clearly bluffing, because if there was CCTV everywhere in the school they would know who Big Red is by now. 'This has gone too far. We will find out who is behind this. And whoever did this can rest assured the punishment will be severe. *Do you hear me?* Now get back to class – all of you, before I start issuing detentions.'

Which is warning enough to send everyone else hurrying back inside.

But I can't move. This painting has latched on to my insides. I don't know if it's because I'm feeling particularly vulnerable today, but when I look at the angel's face painted on the sports hall, the building in school where JJ spends most of his time, I think of him being attacked. I see him battered and bruised, broken and bent, just like the angel's wings.

And what makes it worse is everyone at school believes I could do this to someone. They believe Wynter's rumour. They believe I broke JJ. They believe I'm the villain, just because of who and what I am.

'Ryan?' says Mrs Duncan.

'Sorry. I'm going.'

'Is everything OK?'

'I didn't do it.' I feel like I need to say this.

She nods, and it's not like the nod she gave me before, after the face appeared on the art block.

This time, I think she hears me.

THIRTY

By last lesson, Mr Kirkup, the school caretaker, has painted over the entire sports hall wall. This time Mrs Duncan isn't pulling any punches. She's made sure there wasn't time for a conversation about keeping this painting.

Big Red's angel is gone.

But I don't think I'm going to be able to forget it so easily.

'I don't know how JJ managed to do it when he hasn't been here,' I say to Adam, as we walk to class together.

'Do what?' he says.

'The painting on the sports hall.'

He turns to look at me. 'You're not being serious?'

'He must have done it today. But he hasn't been at school all week. It makes no sense. Maybe he did it last night . . .'

'Roman,' he says, splaying his hands for emphasis. 'Just to be clear – you think JJ Dixon painted the sports hall?'

It feels like things are getting out of hand: the paintings are getting darker; JJ has been attacked; I'm potentially going to prison. These are all super-serious things and I need to talk about them. I've managed to keep the Big Red stuff secret this far, but if I don't talk about this stuff now it's just going to fester inside my head, and I really don't want that. Beau Greene pretty much disappeared straight after English class, so, though he probably doesn't want to hear it, I have to tell Adam.

I nod. 'Yeah. JJ did this.'

'Seriously?' he says.

'I've known for a while. He's Big Red.'

We walk a little further, neither of us speaking. I'm feeling scared right now, like I'm not safe here, or something. The new painting has made me doubt everything all over again. The angel's face looked so pained. It's entirely possible this stuff isn't about romance after all, but about tearing me down. What does JJ want? Why is he targeting me?

'Do you know what?' says Adam, as we walk into the history block. 'I think I'm done.'

'What?' I say.

'Yeah. I'm done with this whole thing. I mean, how many times does he have to make a massive fool out of you, before you get the message?'

'Wait. Who's made a massive fool of me?'

'Do you realise that JJ Dixon has never once set any of the rumours about you two straight. Never once. It's almost like he enjoys seeing you upset. Shit. It's so weird.'

'That's not true.'

'Oh, for God's sake, Roman, why are you such an idiot?'

'I'm not an idiot.'

'OK. You're not an idiot. You just enjoy being made a fool of by some straight boy who literally couldn't give a crap about you. Is that better?'

He continues along the corridor and I follow, charging behind, blood pumping in my face.

'You don't know everything about JJ and me,' I say.

173

'I know that most of the relationship exists inside your head.'

'Shut up! You're being beastly!'

He laughs, and it's totally annoying. 'Beastly?'

'You don't know all the things JJ's done for me.'

'I know he's made you look like a crazy person. Or did you do that to yourself?'

'Stop!'

'You're such a bloody cliché, Roman, falling for the straight captain of the football team. You're setting back the queer rights movement by, like, thousands of years.'

'I'm not!'

'It's so frustrating.'

'Why are you so mad?'

'I'm not mad,' he says stonily.

'You are! You know you are.'

'I'm not.'

'You've been a complete arsehole since I got invited to Wynter's party.'

'What? No I haven't.'

'Yes you have! You're constantly having a go at me about something.'

He stops. 'That's not it.'

'Then what is it, then?'

He looks away from me, shaking his head, clenching his teeth together so hard the muscles in his jaw begin to pulse. He's clearly angry about something. 'I've tried so hard,' he says. 'Solange has tried so hard, but it's like you can't hear us. Everybody knew why she invited you to that party. She wanted you to see her and JJ together, wanted your reaction on show for everyone. We tried to stop you going and making a huge tit out of yourself, but you're just so blinded by their popularity, and good looks, and whatever else, that you couldn't hear us – and we're supposed to be your best friends.'

'You are my best friends! I'm not blinded by anything – I just wanted to be included.'

'Well, you got what you wanted, Roman – you got included by the pretty people in the only way they include people like us – as laughing stocks. Congratulations.' He aggressively sticks his thumbs up when he says this.

My mouth drops open because, even though I know this is partly true, I can't believe he would say this to me right now when I already feel so crappy. I would never say anything so mean to him. Never.

'I can't believe you're being like this,' I say.

'I'm not being like anything,' he says. 'I'm just telling you the facts. Fact: JJ is with Wynter. Fact: JJ ignores you every day. Fact: JJ doesn't give a crap about you.' He claps every time he says *fact*, which is totally aggressive. 'Stop obsessing over him. Just stop. It's not normal, Roman.'

His words push me back until I'm leaning against the wall.

It's not normal.

I'm not normal.

Even to my gay friends I'm not normal; I'm the villainous freak.

And I'm so sick of feeling this way.

Do you know what?

OK.

Fine.

So, you want a villain?

Then a villain you shall have.

(Sharpens claws.)

'Oh wait, is this because I actually have someone interested in me?' I say.

His face instantly drops, because I've totally gone there.

'*Omigod*,' I say, loudly enough for the group of Year 7s walking in front to turn round. 'You're jealous of me.'

'Oh, dream on.'

He rolls his eyes, and I feel venom rising inside of me. 'Look, I can't help it that I've got some totally hot guy leaving totally romantic paintings for me, and you're going to die sad and alone with about twenty cats.'

His mouth opens wider; he looks like he could catch about twenty flies in there.

'Facts are facts,' I say, shrugging. 'I mean, who loves *you*, Adam? Have you ever even kissed anyone before? I think you need to take a look at your own love life before you start criticising anybody else's, hun.'

He takes a step towards me. 'What did you say?'

I take a step towards him. 'You heard me.'

We stare at each other, my heart pulsing through every part of me because I'm so mad right now, and I'm not going to back down to him because this argument needs to happen; it's been brewing for ages.

'Do you know what,' he says, 'I've wanted to say this to you for months, but I didn't want you to go crying back to your bedroom. Well. Now I couldn't care less . . . I'm the only person who has stood by you through this whole thing! Even

Solange had a summer holiday, but I've lived with this bullshit nonstop since last term, and all I've come to realise is that you are the most selfish, self-centred arsehole I've ever known! Everything always has to be about you; everybody always has to fa-la-la to your tune. Well, I'm not doing it any more, Roman. I'm out. You can call me sad for never being in love all you like. Fine. I don't care. Because if you seriously think that what you have with JJ Dixon is love, then, really, you're the sad one, because you don't have a clue what love is.'

Then he turns around and bombs along the corridor, leaving me standing alone in a crowd of grey blazers.

THIRTY-ONE

Mam walks into the bedroom, stepping over me because I decided the carpet was far more suitable than the bed. Life has, quite literally, floored me.

Behind the curtains, the sky flashes orange and pink, popping like bubble wrap when you twist it, as the annual village firework display kicks off on the beach. The world is partying, bridging the gap between Halloween and Christmas with Bonfire Night.

And I'm spiralling.

'I think you need to talk to me,' Mam says.

I shake my head. There's nothing she can do or say to help me. Today was a bad day. And I don't think hearing *I'm so sorry to hear that your entire life sucks* is going to make me feel any better.

'Come on, Roman.'

Another head shake.

'I'm officially worried about you.'

A loud whistling sound screeches through the sky and my bedroom lights up green.

'It's the fireworks tonight,' she says, unnecessarily. 'You usually love to watch them.'

She's right. I do. Usually, there's nothing I love more

than seeing the sky outside my window given the Disney treatment.

But tonight, all it's doing is reminding me of what I don't have. With each loud bang and explosion of colour, I'm reminded of how the world is just one big party that I'm not invited to. Parties are for winners. For normal people. Whenever I turn up, brooms get thrown and hearts get smashed.

'What's happened?' she says.

'I feel bad,' I say into the carpet.

'Why?'

'I had an argument with Adam. I was pretty mean.'

'How mean?'

'I said nobody loved him. I told him he was going to die alone with twenty cats.'

'Oh, I see. *Mean* mean.'

'Oh, and I'm Chrissy Teigen – I've been cancelled.'

'I don't know what that means.' She takes a seat on the edge of the bed, the springs in the mattress bouncing as she sits.

'It means my life isn't worth living.'

'Never say that, Roman.'

'It's true.'

'Come on, what's really going on? Why did you fight with Adam? You haven't been yourself for weeks.'

She begins to stroke my hair, and it feels nice. Just being touched by someone makes me human again, makes me more than a lowly bedroom-carpet-dwelling dust mite.

This would be the perfect time to tell her everything: the truth about JJ, and Big Red, and what happened at Wynter's party. This would be the perfect time to get everything out in the open and move on from the absolute shitshow that is my life. But this stuff feels so heavy; telling her would only burden her with it as well, and she already does so much for Mikey and me. She doesn't need to take on this thunderous crap.

'Everybody hates me,' I say instead.

'I'm sure they don't.'

(You've got to love mams. I'm literally the most hated person in the world right now, and she thinks I crap glitter.)

'Can I ask you something?' I say.

'Anything, lover.'

'Do you think I'm selfish?'

She pauses for a little longer than I would have liked. 'No.'

'You paused.'

'I was thinking about why you'd be asking me that. I'm guessing this is something Adam said?'

'Yeah. He called me a selfish arsehole.'

'Ouch.'

'You don't think I'm a selfish arsehole, do you?'

'No, Roman. I think you're thoughtful, and caring.'

'You do?'

'Yes.'

'But do you ever wish I was just . . . normal?' The word comes from a place way down deep, a place I don't like to visit. Right away I feel sort of shy that I've even said it.

'Normal?' she says.

'You know, like other boys.'

'No.' She doesn't miss a beat. 'Absolutely not – what is normal anyway? You're wonderful just as you are, Roman.'

I shake my head. 'That's not true.'

She kneels down on the carpet and grips my shoulders, holding me directly in front of her face. 'Do you trust me?' she says. I nod. 'Then believe me when I say this – you're special, Roman. Your life is going to be magical, full of laughter and fabulous things. I know that.'

'You can't know that.'

'Well, I do.'

She pulls me in hard and we hug, as a blue palm tree explodes over our heads.

'I hate the world,' I say into her shoulder.

'When I was a teenager, I hated the world too.'

'You did?'

'Of course I did. There was always something to hate – boys, my hair, some bitch at school, boys—'

'You already said boys.'

'It needs a double mention for emphasis.'

This makes me smile.

'Look, being a teenager is bloody horrible. You're just a kid and you've got a pharmacy-load of hormones coursing through you. It's a crazy time. Everybody goes through hell—'

'No they don't.'

'They do. Even if it looks like they don't, they do.'

'I don't know anybody else who has to deal with the stuff I do.'

'I get that. I know you're different, Roman. I know it must be so much harder for you. All I can say is – it gets better.'

'Does it? It's been four years of not getting better.'

'It's been four years of high school. High school isn't for

ever. You'll be done by the summer, and then you have your whole life ahead of you.'

'Summer feels like a lifetime away.'

'OK. I'm listening to you. I am. What do you want me to do? I can make the call right now – I can pull you out of school, and you can do the rest of the year at home. I'll find a tutor. God knows where, but if we need to make it work, I'll find a way.'

I feel her heart beating through her jumper. And it's a really comforting feeling, just knowing she cares this much. I know how lucky I am.

'No,' I say. 'You don't have to do that.'

Being home-schooled would only make me even more of an outsider – like Lindsay Lohan at the beginning of *Mean Girls* ('*Jambo*'). That's the last thing I need right now. And Mam definitely can't afford to pay for a private tutor. We're not the Kardashians. (Facts.)

'How about I make you some hot chocolate,' she says.

'No, thanks.'

'We could watch a film, then – they've got *Steel Magnolias* on Netflix now. "My colours are blush and bashful"?'

'I think I just need to be on my own.'

'Wow – I don't even get a movie quote response?'

'"Your colours are pink and pink",' I quote half-heartedly.

'We can watch it up here. I'll put Mikey to bed and we can have a girly sleepover?'

'I'm OK. Really.'

'You sure?'

I nod my head.

'OK,' she says, cupping my jaw with her hand. 'Well, I'll be downstairs if you need me. Remember what I've said. No problem is too great for us to fix, Roman. I love you.'

'I love you too.'

After she leaves, I use the remaining fragments of my wavering strength to climb into bed, shuffling under the covers, pulling the duvet right up to my chin.

My TV hangs on the wall opposite, the screen so big, and blacker than black, and empty, it's like staring into the abyss. Staring into my soul.

I need to fill it.

I reach for the remote and click it on.

And there it is, recommended for me by Prime Video, because Prime Video probably knows me better than anyone else right now. Prime Video is the only friend I have left.

Grease – the movie musical spectacular.

And I know I probably shouldn't watch it. I know there are parts that will confirm how tragic my life is right now. But I don't think anything else is going to cut it. Prime Video is absolutely right: I need to fill the void with poufy A-line skirts and pink hair and teenage pregnancy storylines. I need them now more than ever.

So, I press the play button (which shall henceforth be known as the 'self-destruct' button). Maybe if the screen fills with colour and joy, my soul will do the same.

Cue opening scene.

The beach.

I've watched this film so many times recently, obsessing over the Danny and Sandy storyline, as if this would somehow make it my own.

But.

This time I feel differently.

And it comes as such a surprise that I have to sit up. Because, as I watch the story unfold from the comfort of my duvet, as I stare at the girls vs the boys in the musical number 'Summer Nights', as I notice how pink the girls are and how macho the boys are, I realise something.

And that is . . .

I'm not a Rizzo.

I'm not a Sandy, or a Frenchie either. Hell, I'm not even a Patty Simcox – the Pink Lady wannabe, the outcast, the most tragic of them all.

I don't see myself anywhere in this film.

I'm not here.

I don't exist.

And that's a light-bulb-moment-sized problem.

Just like at St Anselm's, there is no place for non-binary queer kids at Rydell High. As far as *Grease* is concerned, high school is just a buffet of straight cisgender clichés, and even the most ridiculed kids, even the geeks like Patty and Eugene, are better than me, because at least they exist. No wonder I don't think I'm normal.

I slap my hands to my face as if a ton of strawberry milkshake has just been poured over my head.

What a load of tight-jean-squashed bollocks!

Well, this spiralled quickly.

I click the film off.

Prime Video has joined the list of others who have betrayed me.

Prime Video is dead to me.

RIP Prime Video.

I change to Disney+. This won't let me down; it's physically impossible, like sneezing with your eyes open.

It isn't long until I come to *The Little Mermaid* because all roads lead to *The Little Mermaid*. I should have started with this, my OG favourite, my safe place. My people, the magical non-binary mermaids of the world, are exactly what I need.

Play.

Cue Disney choir.

Cue magical underwater kingdom, where fins and shell bras are de rigueur, and 'normal' looks nothing like it does in Tynemouth village.

Yup.

I'm definitely feeling like I could crawl out of bed and through the screen right now. This was a brilliant idea.

Until – and I'm going to use the word *inevitably* – it turns out it totally wasn't a brilliant idea.

Because, when Ariel, the little mermaid, has to make a decision – stay a magical non-binary creature for ever, with green fins and a totally cute purple shell bra or trade in her voice to appear 'normal' for a prince – she makes the wrong one.

Am I the only one who thinks that it doesn't matter how charming, and chiselled, and dreamy-eyed Prince Eric is, Ariel should never have had to trade in her voice – or identity – to stand beside him? Her queer identity is who she is. She shouldn't change just to fit in. Nobody should. That's totally screwed up.

(It turns out even in fairy tales, binary gender roles win the day.)

I get so pissed off, I throw a cushion at the screen.

Now, I can't even rely on films to pull me through.

Off button is firmly pressed.

BOOM!

A huge explosion right outside my window signals the climactic ending of the firework display.

Then, suddenly, the world is totally quiet.

No fireworks.

No films.

My room is completely dark.

I'm back here, in the place I swore to myself I would never be again, lying in the black silence of my bedroom with nothing but the ticking of the star-faced clock on my bedside table for company.

I can't stand it, not even for a second.

I reach over the bed for my phone, and before I know it, I'm scrolling to the last WhatsApp conversation we had. Then, I'm messaging the one person who understands what it feels like to be this much of an outsider, because I think I need to see him tonight.

WhatsApp Chat

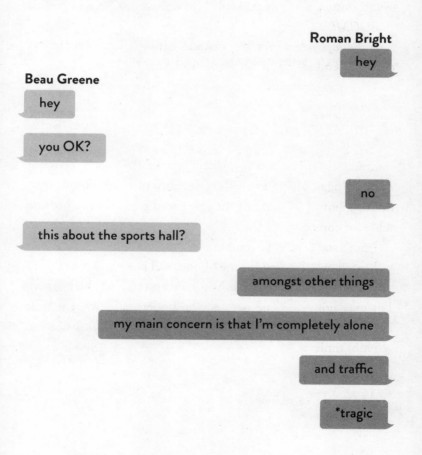

Roman Bright

hey

Beau Greene

hey

you OK?

no

this about the sports hall?

amongst other things

my main concern is that I'm completely alone

and traffic

*tragic

187

you're not alone and you're not tragic you've got me

😊

that's actually helping

never underestimate the power of an emoji

🙏

😃

😍

👍

😃

OK enough now 😇

i know you're smiling

not fully. it's a Mommy Dearest side smile

Mommy Dearest?

a side smile is better than no smile

what u up2

on way home

been watching fireworks

I watched from my room

you wanna do something?

???

like what?

hang out?

ok

i'm close to your house

give me 5 mins

THIRTY-TWO

I'm lying in complete darkness when I hear a tap on my bedroom window.

I sit forward and swipe the curtain to one side, glancing down at the backyard. The only light out there is coming from a street light at the end of the alley. I squint my eyes to see if I can make anything out, and another tap comes, right in front of my face.

I shunt the window open and poke my head out into the cold.

'Roman,' says a voice from below.

'Who's that?' I ask.

'Three guesses,' they say, and right away I know it's Beau Greene.

'Beau. What are you doing?'

'I'm vying for your attention.'

'Couldn't you have done that at the front door?'

He steps into orange light and smiles at me. 'Hi,' he says, waving his hand. 'I was going to come round the front, but I was passing this way, and I knew you'd be in your bedroom.'

'So you decided to throw stones at my window instead?'

'Um . . . yeah? How are you?'

I take a deep breath of freezing, smoke-scented air. Usually when somebody asks this question, the custom is to answer 'fine'. Basically, the custom is to lie. But, as I look into Beau Greene's truth-searching eyes, I don't feel like a lie is going to cut it with him. And I don't want to lie anyway. I sort of need to talk about how I'm feeling right now. That's why I messaged him in the first place.

'I don't know,' I say. 'Not good.'

'Why not good?'

'Aren't you going to come in?' I say, looking up and down the back alley. 'I don't really want the whole street to hear about my personal problems.'

'Right,' he says. 'Hang on.'

He disappears but I can hear his footsteps, and then I hear grunting and scratching, before he appears on top of the back wall.

'That was surprisingly easy,' he says.

He swings his legs over so he's perching on the wall like some character from a nursery rhyme and then jumps into the backyard.

'Be careful!'

'I'm OK,' he says, ducking under the kitchen window as he walks towards the wisteria, which climbs up the wall all the way to my bedroom.

He looks up at me, still smiling. He looks sort of cute tonight, his frostbitten face all flushed as it pokes out from under his curls, which, in turn, poke out from underneath a chunky knitted hat.

'That hat is quite fabulous,' I say.

'Thanks,' he says, shrugging. 'And it keeps my head warm.'

'Stylish and practical – will wonders never cease?'

He laughs, and a cloud of hot air shimmers out of his mouth and floats up to my window.

'So what's up?' he says.

I take a deep breath and sigh, my own cloud tumbling from my mouth into the night. 'I had an argument with Adam Chung. And now, on top of everything else, I feel like the world's worst friend.'

'Why – what did you say to him?'

'I basically told him he was tragic because he's never been kissed.'

'Wow. That's pretty mean.'

'In my defence, he started it. He told me I was pathetic for still having feelings for JJ.'

'Hmm,' he says.

'What?'

'He has a point.'

'Hey!' I say, loud enough for the sound to go galloping along the back alley.

'Shh,' he says, holding a finger to his mouth. 'You don't want the whole street to hear your personal problems.'

'*Very funny.* Are you going to come in now – I can let you in the back door?'

'No need,' he says, eyeing up the wisteria as if it's his next challenge.

Then he dives in, hands first, and begins to climb, biting his lower lip as he navigates his way with surprising surety from branch to branch, all the way to my bedroom window.

'Give me a hand up,' he says when he's at the edge.

I offer him my hand and he grips my wrist. His grip is strong. I lean back as I heave him up, and he pulls himself on to the window ledge.

Right away, I climb out so I can sit beside him.

'It's cold,' I say.

He shuffles closer to me and begins to rub my back to keep me warm.

It feels nice being this close to someone, to him.

'Thanks for coming over,' I say. 'I didn't want this to be another night I spent alone and sad in my bedroom.'

'Thanks for asking,' he says. 'I'm glad you thought of me.'

'You're the only person I'm vibing with at the moment. My other friends either want to give me a life lecture or call me selfish.'

'They just care about you, Roman.'

'Doesn't feel that way,' I say. 'The way Adam spoke to me today – I've never seen him like that. He was like a different person.'

He goes quiet, and right away I feel self-conscious and stupid.

'What?' I say.

'Nothing.'

'You think he's right – you think I'm a selfish arsehole too, don't you?'

'Only some of the time,' he says, smiling.

'Stop! Really?'

'I'm joking. You're not selfish, Roman. I actually think you care a lot about other people. Though sometimes I think you care a bit *too* much about what other people think of you.'

'It's hard not to when they feel the need to tell you so freely on a daily basis.'

He begins to laugh. He's all dimples and flushed cheeks tonight, curls and chunky-knit headwear. 'You are funny.'

'I'm glad you find my life tragedies so amusing.'

'I don't mean it like that, I mean – in the way you talk. You have a real way with words, Roman. You can dramatise anything. I think that's a real skill.'

'You do?' I say, sitting up a little taller because compliments are like oxygen to screen legend goddesses like *moi*.

He smiles at me, and it's like his whole face is smiling. I can see the smile in his cheeks as they fold, his eyes as they sparkle, his forehead as it creases. He looks happy. And it's sort of changing the way I feel.

'Stop it,' I say.

'What?'

'Smiling at me like that.'

'OK. I'll stop.' He does this weird pouty face, and I can't help but snort.

'Anyway, tell me about your night,' I say, extra conscious of not being self-centred like Adam accused me. 'How were the fireworks?'

'They were good,' he says. 'They went on for ages.'

'We take Bonfire Night very seriously around these parts. Who did you go with?'

'Just Cindy and Mum. It was nice. I like doing things the three of us. We're like a proper little unit these days.'

'I feel the same about Mikey and Mam. We probably

should have gone tonight. I feel bad they missed out because of my misery.'

'There's always next year,' he says.

He rubs his hands together and blows in between them to warm them up.

'Come in,' I say. 'It's freezing out here.'

'Nah, it's OK.'

'Beau, come in,' I say, stepping through the open window. 'We don't want you catching pneumonia now, do we?'

I step on to the bed, and he follows me in.

Right away I grab a blanket and throw it around my shoulders, then I snuggle into my cushions as he takes a seat cross-legged on the opposite end of the bed.

'I thought you'd be watching a film,' he says, looking around my bedroom, and – no doubt – at how dark and lifeless it seems.

'I tried. I went straight for the big guns – *Grease* and *The Little Mermaid*. Neither worked. It turns out I can pick fault with even my most steadfast coping mechanisms right now.'

'Things must be pretty serious.'

'Yeah. I suppose they are.'

'Is this because of what Adam said? I'm sure you guys will make up—'

'It's not just that,' I say, cutting him off. 'It's everything. It's school, it's Halloween, it's JJ . . . I'm trying to be stronger, but it feels pretty much impossible right now.'

'I thought you were trying to get over JJ?' he says.

'I was. I am. I don't know any more.' I run my hands down my face. 'Urgh. This is so confusing. I thought I was over him, and then all this Big Red stuff happened, so then I wasn't over him, and then Halloween happened, and it was sort of shocking, and I knew I *should* forget about him after that, but then he painted the sports hall today, even though he's been AWOL all week and—'

'You still think JJ is Big Red?' he interrupts.

'Yeah. It has to be him.' As I reaffirm this out loud, my mind jumps into action, presenting the reasons why Big Red has to be JJ: the painting of the face with two sides, one for the true face he showed me, one for the false face he showed everyone else; the Coke explosion, a clear act of revenge – an apology, almost – for what Tyler did to me last term; the wings on the wall at the beach, a physical representation of romance in *our* place; the broken angel (representing JJ post-attack) on the sports hall, the building in school where he spends most of his time. It has to be him. 'But I don't understand why,' I say. 'I thought this Big Red stuff was all about romance, but now I'm not so sure it is.'

He goes quiet for a moment as he looks out of the window, down to the backyard, pulling at his lower lip with his thumb and forefinger.

'You think I'm pathetic, don't you?' I ask.

'Not at all,' he says.

'I wouldn't blame you if you did. Cosmopolitan.com is totally right – I should have deleted him from my life months ago.'

He nods. 'Yeah. Well, you know what I think about the guy. I think you can do a lot better.'

'You do?'

'Course I do! You should totally forget about him.'

'You sound like Adam.'

'Well then, maybe Adam's talking sense.'

'Oh, that's right,' I say, throwing my hands out as if playing to the upper circle. 'Everybody gang up on me. Kick a girl when she's down, why don't you?'

'I'm not ganging up on anybody. I just . . . wish you could see yourself like everybody else sees you. That's all.'

'*No thanks*. Everybody else hates me.'

'No, they don't.'

'Trust me, they do.'

'Well, I wish you could see yourself like . . . I see you, then.'

Even though my bedroom is dark, I can feel his truth-searching eyes searching me for *my* truth. And right away I feel like I want to hide behind one of my (fabulous) scatter cushions. Right away I don't know what to say, because it sounds like Beau Greene is telling me that he sees me in a certain way, and for some reason this makes me feel weird.

'What?' he says.

'Nothing,' I say.

'You went weird for a second.'

'I didn't. Not at all. There's zero weirdness here.'

'OK . . .'

'It was just a nice thing to say. I guess I'm not used to people saying nice things, that's all.'

He chuckles to himself. 'I always say nice things to you, Roman. You just don't want to hear them.'

I can feel him looking at me again, and this strange feeling starts to rumble in the bottom of my stomach, as if the wings down there, which have been lying dormant for a good few weeks now, are stirring back into life. I know this feeling – it's the feeling that exists in the grey areas of life, that thrives off confusion and mixed signals and sleepless nights. And I'm super-aware that I absolutely shouldn't be feeling this way about my friend. I mean, we're in my bedroom, and we're alone, and we're friends, and I shouldn't be feeling anything other than friendship-related feelings.

'Can I tell you something about me?' he says.

'Why?' I say.

'I just want you to know.'

'Sure.'

'I have a condition called synaesthesia,' he says. 'Do you know what that is?'

I shake my head.

'It means I experience senses differently to most people. There are loads of different variations, but for me how it manifests is with colours. Specifically, I strongly associate people with colours, and sometimes shapes. Crazy, right?'

'It sounds sort of fabulous,' I say.

'For all my life, people have appeared the same – brown, peach, beige, grey . . . very rarely someone was yellow, the colour of lemon sorbet, or green, like peppermint creams . . . and then I met you. You're not like anyone else, Roman. Trust me – you're special. Don't let anybody make you feel differently, OK?'

'OK?' I say but I'm confused.

He begins to tap out a rhythm with his fingertips against the window ledge, which I'm guessing means he feels a little bit awkward because he's just shared something deeply personal with me. I think this means it's my turn, and I now have to share something with him. I don't really want to, but I feel like I should.

'Um . . . I was born with a heart murmur,' I say. 'I mean, I grew out of it when I was, like, two, but it still happened.'

'Interesting,' he says.

'You're such a bad liar.'

'I'm not lying – that is interesting!'

'Oh, and I've broken my arm twice in the same place . . . and I have a scar on my leg from climbing a barbed-wire fence when I was ten, and I chipped my front tooth because I headbutted someone when I was six . . .'

'You headbutted someone?'

'Accidentally.'

'I knew you were a rebel.'

'I would never do that on purpose! I hate violence.'

He lifts his eyebrows as if to say, *OK – whatever*, and I firmly cross my arms across my chest to feign annoyance. But I'm not annoyed. I'm so far from annoyed. Having him here has helped to diffuse some of my negative feelings, which is pretty amazing. I like that I can be so relaxed around him. I like that he doesn't judge me for all the mistakes I've made, when it feels like the rest of the world absolutely does. He's the type of person who, when he asks how you're doing, actually wants to know. That's pretty amazing too.

'Thank you,' I say.

'What for?' he says.

'For coming over – it's really nice of you.'

'Ah, don't mention it,' he says. 'I probably should get going, though. Mum will wonder where I am.'

'You don't have to. We could watch a film, or something?'

'I mean, I'd love to,' he says. 'Maybe some other night?'

He grips the edge of the window and lifts it up.

'You can use the front door, you know,' I say.

'This way feels like more of an adventure,' he says.

He shunts the window fully open, and my bedroom instantly fills with a cold burst of outside. Right away I smell woodsmoke, and mulled cider, and the synthetic scent of fireworks. I take a deep breath. I really do love Bonfire Night.

'Good night,' he says, before he climbs on to the window ledge and out into the dark.

I stay in my corner of the bed, listening to the rustling of wisteria branches, and the sound of footsteps across the backyard. It isn't until I know he's reached the back wall that I slide over to the window and poke my head out.

'Night, then,' I say, as I watch him jump down to the back alley.

He answers with a raised hand, and then I hear the sound of his footsteps heading towards the end of the alley.

I watch until I see him turn the corner, then I close the window and throw myself back, starfishing on top of my bed. Weirdly, I can still smell him in here. Along with the smell of Bonfire Night, my room now smells of something that is uniquely Beau, a mixture of salt wind, cut grass and fresh bedding.

I take a deep breath, rubbing my cheek against the duvet in the place where he sat, enjoying the soft feeling and the smell of him brushing against my face.

And right away I know that messaging him was a good idea. Because, for the first time today, I'm smiling.

THIRTY-THREE

It's three rainy days later when the moment I've been waiting for finally arrives.

I'm shaking out my brolly in the hallway when I notice a group of guys all clumped together by the Year 11 lockers, because, you know, everything happens by the Year 11 lockers. The grunting and excitement of a group like this would usually leave me backing away to the nearest cleaning cupboard. But I've become quite devil-may-care recently. Recently, backing away feels like a waste of time.

A quick surveillance of the corridor tells me this group is made up of the sporty guys, the guys on the football team, the ones that seem to be above the usual pitfalls of teenage life. With unblemished skin, perfectly faded haircuts and the very latest Nike Air Whatevers, they're as intimidating as Tyler and his henchmen, but for different reasons: mainly because they're all beautiful. (I guess this makes them the male counterparts to Wynter and her harem of broken dolls.)

As I hurry past, careful to avoid the gathering puddles of rainwater on the overly polished floor, I sense one of them is staring at me. Which is never a good thing. I flick my eyes across the hall to see who it is, and the hairs at the back of my neck turn into pins under my collar. The face I see may be a little scuffed around the edges, with yellowish bruises around one eye and scratches around the other, but it's still as handsome as ever.

That's right.

JJ Dixon is back.

Without slowing down, I bury my chin deeper into Marlene, and hurry to form class, trying my best to stop my heart from exiting my body through my backside.

I don't know why I thought he'd be out for longer. I guess I got so swept up in the rumour mill that I actually started to believe that I *had* broken his jaw, and, according to Dr Google, that can take anything from eight weeks to several months to heal. But at least now it's clear for everyone to see that I didn't. It's clear for everyone to see I didn't break his arm or leg or any other bone either, because I'm not a back-alley-lurking villain, and today could be the day this finally gets proven.

At break time I don't hide out in the art block bathroom, which has become a bit of a habit of late; instead, I head straight for the hall. Brave, I know, but he'll definitely be here. And, because of the wet weather, most of the rest of school will be too. Now that he's back, JJ is going to have to set the record straight (oh the irony), and doing it in front of the entire school is exactly how it needs to happen. Once he tells the truth about the attack, my name will be cleared, and the apologies and giant cookies and chocolate bars will come flooding in. (I've already decided I'm going to forgive them all. I know it's not what they deserve, but I'm far too fabulous to hold a grudge.)

I keep my head held high as I walk in, making sure everybody sees me arrive, making sure everybody knows exactly where to send the giant cookies. With pouted lips, I stand in the threshold for a suspended moment, being the most Marlene Dietrich I can possibly be, before finding a chair in the nearest corner.

Adam and Solange are at their usual table. I can't wait for them to hear JJ's almighty apology. I can't wait to see the looks on their faces when they realise I've been right all along. (Is it wrong that I'm enjoying this right now?)

As I sit cross-legged, listening to the conversations around me, I notice the crowd parts and something moves towards me, a monster with several sets of arms and legs, and several heads (but only one brain).

It's the harem of broken dolls.

They shuffle as one to my chair, where they open like a flower to reveal their queen bee.

'Hi, *Ryan*,' says Wynter Brown.

JJ is standing at her side, holding her hand, their beautiful fingers interlocked. Looking at him now, I can't see why his injuries warranted even a week away from school. I mean, apart from the tiniest bruise on his eye, he looks pretty damn healthy to me.

'Can I help?' I say.

She's come to apologise, and rightly so. It's absolutely fitting that she should offer me the very first apology after everything she's put me through.

'I would just like to say something,' she says.

'Yes?'

'I think you're the worst person I've ever met.' (Wow. Harsh.) 'Look at what you've done – look at John Jo's face.'

So he hasn't told her yet. OK. Well. She's about to feel really stupid in a minute when her 'boyfriend' opens his gorgeous mouth. (BTW – I've kissed that.)

'I'm looking,' I say. 'But I don't see anything I've done.'

I imagine she thinks that by coming over here she's making things really difficult for me, but she's actually doing me a favour. There's no harm in a little dramatic tension in this scene; it's actually helping to gather more of an audience, which is what I need for when JJ issues his almighty, life-changing apology.

So, thanks, Wynter.

'Are you being serious?' she says.

'Deadly,' I say. 'Why don't you ask your boyfriend to tell you the truth – *for once.*'

JJ's mouth falls open, and I can see his neck muscles begin to move as deep, apologetic words begin to form somewhere in there.

And here it comes.

Here we go.

(Drum roll please.)

'*Ladies, gentlemen and all my enby family, I present to you the moment we've all been waiting for – I present to you, JJ Dixon's truth . . .*'

But.

Nothing.

Happens.

He shuts his mouth. The apology doesn't come. He just

stands there, a step behind Wynter, like a skulking kid.

'He's told me the truth!' says Wynter. 'He knows it was you.'

I look at him. Then I look at her. Then I look back at him, his eyes seem vacant, just like they did last term when I had a bottle of Coke emptied over my head in this very room.

'He can't,' I say. But I don't sound too sure. I'm all muffled and woolly, like I'm talking in a memory. I lick my lips and swallow hard, because I want to be as clear as I can. I'm not going to shut up. I'm not going to take this. Not again.

'Tell him, John Jo,' she says, 'tell him what you've just said to us.'

Her words seem to grow bigger, stretching out across the room, because the background noise has dimmed, the rest of the school really listening now.

'Just leave it, Wynter,' I hear him whisper, in the most pathetic, barely audible voice imaginable.

'No, I won't leave it, John Jo!' she says.

'I didn't do it,' I say. 'He knows I didn't.'

'He says you did,' she spits back.

'Can't he speak for himself?' I ask.

'Tell him, John Jo!'

'Yeah, tell me, John Jo – tell me exactly what it is I'm supposed to have done.'

I'm staring at him, and Wynter's staring at him, and I'm pretty sure the entire hall is staring at him now, because we're all waiting to hear what he's going to say.

'Well . . .' he mumbles, 'I guess . . . well . . . it could have been Roman.'

And my heart drops right out of my arsehole to the floor.

'See?' says Wynter, in a voice that cuts the air in half. 'It's true – he did it.'

The entire hall audibly gasps, and the sound pins me to my chair. I'm suddenly aware of how many of them there are. I'm suddenly aware that it's hundreds united against one.

I quickly stand. 'I didn't do it!' I shout. This turns the gasps into laughter. 'Listen to me – I'm not the villain you think I am. I wouldn't do that! I'm telling the truth!'

Wynter throws her head back, her brilliant curls bouncing so perfectly against her shoulders. 'No you're not, Ryan,' she says. 'We all know you've been obsessed with him since last term. We all know what you did because he doesn't fancy you, and we all know you attacked him on Halloween because you found out about us. Just admit it. Do you realise how desperate you look?'

Each one of her particularly harsh words shivers in my guts, as if I'm hearing them there instead of in my ears.

My face starts to feel really hot, and my chest becomes tight. And Rizzo's song from *Grease*, 'There Are Worse Things I Could Do', begins to play in my head because this is so frustrating I could cry. I've got this hot ball in my chest, and I'm worried that it's a knot of tears, because crying in front of him really is the worst thing I could do.

'You're all arseholes!' I shout, barging through the gathering mob, running towards the door. And I've almost made it there when I feel my feet slip from under me and I go flying forward, my arms and legs flailing before I hit the ground.

The laughter that follows is like being inside a nightmare, consuming and breathtaking and sharp, stabbing into me.

I try to stand but slip again.

'*Shit!*'

More laughter. Harsher. Sharper.

Part of me wants to just play dead. Part of me can't face moving any bit of my stupid, awkward body, because it's only going to make them laugh even more.

But I have to get out of here.

I have to.

So, with the last strength I have left, I pick myself up and run out of a hall full of laughter for the second time in my life.

THIRTY-FOUR

I instantly regret running out. Every footstep across the yard feels like a mistake. By running, all I'm doing is giving up. I'm allowing them to write my story, filling in the gaps with whatever lies they like. With every step I take, my boots splashing through puddles, I feel myself become a little messier, a little crazier. But maybe I need to embrace messy and crazy. Because trying to keep myself together hasn't worked so far.

I head for the art block, but I don't go to the bathroom. There's nothing waiting for me in the bathroom. Instead, I go into the studio, into paint-splattered windows, paint-splattered benches and paint-splattered mugs filled with paint-splattered brushes. This feels right. Messy and crazy. Exactly what I need right now.

As I pace from one side of the room to the other, wall to window, easel to door, the tick-tick-ticking of the clock on the wall ten times louder than I've ever heard it, my thoughts grow teeth, claws and beating hearts inside of me. They become free, wild things and I let them. I'm not going to stop myself from being as messy as I need to be right now. I'm going to ride these feelings out, with clenched fists and dry lips and a whole load of adrenaline guiding me. My thoughts keep coming back to the painting still on the wall outside. It flickers in my mind like a pixelated film. This is what started everything. I wish it would leave me alone now. I wish this whole Big Red thing never happened. Adam was right. Everything he said is true. JJ doesn't care about me; someone who cared about me would never keep hiding behind his secret, letting others turn on me. I still don't know why he painted it but I don't care any more. He's a liar. He's a tormentor.

I wish there was a way to make him stop.

I see the paint cupboard door is ajar, and without giving it another thought I dive in, into a mess of coloured tubes and tins and palettes. On the bottom shelf there's a box of spray paints. I pull out the nearest tin. I twist it around in my hand. It's the colour black (which feels totally appropriate). I give it a shake, the ball inside rattling around, and I feel this sudden rush of power, like this tin is a weapon, a grenade I can throw into the thick of the battle.

When JJ painted that wall, he became way more powerful than any individual Year 11 student. He became this noisy, colourful being, always present, shouting at me whenever I walked past. He made Big Red huge and untouchable by painting rather than talking. Talking is over as soon as it's begun. Hot breath rises into the air and disappears. But paint. Paint has power. I see this now.

The bell to signal the end of break explodes into the studio, and the corridor outside begins to fill with noise. The yard is about to become the thoroughfare of every single kid at St Anselm's. I can't think of a more perfect time to make a statement of epic proportions, one big enough to bring even the most popular boy in school to his knees.

I leave the studio, and as I walk into the crowds of grey blazers, everything seems still. It's like I've pressed the pause button on the rest of the world and only now really have time to observe it all. Where only a few moments ago, this place, this yard, these buildings, seemed so important and loud, it all feels less so – just a few random bricks, standing around a square of tarmacked yard. Rusting fences. Sepia background.

I turn and see it immediately.

Colour.

Noise.

It's as if I've just woken up from a long sleep, and I'm more awake than I've been in months; all I want to do is burn this thing to the ground. I grip the cold metal tin of spray paint – the grenade – tighter in my hand, and I walk right up to the wall, pressing my hand flat against the cold bricks, allowing my fingers to fall into the grooves. I feel so rock 'n' roll right now, electric guitars playing in my head, underscoring the moment I light this bitch up.

I take a deep breath. Then, as easily as exhaling, I press the top of the tin and write . . .

JJ DIXON IS BIG RED

My words dance across the two-sided face, covering the vibrant red and acidic green, black paint weeping down the wall like tears as it mixes with rainwater.

And I can feel the crowd gathering behind me. I can hear their shock. I can feel them listening, feel myself being heard for maybe the first time since I started this school.

It feels incredible to fight back like this.

When I'm finished, I turn to face my soaking wet crowd. I'm like a rock star at Glastonbury, just about to finish an iconic set; I'm Stormzy, I'm Beyoncé, I'm Gaga. The band is still playing, drums and guitars going wild as they wait for the final gesture from me to signal the end. I walk forward, holding my arm out straight in front of me, and I drop the tin. It's over.

Mic drop

THIRTY-FIVE

'What *on earth* were you thinking?'

'That it's the truth!' I say, every inch of me still beating with adrenaline. 'JJ Dixon *is* Big Red.'

Mrs Duncan stands on one side of her desk, hands planted firmly on her hips, and I stand on the other. I'm in huge trouble, but I don't care; I won't back down now.

'*If* that's true, why not come to me and tell me? You didn't need to vandalise the school—'

'Yes I did! Nobody listens otherwise.'

She clenches her teeth. I can see a tiny plum-shaped muscle pulsing in her saggy jaw. 'That is not true.'

'Yes it is. I had to make sure I was heard.'

'I can see you still have an incessant need for drama, Ryan,' she says, throwing her bony hands out at her sides.

'I don't have an incessant need for drama. I have an incessant need to be heard.' (Though, I realise as I say it, they're probably somewhat related.) 'I just wanted everyone to know the truth!'

'Roman,' says a voice behind me.

I turn slowly and see there's someone already sitting in my usual chair. I didn't notice him when I was called in; I was too busy buzzing my tits off. But now I'm suddenly aware that I'm standing inches away from JJ Dixon for the second time today.

'What's he doing here?' I say, turning back to Mrs Duncan.

'I asked Mr Dixon here to talk about his return to school. This was prior to your little performance. Now I think it's important he stays so we can get to the bottom of this. Don't you?'

'He's a liar,' I scoff. 'Whatever he says, it isn't true!'

'*Enough!* Really, Ryan, we're not going to get anywhere if you refuse to listen. Please.' She stretches out her hand, indicating for me to take a seat next to JJ.

I really don't want to sit. I'm too pumped to sit. But I know she won't listen to me unless I do. And I need her to listen to me. So, I slump into the chair, crossing my legs away from JJ because I don't want to be anywhere near him right now.

'I did spray-paint the wall, but I didn't attack *him*,' I say, because who knows what JJ might have told her before I came in. 'If that's what you brought him here to talk about, then that's all you need to know.'

'Roman,' he says in this weird, caring tone, like he actually gives a crap about me. This warrants one of my death stares, because even in here he's playing his twisted games. 'All I said was it *could have* been you.'

'Are you joking? The whole school thinks I attacked you and that's your defence? That you only said it *could* have been me?' I shunt my chair further away so I can turn my back on him, because leaning away isn't enough. I want to be as far away from him as possible. 'You're so full of it, JJ. It's laughable.'

'Mr Dixon,' says Mrs Duncan, sighing heavily, 'does this mean you *don't* believe Roman was involved in your attack?'

Silence.

Silence so wide I turn to face him.

He's looking right at me, blue eyes searching for something: recognition, sympathy, reassurance? I don't know, this guy should have a PhD in mixed signals.

'What do you remember about Halloween?' he asks me, dodging the question.

'Really?'

He nods.

'I remember being humiliated.'

'And after?'

'JJ, what are you trying to do?'

He doesn't answer, just stares at me with the same mixed signal look on his face. 'What about after the party?'

'Do you really think it was me?'

'Just answer the question, Mr Albright,' says Mrs Duncan. 'Where were you when JJ was attacked?'

'I was at home, in bed, cursing the day I ever met him.' A half-lie. I was at home, in bed, totally obsessing over him. But I'll be damned if I let him know that.

She nods. 'Do you have anything you'd like to add, Mr Dixon?'

He takes a deep breath. 'The person . . . the guy who attacked me, just kept saying, "You know what you've done." I got punched a couple of times. I just thought, because of what happened last year, it might have been Roman . . .' He trails off.

I scoff loudly. 'Well, it wasn't. I would never attack anyone.'

JJ nods miserably. 'I know that.'

'So, just to be clear,' Mrs Duncan says, 'you don't think Roman attacked you?'

He shakes his head. 'It was dark but . . . no, I know it wasn't Roman.'

And there it is: the truth I've been waiting for.

I should be thrilled, but hearing him talk only annoys me even more, because admitting it in here means nothing when he's just lied in front of the entire school. If you want to be heard around here, you have to do it in a totally epic way. You have to yell it out in the hall on a rainy break time, or spray-paint it on to a wall or secretly plant a Mentos mint in a bottle of Coke. And he knows this. In this room, his words are pointless.

'It was over pretty quickly, really,' JJ adds. 'I was more shocked than anything.'

'And yet you've been absent for a whole week,' Mrs Duncan says, folding her arms.

'That was my parents' idea,' he says, sounding embarrassed.

'Very well,' says Mrs Duncan, nodding. 'At least that's one thing taken care of.'

'Is it?' I say.

'Excuse me?'

'Is it really taken care of? It doesn't sound that way to me – he's just told the entire school that I *did* do it.'

'I only told them you could—'

'*Shut up, JJ!* Every word that comes out of your mouth is a lie.'

'That's quite enough, Ryan,' says Mrs Duncan. 'If you want to have an argument, by all means do it in your own time, but

I won't have it in my office.'

I fold my arms across my chest, as everything I wish I could say to him comes bounding into my head all at once with nowhere to go.

Why did you send me those postcards?

Why couldn't you leave me alone?

Why do you think it's OK to mess with me like this?

'Now, what about this Big Red business?' says Mrs Duncan.

'It's him,' I say, without missing a beat.

'Mr Dixon – is this true?'

'I . . . I didn't do it,' he says.

'Liar!'

'I didn't paint any of that stuff. I'm crap at art.'

'He sent me postcards too,' I say. I reach into my bag and pull them out. 'Here. See? They're signed by Big Red.'

'Yves Klein?' she says, taking them from me. 'What's the relevance?'

'Maybe he can tell us.'

We both turn to face him.

He shakes his head, his lips turning down at the edges. 'I didn't write those.'

'It has to be you,' I say. 'You're the only one who would do this to me, JJ. You're the only one who would mess with me like this. You've done it before, so why not do it again?'

'No, I haven't.'

'You know you have!'

Mrs Duncan raises both of her hands to silence us. 'What did I just say about arguing? Any more outbursts and I'm suspending both of you.'

218

My mouth drops open so wide my jaw clicks. 'Both of us – what the hell have I done?'

'We'll come to that in a minute.'

'*This place is a joke!*'

'You're skating on thin ice now, Ryan – if I were you I'd tread very carefully.'

I bite my teeth together as firmly as I can.

'It seems there's been an awful lot going on here that I wasn't aware of,' she says.

'Yes,' I say.

'No,' he says, at exactly the same time.

'Oh, get a backbone,' I say. 'He's been messing me around for months – ever since last summer, ever since we made out.'

Wow.

I really went there.

And it feels sort of good; saying these words in this office is so totally liberating, like swearing in front of your parents for the first time. I never thought I'd be this brave. But here I am, letting rip like never before.

'Big Red is just another way for him to get to me,' I say.

'Roman. Seriously. It's not me.'

'I don't believe you.'

'Do you have any *proof* JJ is Big Red?' Mrs Duncan asks me.

'One of those postcards was in a book he handed to me! Plus the things Big Red painted are all about him and me . . . the art block wall is about how two-faced he was . . . the old lido on the beach with the romantic wings – that's the spot we kissed, last term . . . and then there's the painting on the sports hall – which is basically *his* building. That was about the attack. I think.' Even as I'm saying it, I realise it doesn't sound like very much.

Meanwhile, JJ is sinking in his chair. He's literally deflating beside me, like one of those helium balloons a few days after the party.

Mrs Duncan tilts her head towards him. 'Well?' she says.

'It wasn't me,' he says, and his voice sounds pathetic again, just like it did in the hall.

'He's a liar. He kissed me—'

'What you get up to in your personal life is no business of mine,' she says. 'But what happens in this school is.'

'Fine,' I say. 'Well, let me give you a list of things that have happened to me at this school. I got a bottle of Coke poured over my head. I got laughed out of the dinner hall. I got cancelled. *I could have gone to prison.*'

'And this is all down to Mr Dixon?'

'He could have stopped it. One word from him and it would have stopped, and he knew it. But he lied. Just like he's lying now. You can't believe a word he says. He lies to everyone, most of all himself, because he's ashamed or embarrassed or whatever.'

The silence that follows seems to stretch all the way to Christmas, because JJ has nothing to say to this. He can't defend himself against the whole, unfiltered truth.

'Give me strength,' says Mrs Duncan eventually, her eyes flicking to the crucifix on the wall. 'Do you have anything you'd like to add, Mr Dixon?'

'Don't listen to him,' I say.

She holds her bony hand up to me. '*Anything?*'

He takes a deep breath. 'I'm not Big Red. I . . .' For a moment it seems like he's going to say more, but instead he just trails off and there's a long silence.

'I see,' Mrs Duncan says eventually, standing. 'Very well. You've both had more than a fair chance to speak. Now, here comes the bad news. I'm giving you both detention.'

'*What?*' we say in unison.

'After school tomorrow you'll both clean up the art block. We should have painted over that wall months ago. That's the last time I listen to Colin Sharpe. You'll both be responsible for returning it to its former glory.'

'But I haven't done anything,' says JJ.

'Exactly,' she says. 'You seem to have had many opportunities to do the right thing, Mr Dixon, and you failed to do anything every time. Think of this as your redemption. You can clean up the wall with Mr Albright here, where you can both argue yourselves hoarse.'

'What have *I* done?' I ask.

'You spray-painted that wall in broad daylight,' she reminds me. 'Maybe, if you'd been inconspicuous like *Big Red* – whoever they may be – you wouldn't be here.'

'This is ridiculous,' I say.

'I'm glad we can agree on one thing. I find this whole thing completely ridiculous. Now, get out, both of you. I've wasted quite enough of my morning on this debacle.'

THIRTY-SIX

'ROMAN!'

My name echoes along the empty corridor.

I turn to see Solange bounding towards me, a wild look on her face. Adam is trailing behind her. His look is also wild, but not in the same way. He looks wide-eyed and sort of nervous.

'I've had enough of this,' she says. 'This is not what we're about at all!'

The sound of her Doc Martens thumping against the hard floor rushes down the corridor with her, until she's standing right in front of me, her hands firmly planted on her hips.

'I saw what happened in the hall,' she says. 'And I'm sorry that we weren't there for you. We're your friends, both of us, and we should have stepped in.'

I don't say anything to this because, yeah, she's right, they should have been there for me. Totally. And they should have stepped in. They should have told Wynter where to go. They should have called out JJ for his lie, instead of leaving me to face an entire hall of laughter again.

'I'm so, so sorry,' she says. 'We're so, so sorry. Aren't we?'

She turns to look at Adam and he shrugs his shoulders, keeping his hands firmly in his pockets.

'OK, that's it,' she says. 'I need you two to make up, right now. This arguing is utter bullshit and I'm not having it. We shouldn't be pulling each other down, not when there are so many others who would happily do that for us. United we stand, divided we fall.' She grips her hand into a fist when she says this.

I look at Adam, but he doesn't look back. He turns his face to the window, looking down at the forecourt in the middle of the building, where a load of sixth formers are having an animated discussion about whatever sixth formers have animated discussions about.

'Oh for God's sake,' says Solange, grabbing him by the arm and shoving him towards me so we're facing each other.

He looks at me, and I look at him, and I'll be damned if I'm going to say the first word. After all, I might have been a total arse to him, but he definitely started our epic argument, which means he has to be the first to reach out. It's, like, the rules of friendship, which are written somewhere in stone; they who cast the first stone must also cast the first apology. (Or something like that.)

'Hi,' he says.

I press my lips together into a half smile.

'I'm . . . I'm sorry I called you a selfish arsehole. I didn't mean it.'

I nod. 'OK. I'm sorry too. I never should have said that thing about having twenty cats. It was totally uncalled for.'

'Yeah,' he says. 'It was.'

This makes Solange throw him an infamous Ballerz death stare.

'Sorry,' he says. 'I'm totally over it. Can we be friends again?'

223

'Sure,' I say, trying to sound cool and composed, but really feeling so damn relieved. I need my friends. Solange is right – united we stand, divided we fall. And I'm done with falling. (BTW not talking to someone is sooo draining, not to mention terrible for the complexion due to the general lack of happiness/sleep; I feel like I've aged a decade this past week.) 'I'd like that.'

'Thank God for that,' says Solange. 'Hug it out?'

'No way,' says Adam.

'Not going to happen,' I say at exactly the same time.

'I thought that might be asking for too much,' she says. 'But it was worth a shot.'

She links arms with both of us and we start walking along the corridor together, side by side, and it feels nice to be like this again.

'I have to say,' Adam begins, 'what you did to the art block wall was freaking iconic, sis!'

'I still can't believe I did it,' I say.

'I honestly thought I'd lost you to him,' he says, more serious now. 'It was like you weren't you any more. I really thought you were going to go back there, and it made me so frustrated – but then you did that and my faith in humankind is restored.'

Wow. I wish he'd been this honest with me before now, because this totally makes sense. He felt like he'd lost a friend, and he was upset, hurting, and I was too far gone into JJ Dixon to see sense. I know I've been so obsessed with JJ that I haven't been the best friend to him, to either of them. But now I'm officially out of my JJ Dixon phase, and so we can go back to being sisters. And there really is nothing like a gay sister to ease the stresses of high school – to quote *To Wong Foo* with, talk about boys with and be totally sarcastic with. If the last few weeks have taught me anything, it's this.

'Do you really think he is Big Red?' asks Solange.

'I don't know any more,' I say.

'Even if you don't,' says Adam, 'the whole school does now. The truth never stopped anyone from believing a rumour before. He's about to get a taste of his own medicine.'

'Yeah,' I say. 'I guess he is.'

'And it's nothing less than he deserves,' he says. 'Remember that.'

'I will,' I say. 'Don't worry. I'm not going to go back there. I'm pretty sure all romantic feelings for JJ Dixon have officially left the building.'

'Really?' says Solange.

'Totally! He's a good-looking guy, yeah, but I'm definitely not interested in chasing someone who treats people the way he does. No way.' Saying this out loud to my friends makes this realisation seem even more deep-rooted. I guess these feelings have been building up without me even realising. But it's true – good looks are nice, but I'm starting to see the appeal in other things, like humour, and silliness, and kindness. They seem sort of more important than a pretty face now.

Wow. I guess I'm evolving.

'She's seen the light,' says Adam, raising his hands to the ceiling.

'Good for you,' says Solange.

'Yeah,' I say. 'I really think it will be good for me.'

THIRTY-SEVEN

Apparently, the news that JJ Dixon is Big Red is more interesting than me being a back-alley-lurking villain. (I don't know whether to be really pleased or really offended by this.) My sort of plan has sort of worked. In a totally epic plot twist, spraying the art block wall has redirected the conversation away from me entirely.

The flip side of my good fortune (because there's always a flip side) is, for the first time in his cis-privileged life JJ Dixon is getting a dose of his own medicine. By the end of the day, the building is abuzz with whispers about what he was trying to do as Big Red. This is where the rumours go completely off-piste.

Some say he set up a fake Snapchat profile, just to troll me.

Some say he's been secretly waiting for me outside my house at night.

Some say it was he who attacked me, not the other way round, and that my nose isn't my real nose because I needed immediate plastic surgery afterwards. (Again, I don't know whether to be really pleased, or really offended by this.)

I don't feel the need to correct them. JJ is no longer my problem. I let the rumour mill spin. I let them drag his name through the dirt, because this is exactly what he did to me, and all's fair in love and war.

My plan is to get my afterschool detention with him over with, and then pretend he doesn't exist. I think it's for the best. After everything that's happened, I don't think even an acquaintanceship would be appropriate. Our romance is over. I'm officially dropping the 'and JJ' and making this story all about Roman.

THIRTY-EIGHT

As I walk out of history class the next day, I notice a hooded figure leaning against one of the wall displays in the corridor outside the classroom. The hood is pulled all the way up, the face is pulled all the way down, and if I didn't know him so well, I'd say the person standing in front of a rather questionable sketch of Joan of Arc wasn't Beau Greene at all. He looks like he hasn't slept in days. (Or, alternatively, like he's about to be burnt at the stake for heresy.) Right away I wonder what's happened to him. The boy who climbed out of my bedroom window, out into the cold of Bonfire Night almost a week ago, was all flushed and happy. This boy is neither of those things.

'What's with the sad face?' I ask, bobbing my head down so I can look up into his hood.

'Oh, hi,' he says, as if I've just woken him from a deep sleep.

'Were you waiting for me?' I say.

'I thought I might catch you walking home.'

'I'm not walking home,' I say. 'Well, not until my detention is over.'

'Detention?'

'Didn't you hear what happened?'

'Everybody heard what happened, Roman.'

'I know, right?' I say. 'What have you heard people saying about me?'

'I've only heard good stuff.' He shrugs. 'Well. Good stuff about you. Not so much about JJ.'

'That's what you get for screwing with people's emotions.'

He nods but doesn't say anything else.

There's nothing about him that looks like the guy I've come to know, and everything about him that looks like the person who was sitting at my table on the first day of term. He's back to being hidden Beau Greene again, he's back to being the waster Beau Greene, and it's sort of throwing me. Come to think of it, he has been pretty quiet these past few days on WhatsApp, which I guess is weird. But not, like, *weird* weird. To be honest, I'd put the radio silence down to his general crap-ness at replying to messages. And maybe not finding the latest meme I sent him all that hilarious (although, it was obviously completely hilarious – I mean, when is a goat strutting to 'Good as Hell' by Lizzo ever not hilarious?). But now, looking at his tired and worn-out face, I'm starting to think something else might be going on.

'I was worried you might get expelled,' he says.

'You were worried?' I say. Maybe this is it?

He nods.

'Aw. That's cute.' I rest my head on his shoulder when I say this, looking up at him to see if this has lifted his mood at all. I'm not sure it has. His mouth starts to twitch as if there are words in there but he doesn't quite know how to shape his lips around them.

'Is everything OK?' I ask.

'Why wouldn't it be?' he says.

'You just seem a bit . . . I don't know. I've barely heard from you all week. Have you been ill?'

'Why – what have you heard?'

I take a step back. 'Heard? I haven't heard anything.'

'Right. Good.'

He carries on walking, but I stand firm. 'What's happened?'

He stops, his shoulders rising up to his ears as he turns to face me. 'Nothing.'

'Not buying it. Nope. You need to lie better.'

He does the lip-twitching thing again before he says, 'I need to tell you something.'

And right away my heart starts pounding in my chest. 'Okaaay – something bad?'

'Yeah. Something bad.'

'What's happened?'

He takes a deep breath and lifts his face so I can properly see him for the first time, and I notice his eyes are red and puffy, as if he's been crying.

'Beau?' I ask tentatively.

'Dad's back.'

The words hang in the air while I wait for the rest.

But he doesn't say anything more. There is no 'rest'. This seems to be it.

'Is he visiting, or . . .'

'He's back for good,' he says. 'He just turned up the night of the fireworks, saying he'd "done his time", whatever that means, and now he's back for good and I don't know what to do. This whole thing is a mess.' He hangs his head again, throwing his hands to his face, pressing them so firmly against his cheeks that his knuckles turn white.

'And you don't want him to be back?' I say, trying to work out the source of Beau's despair, trying to remember what Beau said about the argument he'd had with his dad. I should have listened better, but I was so focused on JJ and Wynter's kiss that night that nothing else mattered. Didn't he want his dad to come back so they could resolve their fight? Isn't this sort of a good thing?

He drops his hands away from his face as he says, 'He doesn't get me. He doesn't understand me at all. And I was just settling into life here, and now he's back and everything has to go back to how it was before . . . and I'm not sure I want it to. I'm not sure I want to go back. I'm not sure I want him to be back. I'm not sure I want him to be . . .'

'What?'

'Doesn't matter.'

'Say what you were going to say.'

'No, because you'll judge.'

'I would never.'

'Roman, judging people is your hobby.'

I can't help but laugh out loud at this one, because it's remarkably cutting for Beau Greene. 'Ouch.'

'Sorry. I just . . . I'm struggling a bit with this.'

'OK. Have you told anyone else – have you told a teacher?'

He shakes his head.

'Do you want to?'

He shakes his head again. 'Am I a bad person?'

'Beau – you're like the nicest person I've ever known.

231

It's actually quite annoying how nice you are. Truth be told, I don't even know why I hang around with you – you make me look like a total arsehole you're so nice.'

'That's . . . not true,' he whispers.

I look at my phone to check the time and see that I'm about to be late for detention. 'Walk and talk?' I suggest.

We walk through the emptying corridors, out into the emptying schoolyard, and I try to think of something useful to say. Relationships with parents is such a minefield of a topic. One wrong word and Beau Greene might explode. I decide more information is needed.

'This is totally none of my business,' I say, 'but what actually happened between you anyway?'

'We just . . . drifted.' He parts his hands as he says this to signify a large gap.

'OK,' I say, though this doesn't really give me any more insight than before. 'Well, if you drifted one way can you just . . . drift back?' I clap my hands together and hold them under my chin.

'I don't think we can.'

'And that's because . . . ?'

He presses his lips together, puffing out his cheeks as if the answer is already in his mouth but he doesn't want to breathe life into it.

'I'm sorry,' I say. 'You don't have to tell me if you don't want to.'

'That's the thing,' he says, 'I do want to. I want to tell you everything, it's just – I don't know how. I thought I did, but now I don't. Does that sound stupid?'

'It sounds a bit strange, I'm not going to lie.'

'Maybe writing it down would be easier.'

'Writing it down – like in a letter? How very Ernest Hemingway of you.'

'Who?'

'He used to write love letters to Marlene Dietrich.'

'Right,' he says. 'Um, no, I thought more like in a WhatsApp message, or something?'

'OK,' I say. 'Whatever you think would work.' I'm starting to feel a bit worried about him now. I know Beau isn't the biggest talker in the world, but I've never seen him lost for words like this. Not with me, anyway.

We arrive at the turn-off for the art block, and I really don't want to leave him like this, but then, I also don't want another detention on top of the detention I already have for being late to that detention.

'This is me,' I say. 'I'm going to have to go.'

'OK,' he says.

'You can come and help me paint if you like?'

'I'm good. I think I just need to think about a few things on my own.'

I nod. 'You know where I am if you need me, OK?'

'Yeah. I do. Thanks, Roman.'

He moves to go, turning his face away first, as if he doesn't want me to see him any more. Then he makes his way across the yard, alone, his feet traipsing beneath him, his head directed at the floor.

THIRTY-NINE

As I turn the corner, I see him leaning against the art block wall, a tin of paint and two sponge rollers with troughs at his feet. (I knew I'd get my Naomi Campbell community service moment eventually. I only wish I owned something Dolce & Gabbana to go with it.)

Usually, this would be the moment I hide in the shadows so I could take all of him in for a secret moment.

I don't do this today.

His physical beauty is the last thing on my mind.

The painting looks like a hot mess now, with my black words weeping down it. It's weird; I can still feel my anger as I approach it. It's like seeing a smashed-up car at the roadside after a hideous crash – you don't need to see the casualties, or hear the screaming, or see blue sirens flashing to know all these awful things happened. You feel it, like a ghost.

'Hey,' he says.

I know he's pissed off with me. Word in the yard is he's been suspended as captain of the football team for defacing the sacred sports hall, and Tyler Hudson wants to kick ten shades of crap out of him because the entire school knows that, as Big Red, he was the one who put the Mentos in Tyler's Coke (I think I have Adam and Solange to thank for this information spreading around the school). And – the gag of the century – Wynter and him are over! *Yup.* They are no longer the most beautiful couple in the village. They will no longer be St Anselm's prom king and queen, because, somehow (Adam and Solange again), the entire school knows that Big Red's paintings were totally romantic gestures meant only for me. (I really do have *the best* best friends.)

The queer kids have spoken, and, surprisingly, St Anselm's has listened. JJ's life has taken an almighty battering, and it's all because I exposed his lie.

Is it wrong that I feel so smug right now?

'Is this mine?' I say, pointing at one of the rollers.

'We have to put these on first,' he says, holding up a hideous pair of navy blue, paint-splattered overalls.

'I'm not wearing that.'

He shrugs. 'That's just what I was told.'

'Ah, Roman,' says Mr Sharpe, poking his head around the door. 'Do you have everything you need?'

'Do I have to wear this?' I ask. 'It couldn't be any further from Dolce & Gabbana if it tried.'

His forehead turns into a mush of lines and valleys as he thinks about this for a moment. 'I don't know anything about that. But yes – you need to wear it. PPE and all of that.'

'Fine,' I say, dropping my bag on the ground, my Naomi Campbell fantasy fizzling away at the edges.

'I'll be in the studio if you need anything.'

I step into the overalls, my back always to JJ, and zip myself up.

'I want to talk to you,' he says.

'I don't want to talk to you.'

'I get that. But I just really want to say sorry.'

It takes me a moment to register the word, like he said it in some other language; it sounds that foreign in his mouth.

'I'm sorry.' He says it again, so I know it has to be real. 'I've been a complete arse to you—'

'Yeah,' I say, still not looking at him. 'You have.'

'Look – I did like you, Roman. It wasn't a game. I don't know if that makes it better or worse. I don't know if it means anything. I did like you, but I got scared, and when the lads found out, I had to deny it. I didn't want them to think I was . . .'

'What?'

He shakes his head. 'It doesn't matter. I'm just really, really sorry.'

'I'm sure you are,' I say, picking up a sponge roller and dunking it into the trough of white paint.

I slap it on the wall right in the middle of the painting, and I begin to roll as quickly as I can because I want it gone. Maybe if the messy painting goes, then the messy past few months will go with it.

'I mean it,' he says.

'Do you have any idea how awful this has been for me?' I ask.

'No.'

'No, because you're "straight", you're cisgender, you're "correct". You can change in the changing room with your mates. You have bathrooms you feel completely safe in. You see yourself in every film and TV show you watch, and every book and newsfeed you read. The *whole world* is catered towards you. You've got no idea what it's like for someone like me, and you never will. You've got it so easy, John Jo Dixon. And you still couldn't tell the truth. *God*. It's like the tinsmith forgot to give you a heart, or something.'

I slap another load of white paint on the wall, splashing it all over the place. (Thank God for the hideous overalls.)

'I'm sorry,' he says again, grabbing my arm.

I start to freak out. I think of Tyler Hudson. I think of last term. 'Get your hand off me!'

'OK. OK. But please, can you listen for a minute?'

'Why – what could you possibly have to say that I would want to hear?'

'I'm sorry for what I did to you last year. I'm sorry for not saying anything about what really happened. But I didn't have anything to do with this. Big Red. The postcards. It isn't me.'

'It has to be you! Do you seriously think I'm that stupid, JJ? I've been on to you for months.'

'Please, Roman. It's all anyone can talk about.'

I know exactly what this is about. The whole school is gossiping about him for a change, and he can't handle it. I look into his face, his bruised, pallid face, and somewhere in my head I hear the imaginary pedestal I put him on smash to pieces, like a priceless vase. He's a coward, too scared of what other people think of him to be who he truly is. I almost feel sorry for him. Almost.

'They're talking about kicking me off the team altogether. The coach doesn't tolerate shit like this. It'll ruin my chances of going to a decent college. It'll ruin my life. Tell them. Please.'

I've often dreamt of the day John Jo Dixon came begging at my feet. In my dreams it was wonderful and magical, and I think we were in some fantastical setting, like Mount Olympus, or a champagne-fuelled fancy dress pool party in Mykonos. (Where he's wearing a totally cute toga, and I'm in a leopard-print maxi dress. Obvs.)

This couldn't look any more different.

And it has nothing to do with the hideous overalls.

I take a deep breath and sigh, dropping my sponge roller into the trough.

Of course, this is the moment I should tell him to go straight to hell and walk away; I should throw this bucket of paint over his head like Rizzo – but my own Rizzo, a queer Rizzo (would that be Quizzo?). I should strut off into the sunset with my head held high like I don't care what happens to him at all, because for once in my life I've actually won.

But I suppose I was never that much of a femme fatale.

(Maybe I'm more of a Frenchie – I would totally slay pink hair.)

I'm so over this whole thing. I'm so over the confusion, and lies. I want this to be the end of it. I really do. And if that means I have to clear his name, then I'm fine with that.

'You have to tell the truth, JJ,' I say. 'What you've experienced is nothing compared to what I've gone through. You have to make it right. You have to tell them the truth about last term. I've been accused of the most horrendous things because you weren't brave enough to speak up. What's the point in clearing your name if you won't clear mine?'

'And if I do, you'll tell them I'm not Big Red?'

238

I throw my hands out. 'Sure. Whatever. I mean, I'll look like a huge tit for writing it all over the wall, but when have you ever cared about that? If anyone asks, I'll just say I got it wrong.'

'You did get it wrong,' he says, looking earnest.

God, he's good. I'm starting to believe him. I definitely chose the right person to play the male lead; this guy should be nominated for an Oscar or something.

'OK, JJ,' I say. 'Fine.'

Whether he's lying or not, he's no longer my concern.

We fall into awkward silence, punctuated only by the sound of slopping paint.

And we stay this way until the wall is completely white, a clean slate. You'd never even know Big Red existed. It feels surprisingly healthy; I sort of feel like a clean slate too. With a few rolls of a sponge roller, I am reborn a new Roman Bright.

I'm like Cher.

(I wonder what this new Roman era will mean for my wardrobe – maybe I'll become Disco Roman, and wear nothing but shimmering fishnets, disco ball earrings and roller-skates. Or how about 90s Dance Roman, with a different coloured headdress for every day of the week – I mean, if Cher can do it, then why not I?)

'I guess that's it, then,' he says when we're finally done, stepping back to look at our work.

'Yup,' I say. 'I'll take all of this inside.'

He unzips his overall and takes it off. Then he scrunches it up in a ball and hands it to me. 'See you around, then?'

'I'm not so sure about that, JJ,' I say, taking it.

I watch him walk away across the darkening yard, and as I do, I bury my nose into his overalls so I can smell him one last time.

But I don't recognise his smell any more.

FORTY

Mr Sharpe is sitting at his desk at the far side of the studio, a small lamp shining on a pile of sketchbooks in front of him. Otherwise, the studio is pretty dark, twilight turning the world outside the window from blue to slate grey.

'Where would you like me to put these?' I ask, because I don't think he's noticed me standing here.

'Ah, Roman,' he says, 'just leave them in the sink. I'll sort them out. The overalls can go in the wash basket by the door.'

I wind through the tall tables to the paint-splattered sink.

'That was quite a performance you gave.'

'Sir?'

'I fought long and hard to keep that painting.'

And though it's getting dark in here, I can see the disappointment etched across his prematurely ageing face clearly enough. I realise what getting rid of the painting means to him. I get it – I can't imagine victories are many when Mrs Duncan is your boss. But I also know what it means to me too. 'I'm not sorry,' I say. This takes him by surprise. 'I had to do it.' I weave back through the tables, making my way to the door. 'That didn't come out how I meant it to. I am sorry in a way – specifically to you. You're the best teacher this

241

school has, sir. If it weren't for you – if it weren't for this building, I don't know where I'd be.'

'There'll always be a safe space for you here, Roman,' he says. 'Any time, dear one.'

I leave the studio and cross the hall to the bathroom. It's pretty dark in here now, with most of the light coming from an orange wall light just outside the window. I flick the switch by the door, but nothing happens. I suppose there's no point replacing light bulbs in a disused bathroom.

I walk over to the sink and quickly wash my hands, wiping them down my trousers to remove any residual water, hoping I'm not covering them in paint stains.

As I take a step back from the mirror, hoping to catch a glimpse of my make-up in the orange light, I hear something, something faint, but definitely there. It's coming from the shadowed cubicles on the other side of the bathroom. It sounds like breathing.

I stare over my shoulder at the blackness behind.

'Hello?' I say, my voice multiplying in size as it bounces off the high ceiling.

There's no reply. Of course there isn't. A bathroom-lurking murderer is hardly going to make their presence known.

Until.

SLAM!

The sudden sound of a toilet seat slamming down fires into the room.

'Who's there?' I ask.

There's no reply. I take out my phone and click on the torch, shining instant light on to the cubicles opposite. *OK. Deep breath, Roman*. I walk up to the first cubicle and kick the door open. It's empty. I try the next. Empty. The next. Nothing. *What am I doing?* I should be halfway across the yard by now. I've seen enough horror films to know how scenes like this go. I'm not going to make it out of here alive if I stay.

I shine my phone on the final cubicle. I take a deep breath and kick the door as hard as I can, sending it flying off the partition wall so quickly, so cleanly, there can't be anybody inside. *OK. I'm done.* I can run to safety now.

Although.

I press my hand against the last door and push it open, much slower this time. And I see something on the toilet seat, in the place where I usually crouch when I'm in hiding-from-the-outside-world mode. It's flat and square, like a piece of card.

Or a postcard.

I lean forward and pick it up, shining light on to the blue painting and the name of the artist underneath it.

Yves Klein.

I take a step back and turn it over, slowly.

This time, the message on the back reads:

I attacked JJ – Big Red

The bathroom light flicks on and the door bursts open. A draught suddenly runs cold fingers through my hair, raising the skin at the back of my neck into goosebumps.

'Roman?' says Mr Sharpe.

It's like I'm seeing him at the end of a long tunnel because I'm not here at all. This postcard has yanked me out of the present and dropped me right back into my head, where the noise is climbing so rapidly it's verging on unbearable.

'I heard banging,' he says.

'I was just looking in the cubicles,' I say.

'Why?'

'I thought I heard something.'

'What did you hear?'

'I don't know. Nothing. There's nobody here.'

'What do you have there?'

'This?' I say, stuffing the postcard inside my bag. 'This is just a postcard, for my mam. It's nothing at all really.'

I stride towards the door, hoping that I've done enough to convince him that I'm not losing the plot completely. I need to get out of here before he asks me any other questions that I'll have to make up lies for, because I'm not feeling particularly creative right now.

'Are you sure you're OK?' he asks, just as I pass. 'You look like you've seen a ghost.'

I have, a ghost I thought was gone, a ghost I thought I'd exorcised when I painted over the wall outside.

'Totally fine, sir,' I say. 'That detention has just tired me out, that's all. I think I need to go home.'

'Fair enough,' he says, nodding. 'Take care walking back. There's a snowstorm heading this way.'

'I will, sir,' I say, before diving out of the door and out into the freezing schoolyard.

FORTY-ONE

The house is too quiet when I get in. It's *Disney on Ice* day. Mam and Mikey will be sitting rinkside right now, enjoying songs from *Moana*, *Frozen* and *Encanto* performed in sub-zero conditions. I have no regrets about not going. It's cold enough outside without willingly sitting by an ice rink for a couple of hours. But I sort of wish they were here right now. I sort of don't want to be alone.

I click on the kitchen light. There's a Post-it note on the bench.

Pizza in the fridge, Love you x

But I'm freaking too much to be hungry, because Big Red attacked JJ, and for some reason he or she or they (because I'm totally not sure any more) wants me to know.

This could mean a whole load of things but mainly it means that JJ isn't Big Red. And I was so adamant he was. I wrote it on the wall in letters six feet high, for goodness' sake. I mean, I'd started to doubt it this afternoon, but I figured that was just my residual feelings for JJ clouding my judgement. I suddenly feel really stupid. An hour ago I really thought I was done with this. And now I'm right back to where I was at the start of term. There'll be no clean slate for me, white wall or not. That painting might as well still be there, screaming at me from the art block, because Big Red hasn't gone anywhere.

This means someone at school attacked JJ. I assumed some faceless idiot did it on Halloween night. The village was full of them after all. I never once thought someone at school would want to hurt their golden boy.

I begin to pace the kitchen, thinking about everything I've missed, all the clues that have been there all along but I was too blinded by adoration to see.

The way I see it, there are two sides to Big Red. Firstly, there's the artistic side: the murals, the postcards. Then there's the violent side: the attack on JJ. Somehow, the same person is behind both.

'Who are you?' I say out loud.

I suddenly feel like I'm in a film noir, and I have to channel my inner Joan Crawford in *Mildred Pierce* ('You're cheap and horrible!') so I can find out who the real culprit could be. (I can almost hear the creepy violins playing in the background.)

OK.

So, I know JJ is out of the picture, because he didn't attack himself, which means everybody else is back in . . .

Tyler Hudson. He'd definitely attack JJ. He'd attack anyone, and it would be nothing to him. But the paintings and postcards are too unlike him; I mean, he's the least artistic person I know, plus (and not to be presumptive, but) I don't get the feeling he's the postcard-writing type. The kind of messages he leaves around school are usually black and blue, rather than International Klein Blue.

246

Wynter Brown. From memory, Wynter has always been pretty good at art, though she didn't take it as a subject in Year 10, so she could be behind the postcards and murals. Maybe Big Red is her artistic outlet. Maybe the paintings always were meant to be regular homophobic crap. And she definitely enjoyed accusing me of the attack. Trying to shift the blame away from herself? But I doubt she'd actually attack her own boyfriend. That seems to be a little extreme, even to get at me. She might have just taken advantage of a situation perfectly crafted to set me up for failure.

Then there are my friends, my Ballerz. I don't want to believe they could do such things to me, but I guess I have to. I guess everybody is now a suspect.

Adam Chung. He hates JJ enough to attack him. I can't think of anyone who's consistently hated JJ as much as him. He could have sent the postcards too. But I'm not so sure about the artwork. If I remember anything from sitting beside him in Year 9 art class, he's pretty terrible at it.

Solange Burrell. She's the best artist in our year. She could definitely be behind Big Red's masterpieces. Definitely. And the Yves Klein connection is there too – I mean, Solange is French; she's a French artist. But she wouldn't attack JJ. I know that. Solange isn't violent.

Beau Greene. He's the new guy, which means he could be guilty of anything. There's still so much I don't know about him. We were together for most of Halloween night, until he walked home. Maybe he attacked JJ then. Maybe he sent the Yves Klein postcards. Maybe he's a really good artist. Although, he doesn't take art. Plus, he's the only person I've spoken to about this stuff. He knows my deepest thoughts on Big Red. And never once in all the times I've spoken about this with him did I get the impression he was in any way involved. And I think I know him well enough to know that he wouldn't hurt a fly.

All of them could be Big Red, but then, at the same time, all of them couldn't. Maybe Big Red isn't one person. Maybe Big Red is a collective. Maybe my Ballerz are Big Red together. Maybe Tyler Hudson has teamed up with Wynter Brown. Maybe all of them are Big Red, only they want me to believe it's one person so I lose my marbles completely. Maybe this is how gay non-binary queer kids are dealt with these days – we're tortured into madness just for being who we are.

Olivia Newton-John!

I walk over to the sink and pour myself a glass of water, because I suddenly feel really hot and dizzy. Outside, it's snowing. Thick chunks swirl around the backyard, settling in the shadows. And it's beautiful and frightening, and isn't it weird that wind is invisible until it snows, and then suddenly all these wonderful swirls and patterns are there, and they've been there all the time only you could never see them?

This makes me wonder what else I haven't been able to see.

I swig the entire glass in one and slam it down on the bench.

This is crazy. In a couple of days Big Red has gone from being the love of my life to the person I dislike most in the world to, potentially, one of my friends. What are they going to do for their next trick – pull a rabbit out of a hat?

I open the fridge and grab a piece of leftover pizza. It tastes like cardboard. And this has nothing to do with Mam's cooking, and everything to do with the sickening feeling that comes with thinking that I've been completely wrong about this stuff right from the beginning.

I stalk out into the hallway, heading for my bedroom, and safety, and a quiet place to think this stuff through. But when I reach the bottom of the stairs, something stops me in my tracks, a familiar sound that shudders through the empty house like panic.

The doorbell.

It sounds too loudly, leaving this tinny, ringing sound in my ears.

Mam wouldn't ring the doorbell.

She has keys.

My instinct is to ignore it, because I don't want to be caught on the doorstep talking to someone selling religion for half an hour. But maybe it is Mam and she needs help getting Mikey's chair through the snow. Maybe it's a call for assistance, like when you press that button with the little person icon on an aeroplane.

'Just a minute,' I shout.

I grab my key from the hall table then I turn it in the lock and crack the door away from the frame.

But Mam isn't standing on the other side.

It takes me a minute to recognise who it is, because he looks so unlike himself. This could totally be someone else, someone with wide and wild eyes, staring at me from somewhere inside his hood.

'Beau?'

'I need to talk to you,' he says quietly, like he's scared he'll be heard.

As if there would be anyone else out in this. The world beyond the garden path is white, and I'm not talking just a dusting, like the type that turns to grey slush at the roadside, I'm talking inches piled high on top of everything, every car, postbox and street light.

'Come in,' I say, stepping to one side so he can pass.

Immediately, he dives into the house and bombs up the stairs, leaving a trail of snow and wet footprints behind him.

'I'm not going back,' he says, as I walk into my bedroom after him. 'I won't go back.'

'OK,' I say. 'Go back where?'

'Home. If he thinks I'm just going to play happy families, he can forget it.'

'Are you talking about your dad?'

'Yeah.' It sounds like he's laughing, but it's the type of laughter that's balanced on a knife's edge, and could easily turn into something else, like crying, or shouting. 'He wants us to pretend everything is fine, and it's not. It couldn't be any further from fine. It's a mess.'

'I'm not exactly following.'

'Roman, he's crazy! He'll do anything to control me. Anything. He sent me to my room because I dared to open my mouth at the dinner table. I climbed out of the window.'

'Wait – he doesn't know you're here?'

'No.'

'My God, Beau Greene – and people think I'm the drama queen.'

'He called school today to speak to Mrs Duncan,' he says. 'She told him about us – that we're friends. Now he knows I have gay friends.'

'Why does that matter?' I ask, but even as I say it I can feel the pieces finally starting to fit together.

He does the knife-edge laugh again and his hand automatically finds the back of his head, finds his scar, and he clenches his jaw as if he's in pain.

And the horrible feeling that's growing in my stomach, like the leftover pizza has suddenly turned bad in there, gets even worse. Because he never did tell me how he got that scar, and now I think it has something to do with his dad.

'Beau – what's really going on?' I ask. 'How did you get that scar? Has this got something to do with your dad – did he do that to you?'

I wait for him to deny it. I wait for him to tell me that the horrible thoughts that are running through my mind right now are totally meritless.

But he doesn't deny it.

He nods.

'It happened just before we moved here,' he says. 'We argued. He lashed out.'

'He hurt you?'

'He pushed me. I banged my head. I needed stitches.'

'Did you tell anybody?'

'No. I couldn't tell Mum. He told her I fell over. *Clumsy me.* Then he went back to work – to Cyprus this time, and left me with a scar, and all this anger.'

My hand is covering my mouth, because this is so totally

horrible. I know how it feels to be pushed around. Too many times I've cleaned a bloody lip in the art block bathroom because of Tyler Hudson. But I can't imagine what it would be like dealing with that at home, in what's supposed to be a safe space.

'Why would he do this to you?' I whisper.

'Why do you think?'

'I don't know?' But I think I do. I recognise the frustrated look in his eyes. I recognise in him what I've seen so many times in myself when looking in the art block bathroom mirror – I recognise a person who desperately wants to be accepted for who they are.

'He knows you have gay friends,' I say, repeating his words back to him, approaching my suspicion, but not quite saying it, not quite yet.

'Yeah – and now he knows that, he'll know about me too. He'll know I haven't been trying to change.'

'Trying to change? Beau – you can't change who you are.'

'Try telling him that.'

'So, he found out that you're . . . gay, and he pushed you?' I hold my breath, waiting for his response.

He nods. And all the pieces slot firmly into place.

'What he did was so wrong,' I say. 'You know that, right?'

'It doesn't change anything, though, does it?'

'It changes everything, Beau! You should tell someone – your mam? Or a teacher.'

'Like you did when Tyler hit you?'

'This is different. This is your *dad*.'

'Exactly,' he says, his hands tensed at his side. 'He's my dad.

And I'll never be free of him.'

Suddenly he turns his back on me and walks towards the door.

'Where are you going?' I ask.

'I have to leave. I shouldn't have come here.'

'What do you mean, *leave*?'

'Get out of here. Run away.'

I follow him out into the hallway. 'You can't! Not tonight. It's snowing out there. Just stay here. We can talk more. Mam won't mind you staying.'

But he walks down the stairs and towards the front door without slowing, like he's walking towards his end. The door is still open, snow falling on to the mat, as he creaks along the hallway towards it. He stands in the threshold for a moment, his shoulders shuddering up and down, and for a moment I think he's about to change his mind about leaving or say something that would make sense of what's going on right now. But he doesn't. He just. Goes.

'Beau!' I shout after him. 'Wait!'

An ice wind blasts into the house, sending the door knocking off the wall, and a load of scarves come billowing towards me from the banister, causing me to fall down the last few steps.

'BEAU!'

I pull myself up from the hallway floor and grab Marlene. I grab my hat and scarf too.

'COME BACK!'

I fasten myself up and run towards the door.

And just as I'm about to run out into the night, I hear Mam's voice.

'Roman – why is the front door open?' she says. 'You're letting all the heat out.'

Talk about the worst timing ever.

She wheels a heavily bundled-up Mikey up the garden path, his chair squeaking through the snow.

'I . . . I was just coming to help,' I say.

'This weather! I thought we might get stuck on the Coast Road, but I think we made it just in time. It's come down heavy, hasn't it?'

I step into the front garden, checking each end of the street for him. Nothing. He's disappeared.

'Give me a hand, then,' Mam says. 'It's Baltic out here.'

I grab the front of Mikey's chair and we carry him over the step into the house.

'The show was great. The costumes were fab. It's a shame you couldn't make it. Mikey loved it, didn't you, my gorgeous one? Pop the kettle on, love, and I'll tell you all about it.'

'I'm actually just going out,' I say, making a decision. I can't leave him out there alone.

'What?'

'I'm going out.'

'Where are you going?'

'Just fancied a walk.'

'In this?'

'Yeah.'

'I don't think so.'

'I won't be long, OK?'

'No, it most certainly is not OK. You're not going out in this, Roman. It's freezing.'

'Look, I have to go now,' I say, wrapping my scarf around me. 'I'll explain everything later.' I kiss her on the cheek. 'I love you, Mam.'

FORTY-TWO

His footprints are deep and clear in the snow, presenting a trail for me to follow. They lead me to the end of our street, and then disappear across the field – the same field where JJ was attacked on Halloween night. But there are no hiding places for hooded attackers tonight. The snow has brought to light things that usually live and breathe in the dark. Still, there's a part of me that wants to turn back, that wants to fall into the warmth of home, and slide into my Ugg boots, and listen to Mam's stories about *Disney on Ice*.

But there's another part of me now, a stronger part, an unexpected part, solid as concrete and just as heavy. It's the part that ties me to Beau, the part that's made up of all these feelings I have for my new friend, the part that needs to know he's safe. It's all too obvious out here in the cold, like, I didn't know I felt so strongly about him until I was chasing him across a snow-covered field.

On the other side of the field, there's a lamp post. I stop here, because I think he stopped here. The snow has been flattened where the orange light hits, as if he trampled the same path over and over, towards and away from the lamp post, towards and away. I can almost follow his thoughts; he's left them here for me, written with shoeprints in the snow. Towards and away.

His is one of the houses across the road; there should be a trail from here to there. This is what I'm looking for. But I don't see it. I don't see his footprints going in that direction. I don't think he went home.

To my left the snow is unspoilt, smoothing over the pavement all the way back into the village. To my right the path leads downhill, to Longsands beach. I take a few paces this way, stepping beyond the reach of the street light.

This is where his footprints reappear. I was right; he didn't go home.

He went to the beach.

I run, crunching through snow piled ankle high, heading to the edge of the world, where the frozen land meets the dark water. It's like I'm living in some black and white film, where the snow looks too white, and the darkness too dark – a film made sadder by its lack of colour, like *It's a Wonderful Life* ('Remember, no man is a failure who has friends').

I arrive at the promenade, wrapping my hands around the metal railing as I look down. It's a high tide tonight. Where there's usually enough space on the sand for volleyball courts, and windbreaks, and every dog-walker in the village, tonight it's just a thin snow-covered bank, clawed away by the sea as it tries to reach the dunes. It's strange to see snow on top of dune grass and sand and boardwalk decking, all the things I associate with summer. It's like two extremes have been forced together: black and white, sea and snow, summer and winter.

If Beau wanted to run away, I can't think why he would come down to the beach. The beach doesn't lead anywhere. There's only one place to go from here, and that's into the sea . . .

Wait.

The sea.

Oh my God. *Oh my GOD*. Is this what he meant by 'run away'?

My heart begins to beat so fiercely in my chest it could tear through my skin, as I think of Beau Greene joining the list of names of people who walk into the sea at night and never come out – his photograph in the local newspaper, someone from Tynemouth RNLI interviewed on the local news as they talk about calling off the search because they couldn't find his body. (This is one of the not great things about living by the sea, one of the things that people who only visit during fair weather never think about.)

Shit. Shit. Shit.

This can't happen, not to him.

I dive at the steps, which cut a path through the dunes to the beach, swiping spiky grass out of my way as I descend into darker places where the orange light from the street lights can't reach.

As soon as I get to the bottom, I jump on to snow-covered sand and run the short distance to the water's edge. This is where his footprints stop, as if Beau has been washed away. It's like he was never here at all, like the past few months never happened. All I can see is endless black, like staring at the TV at the end of my bed.

'Beau!' I shout, cupping my hands to my mouth, looking up and down the beach. My voice sounds tiny. 'Beau! Where are you?'

A wave comes crashing towards me, white spray dancing off it like snow, and I see something in the water, something long and dark, something motionless.

'Oh my God!' I shout, unfastening Marlene and throwing her behind me. 'Beau! Beau, I'm coming!'

Without needing to think about it, I run straight into the freezing sea.

'Beau!' I shout, as I splash into the shallows. 'Hold on!'

I should never have let him leave. I should have made him stay with me. I should have tied him to the banister if I had to because now he's walked into the sea, and he'll be fodder for the local news, another name on the long list of poor unfortunate people, and it's my fault for being such a shit friend.

'Beau!'

I wade in up to my waist, jumping as every wave comes towards me on its way to the beach.

'Beau!'

How am I going to explain this to his mam – his perfect, everything mam? It can't end this way. He can't end this way.

'Beau! Where are you?'

'*What are you doing?*' someone shouts behind me.

I turn around to look and a wave surprises me from behind, washing over my head, pulling me under, and over, and upside down. My mouth fills with salt and sand. It scratches and burns behind my nose as I cough. 'Beau!' I shout as I break through the surface, still trying to push forward though I don't know where forward is right now. 'Beau!'

I feel a hand grab me and pull me towards them.

'Roman, for God's sake, what are you doing?'

'Beau?' I say, wiping my hair out of my eyes.

'Yes. It's me.'

'You're alive! You didn't drown. I'm not the shittest friend in the world!'

He pulls me towards the beach, into the shallows, where my feet find the seabed again. And all at once everything becomes real. Straight away I fall on to my hands and knees and cough up a lungful of salt water. It burns everywhere as it leaves my shaking body, as my hands disappear into wet sand.

I'm cold.

Really bloody cold.

'I thought you . . . were in the . . . water,' I say, in between wheezes. 'I thought you'd drowned . . . and you were going to be on the local . . . news.'

'Come on,' he says, pulling me towards him. 'You need to take this off.'

I just stare at him.

'The jumper, take it off, or you'll freeze!' He helps me out of it, and then pulls his dry hoodie over my head.

I'm instantly wrapped in the smell of him: warm, alive, wonderful him.

'What were you doing?' he says.

'I thought you'd . . . gone into . . . the sea,' I say, my entire body shaking.

'And you went in after me?'

'Of course . . . I . . . did.'

'You would do that for me?'

'Of course . . . I . . . would.'

'Come on, you're shivering. Where's your coat?'

'She's . . . a . . . cape. She's . . . over . . . there.'

He runs over to the water's edge and grabs Marlene, and then throws her around my shoulders, along with my scarf and hat. Then he carries me across the sand to the fish shack, and out of the snow.

I sit down on dry wood, and he slumps down beside me, rubbing my back, holding me close.

'Why did you come down here?' I ask.

'I always come down here to think,' he says.

'Even at night?'

'Yeah.'

'You weren't going to go into the water? That's not what you meant when you said *run away*?'

'Maybe. I don't know.'

I lean further into him, resting my head on his chest. 'Running is never the answer, Beau. Trust me. It only makes things worse.'

'I just had to get out of there,' he says. His lips are close enough to the back of my head for me to feel his warm breath. 'I can't pretend any more. I can't lie. I feel like it's all I've done since we came here.'

'OK,' I say. 'Then tell the truth.'

'You make it sound so easy.'

'It sort of is,' I say. 'I've met your mam. She's lovely. You can talk to her, right?'

'Yeah.'

'Then tell her. You have to tell her, Beau. What your dad did is so wrong – and you shouldn't feel bad about anything. You are an amazing person. Really. You're so warm, and

261

sweet, and silly, and you deserve to be happy just as much as anybody – actually, I'd say you probably deserve it more than about ninety-five per cent of the population.'

'Do you really think that about me?'

'I just said it, didn't I?'

He grips me tighter, which means we're hugging, and it's really nice.

'We shouldn't be out here,' he says, shivering. 'Let me walk you back.'

'Will you stay?' I say, because I need to know he won't do anything stupid. 'Stay at mine? Mam won't mind.'

'Not tonight,' he says. 'I think there's something I need to do first.'

He stands and holds out his hand. I grab it and he pulls me up. Immediately the wind pricks off my face as it comes off the sea like knives. I shudder, and he pulls me closer so we're hugging again.

It's weird because right away I'm reminded that I've done this before, here, in this fish shack. I've held someone close to me. I've felt the warmth of another. Although this time definitely feels different to the last. Maybe it's because I've thought about that day so much ever since that it's become more like a scene from a movie than a memory, something I watched in my head but couldn't truly feel, and being here right now, wrapped in Beau's warmth, is so tangible and real. Or maybe it's because the way I feel about Beau is different to the way I felt about JJ. Maybe it's because, for a very real moment, I thought I'd lost him. I don't know. But, holding on to him, my hands splayed across his back as he grips me close, makes me feel like I'm exactly where I'm supposed to be right now.

'What do you need to do?' I ask into his shoulder.

'I need to go home,' he says. 'I need to tell the truth.'

I squeeze him extra tightly, because I need one more moment of us, just like this, before we move on to whatever happens next.

Then we head back out into the snow, making our way back up the bank towards the village, keeping right at each other's side.

FORTY-THREE

I lie awake, shivering under a pile of extra blankets and towels and anything else I could find in the laundry cupboard that would help me thaw out. I know it's already past midnight, but I don't feel sleepy at all. My toes wriggle at the bottom of the bed, as I flip from one side of the pillow to the other and back again, my mind supercharged with thoughts of him.

My phone is right next to me, face up on the bedside table. I've turned it up to maximum brightness and volume because I don't want to fall asleep before Beau messages. I made him promise he would, and then he left, walked back out into the snow and across the field to his house to tell his mam everything he's been keeping from her. He seemed pretty set on tonight being the night he stopped hiding. This makes me super nervous.

I don't want to miss the moment he needs me.

As I lie here, my arms folded across my body for extra warmth, I think about everything he told me tonight: his relationship with his dad, how he got his scar, his sexuality. Though the circumstances are messy and troubling, I can't help but feel pleased that he's been honest with me. It's like, the extra blankets and towels are great, but nothing can beat the warm feeling that comes when someone opens up to you like this, when someone allows you *in* like this. I've never had this before. It makes me feel really close to Beau right now, like he's still here with me, right by my side.

I tap my phone screen. Still nothing.

I shuffle further down the bed, further into his hoodie, and right away his scent fills my head. My mind leaps into action, showing me an enchanted beach scene where there's no sunshine, only snow and darkness and stars, which somehow makes it seem all the more magical. Though the backdrop is cold, I feel warm when I picture it. I feel *happy* when I picture it. I mean, all drama aside, tonight was pretty epic; I've never hugged anybody like that before, or been hugged in that way in return. Yeah, I've been physically close to someone, but tonight felt different. With JJ – my last beach scene partner – it was all an act. There was never any truth in what we had. I see that now. But with Beau . . . what I have with Beau is nothing like what I had with JJ. We mean something real to each other. We're honest with each other. I guess Beau's openness tonight has sort of cleared a path for me to be open too, and right now, picturing that magical winter beach scene in my head, I can't help but feel like I'm . . .

Well, I'm . . .

I spring forward, sending a load of towels tumbling to the bedroom floor. I don't know if I can admit it, but now I've had the thought I can't un-have it.

So I guess I have to.

'I'm . . . crushing on Beau?'

I sit in the darkness of my bedroom, the air buzzing with the sound of my words. Now they're here, spoken into being,

265

I'm realising how 'normal' they sound; this isn't just a random thought that's slipped out. This has been here for a while, quietly happening in the background while other more dramatic things played in the foreground. But now Beau is in the foreground. He isn't hiding any more. I can see every part of him.

'I'm crushing on Beau!'

I say it more loudly because I want to hear it again, and as I do I'm reminded of all the times he's made me smile, or laugh, all the times when seeing him – even over my very best friends – was exactly what I needed. (Which is textbook crushing behaviour BTW.)

I lie – no, collapse – back on to the pillows and squeeze my eyes closed so I can relive how our storyline unfolded. I see him changing in my bedroom before Halloween, I see our hands touching when we placed the candle on his sister's birthday cake, and I see us together on Bonfire Night, the night he was totally and completely there for me. Why couldn't I see it before now? This is so the stuff great crushes are made of!

Before I know it, I'm rubbing my nose in his hoodie so I can take in a deep breath of him, because now I've admitted it to myself I can't pretend this doesn't feel completely amazing.

Because, now I think about it, Beau does have so many excellent 'male lead' qualities, but in a 'new-look male lead' sort of way. I thought muscles and a handsome face were all it took to sweep me off my feet, but now I know better. Muscles and good looks get boring after a while. A male lead should be dependable. Honest. Caring. These things are way more important than all that Danny Zuko crap. I'm so over that. Just the thought of it makes me shudder. Beau isn't like Danny Zuko; he isn't out to impress; he isn't trying to be cool. Beau is dependable. Beau is honest. Beau is sweet and kind and funny and so caring, which, by the way, actually *makes* him totally cool and impressive anyway!

Wow.

This is so . . . wow.

I want to savour every part of this moment, this electric, coruscating feeling that's rushing through my insides, because this has the potential to be the most amazing thing that's happened this term, because this time the crushing feeling isn't frail and uncertain like it was with JJ. This time the crushing feeling won't lead to me actually being crushed. This time it's sure, strong and so . . . so *everything*. Because this time? Well, I have a feeling there's a chance Beau feels the exact same way.

At 02.01 my phone lights up and the message sound rings in my ears so loudly I jump forward. At some point between constantly tapping my phone screen and imagining a new movie in my mind about Beau and me, I must have fallen asleep. I'm completely twisted up in old blankets and towels, sweating under the pile of stuff from the laundry cupboard.

I shuffle my arms free and tap my phone open.

Beau Greene

told mum everything, dad has gone x

Roman Bright

OMG

he's gone?!

you're awake

course I am!

what happened?

r u ok?

i'm ok, just drained

he and mum argued, he admitted to pushing me, he left

mum has been supportive

is he coming bak?

dnt know

how you feeling about it?

i'm glad I told mum

can I do anything?

you've done more than you'll ever know Roman

i'm here for you Beau

i appreciate it

off to bed now still freezing

night x

OK

night

call if u need me

dnt leave the house again!!!

I can't help but feel bad for him. I'm happy he's finally spoken to his mam, but I'm sad this is the price he's had to pay. More than anything, though, I want to go over there. I want to see him, if only just to make sure he's OK. I want to be the best friend I can possibly be right now, but 2 a.m. is way too late to cross the field, even if the snow has stopped.

So, for now, my efforts will have to wait.

FORTY-FOUR

I wear Beau's hoodie all night. Is that weird? It doesn't feel weird. Actually, since my revelation, falling asleep with the hood pulled up sort of feels necessary right now. There's something about being wrapped up in the warm smell of him that makes me feel protected. Safe. The guy ran into the North Sea in winter for me, for goodness' sake. That's sort of crazy, and magical, and it's making me feel all these really big feelings for him, which the hoodie is definitely helping to make sense of. Like – *Look, he gave you his hoodie – he definitely likes you too*, sort of thing.

Before I know it, the hoodie becomes part of my nightly ritual, as important as brushing my teeth and slapping on Mam's Clinique Moisture Surge moisturiser.

He knows I have it.

It's not like I've stolen it or anything.

With the ridiculous amount of homework I've accumulated thanks to the most dramatic few weeks of my life, and Beau Greene's general crapness at replying to messages, the week just sort of passes by without me realising I haven't heard much from him at all. Before I know it it's Saturday and I haven't seen him, not even in English class, which is totally strange.

So I decide to pay him a visit. I get up early and search my wardrobe for something totally cute, but not too cute. I don't want to seem like too much of a try-hard. In the end, I choose some vintage combat pants and a lavender asymmetric cable-knit jumper, but I add my faux bearskin hat, which sort of screams try-hard just by existing. Oh, and Buffalo boots. (What can I say? I just can't turn it off.) Then I make my way out into a winter wonderland full of kids with sledges, who are heading for the hilly inclines of Tynemouth golf club to make the most of the snow.

As I approach Beau's house, I notice all the curtains are closed, even though it's not that early. Maybe the Greenes are late risers. (I don't have that luxury living in a house with Mam and Mikey – the chaos kicks off at around 5 a.m. at mine.) There's a wreath on the door. It's quite extravagant, made of pine branches woven with dried citrus fruits and feathers. I imagine this is Beau's mam's doing. She, like the wreath, really is quite fabulous.

I walk up the path and can see some lights are on beyond the closed curtains, so decide someone must be up. I press the doorbell.

When the door cracks open, it's her face I see. She looks more like Beau than ever.

'Roman?' she says. She's wearing a pale blue cashmere jumper over a pair of classic Levi's 501s. Her cheeks are bronzed and her hair is tousled into a beach wave. Even though the world is freezing and snow-covered, one look at her and I feel instantly warmed; it's like she carries summer with her wherever she goes. I think I'm officially obsessed.

'Morning,' I say. 'Is Beau in?'

'Yes,' she says. 'Yes – he's in, but I don't know if he's well enough to see you, I'm afraid.'

I inhale so suddenly I begin to choke on my own saliva (I hate it when that happens – it's like my body is self-sabotaging). 'Sorry,' I say, the word clearing my throat at the same time. 'When you say "well enough" . . . ?'

'I'm afraid he's been quite poorly.'

Wait.

What?

'When you say "quite poorly", what are we talking about here?'

'Come in out of the cold,' she says, standing to one side.

I stomp my Buffalo boots on the mat before entering the house. 'What's wrong with him?'

'He has a fever. He's been in bed all week.'

'Oh my GOD!' I say, my hand flying to my mouth as I realise that this must be the reason I haven't heard from him. He's ill. And it's completely my fault; Beau ran into the freezing sea after me, and then gave me his hoodie to keep me warm. I'm such a selfish-bitch-arsehole that I didn't even think about him being cold or the possibility of him getting ill.

'Grab a seat,' she says, indicating for me to sit on one of the plush sofas. 'I'll go up and check on him.'

My head falls into my hands as I think of Beau, bedbound, and all because of my selfishness. I shouldn't have taken his hoodie. I should have given him Marlene, or at least my scarf. *Why didn't I do that?* He walked back to my house in sub-zero conditions in a bloody T-shirt. Of course it's made

273

him ill. He could be upstairs dying of pneumonia right now and it's my fault!

'He's sleeping,' says his mam, reappearing behind the door.

'Is he dying of pneumonia?'

'It's not as bad as that,' she says with a smile.

'Can I see him?'

'He's sleeping, Roman.'

'I know, but can I just sit with him? I promise I won't wake him. I'll be like Beyoncé in the lift – he'll never know I'm there. Please. I want to be there when he wakes up.'

I can tell she doesn't quite know how to take my Beyoncé comment, because she stares at me, open-mouthed, for an awkward moment.

'Sorry,' I say. 'I just *really* want to see him.'

'Oh, OK,' she says, smiling Beau's smile. 'I'm sure he'd want you to be there too. But try not to wake him. We've been through a lot this week – he needs rest.'

I nod because I know exactly what she means by this. I know that her family has sort of been wrenched apart by the secret Beau has been keeping since before they moved here. (For someone who's going through so much, her complexion is remarkably smooth. Her skin tone against the colour of the cashmere jumper is giving me everything right now.)

'The cashmere is periwinkle blue, right?' I say as I follow her up the stairs.

'I think so,' she says. 'You're very observant.'

'I am. And I appreciate a timeless garment when I see one.'

She walks across the landing and slowly pushes the door, then waves me in, departing silently.

The room is dark, save for a sliver of light beaming in from behind drawn curtains. Beau is under a pile of duvet, his thick curls tatted into a nest somewhere near the top. I make my way to the armchair in the corner, and sit down slowly, carefully, making sure not to make a sound. Then I wait, listening to him breathing, checking for any signs of pneumonia-related symptoms, like laboured breaths or coughing (I googled it). He doesn't seem to have any.

On the bedside table there's a bottle of water and a packet of tablets. Most of them are gone, silver foil snapped and curling away from the plastic tray. Next to this is his copy of *Jekyll and Hyde*.

My copy used to stay on the bedside table too. Now it's buried somewhere at the bottom of my bag. The book JJ Dixon handed to me, much like JJ himself, doesn't feel important enough to take pride of place in my bedroom any more. It's sort of strange Beau's is out, considering he hasn't been in English class all week.

I reach over and slip it off the bedside table.

Immediately a bunch of pages fall out and splay across my lap. I slap my hand down quickly to stop them falling on the floor, making a loud thumping sound against my thigh. The mountain of duvet stirs and I freeze, still as a Victorian statue. I can't be the person who wakes Beau from his much-needed rest. Only an arsehole would do such a thing. I wait in the silence of his bedroom, my breath high in my chest, until the duvet is still and I'm sure he's sleeping again.

OK.

I gather up the pages so I can silently slide them back into the book as if I never started going through Beau's personal things at all, and as I do I realise something: they're not pages. They're too glossy to be pages.

They're postcards.

They're Yves Klein postcards.

All of them blank.

The duvet stirs again and I shove them inside the book, because maybe if I shove them back in there I might forget I ever saw them. I place the book down on to the bedside table and it's then that I see there's another book right next to it, a sketchbook, well used, and curling at the edges. I should probably ignore this too, but before I know it's in my hands, open at the first page.

The page is full of faces, bubble text and shapes, all drawn in different colours, the most familiar being an angry red circle in the corner, drawn over and over until the page is so worn it's nearly torn. On the next page there is a sketch of a face with two sides, one red and the other green. On the green side the words *truth*, *hope* and *freedom* twist around across the head and down around the chin where they join with the red-side words: *liar*, *failure* and *shame*. This is a sketch of the painting on the art block wall, Big Red's first painting.

The duvet mountain scrunches and gathers together, and Beau's face appears through the top of it.

'Roman?' he says, smiling. 'What are you doing here?'

'I came to see you,' I say. 'Your mam told me you've been ill.'

He blinks a few times, blinking the sleep away from his eyes. It takes him a moment to realise what I have in my hands. When he does, he stares blankly at it, stares for way longer than an awkward moment.

'Did you look in it?' he says.

'A bit,' I say.

'So then . . . you know?'

I swear my heart stops beating, as if time itself has stopped. Because, yeah, I do know. And out of all the people I thought it could have been, out of all the people who so obviously want to make my life a living hell, the last person I thought would do this to me is him.

'It was you,' I say. 'You're Big Red.'

He nods. 'Yeah. It was me.'

'Why?' is the first word that comes out of my mouth.

'I did it for you,' he says. 'I know how effed up that sounds, but I promise it's the truth.'

I smile, even though my heart is smashing my insides to pieces right now, even though I'm internally turning to sand. I smile, and I know it's a totally weird reaction to have when finding out that your friend has been the villain all along. *Why am I smiling?* This scene isn't about smiling. This scene is about treachery and betrayal. Who the F smiles at a time like this?

'Roman – why do you look like that?' he says.

'Like what?'

Like the bloody Cheshire Cat, you weirdo.

'Why are you smiling?'

'I'm not,' I say, standing.

As I do the sketchbook falls off my lap to the floor, falling open at a pair of blue wings, the same wings that he, *Beau Greene* – not JJ Dixon, or the mythical Big Red – painted on the wall of the old lido.

I walk towards the door and he throws off the duvet.

'Where are you going?' he says.

'I told you it was JJ,' I say, turning around sharply. 'I very specifically told you that . . . you were the first one I told . . . the first one I trusted . . . the first one.' My voice sounds lower. Slower. I'm shaking.

'I know.'

'We spoke about it, and you didn't say anything.'

'I know. I'm sorry.'

'You . . . lied to me.'

'It wasn't like that.'

'You knew. All the time you let me believe it was JJ, you let me make a complete arse out of myself, and you knew. How *could* you do this to me?'

I turn and grab the door handle. But he's leapt out of bed and presses his hand against the door so it bangs shut.

'What are you doing?' I say. 'Let me out!'

'Roman, let me explain.'

'Beau, get out of my way.'

'Please. I want you to understand.'

'What's left to understand? You've won. Whatever little game you've been playing is over. Congrats. You're the winner. Your medal's in the post.'

'What?'

'Who put you up to it – was it Wynter? No – she'd take too much pleasure in doing this herself . . .'

'I don't know what—'

'I suppose it could have been any of them. Or maybe this is just the real you. *God*. I'm such an idiot. Of course it's you. *Of course it is.* You're the perfect casting – the weirdo new kid who nobody really knows. Why didn't I work it out? Oh, well done, Roman, you complete arse! Why do I always put guys I like on such a freaking high pedestal?'

'Stop, Roman! This wasn't about anyone but me and you.'

'Wow.'

'What?'

I start clapping my hands together. 'Get this guy an Oscar – you don't have to keep playing now, Beau. I've found you out. The jig is up.'

'Please – just listen to me.' I go to grab the handle again and he swipes my hand away. 'I want you to know why I did it. I want you to know how I feel about you.'

'Oh, don't worry. I've got the message. Loud and clear.'

He grips my shoulders, and I cross my arms against my chest.

'Roman. Listen to me.'

'Why should I?'

'I did it for you.'

'Liar!'

'I didn't mean for any of it to hurt you. I wanted to show you how special you are. That's all.'

'I don't believe you.'

'Then look!' He bends down and picks up the book, holding it open at the lido wings. 'Look. Let me show you. Every painting meant something. Take these wings for example – they represent how I see you, and how amazing you are to me. I painted them on the beach because, after what happened there, I wanted to give you a new memory of that place—'

279

'Get that villainous thing out of my face!'

'Please. Let me at least tell you why I did what I did.'

I start to laugh. 'OK. Sure. Tell me. Come on. Tell me why you thought it was a good idea to screw with me like this. I'm *dying* to know.'

He takes a moment before he speaks again, as if he wants to be sure of everything he's about to say. He runs his hands through his curls, holding them at the back of his head. Then he starts to talk.

Words come spilling over his lips like water, like he can't get them out quickly enough. He stumbles and trips as he tells me about how he saw what happened to me in the hall last term, and how it reminded him of the argument he had with his dad. I listen as he talks about it making him angry enough to take action. I listen as he talks about seeing so much of me in him that day. I listen as he talks about his synaesthesia, and associating his dad with an angry red circle, and how he created Big Red because he wanted to turn his bad feelings into something beautiful by creating art. He talks about the face with two sides, green for Beau Greene, red for Big Red – and how obvious that message was supposed to be for me, even though I didn't even know him at the beginning of term, so how could it be? – and the broken wings on the wall right outside English class, the wings he hoped would start a conversation between us about everything he was going through at home, and what really happened on Halloween, and, eventually, about Big Red. But what seems to make complete sense to him makes absolutely none to me. And I'm only half listening anyway, because I can't actually believe this is happening right now, because he's supposed to be my friend, and friends don't try to ruin each other's lives like this.

'I need to go,' I say.

'Will you just let me finish?' he asks desperately.

'Beau, I don't think this is going to change anything.'

'I told you I see people as colours, well – I need you to know you're unlike any person I've ever seen before. You're blue, Roman. *International Klein Blue.* You're so rare and special and specific, and all I wanted was for you to see that. All I wanted was for you to see what I see. That's what the paintings were supposed to mean. I wasn't brave enough to tell you as Beau Greene. But I knew Big Red could do it because Big Red was powerful, and I'm not.'

I look right at him, right at his huge, truth-seeking eyes. I don't know if he deserves any more of my time. I don't know if I'm overreacting. I don't even know whether to believe him or not. But then I realise something else.

'Big Red attacked JJ,' I say. 'He was off for like a week. That was you. You gave him a black eye.'

'No . . . he came at me . . . I got scared . . . it was an accident.'

'People don't just accidentally punch people in the face, Beau,' I say, reaching for the door handle. This time he doesn't try to stop me. 'Even if I can make sense of all the other stuff, I can't be OK with that.' I pull the door towards me. *'Jesus.* It's like I don't even know you at all.'

And then I leave.

FORTY-FIVE

Out of everyone I thought it might be, I suspected him the least. Which feels like the biggest joke of all. Even if I could get my head around his reasons – his awkwardness, his relationship with his dad – I can't move on from the almighty lie he's been feeding me for all the time I've known him. He's not the Beau Greene I know, because that person doesn't exist. And that's so unbelievably shocking. I've been friends with a lie, a mirage, a facade. He's a liar, just like JJ is a liar, just like Wynter Brown is a liar. He was never the sweet, caring guy who wore a silly hat to his sister's birthday. He was never the brave guy who came with me to Wynter's Halloween party and stood by my side when she threw me out on to the street. He was never the guy who ran into the sea to save me. He was never the male lead. Beneath it all, he was always Big Red, the villain, the one who's made my life so difficult these past few months.

My initial feeling is anger, loads of it, enough to demolish a block of flats. I stomp across the snowy field, past happy families with excited faces like I'm the Grinch who stole Christmas. I clench my jaw so tightly my back teeth start to sting, because I'm feeling so feral right now I can't guarantee I'm not going to bite a chunk out of somebody's sledge. And, the worst part is, it's a familiar feeling. The piece of anger Tyler Hudson left with me the day he poured Coke over my head, which I thought I'd exorcised when I sprayed JJ's name on the art block wall, was just sitting there waiting. It's still there, the piece of glass; it's sticking right in my heart. I feel it now more than ever.

I stomp along my street, swiping the snow off front garden walls as I pass for no other reason than it looks pretty, and I don't want to see anything pretty right now. I'm so unbelievably pissed off I want to break something. This betrayal is too much. JJ might have been an arse to me, picking me up and dropping me whenever he pleased, but this is worse. This was calculated. Smart. This was truly villainous behaviour. I feel sick when I think of all the time Beau and me spent together in my bedroom, and all things I told him, and all the ways I opened up to him, when the whole time he was secretly making my life hell with every painting and postcard he left.

I know Mam has taken Mikey to Grandma's house, so when I get in, I slam the door as hard as I can, because I can't make loud noises when he's here, and I need to make loud noises right now. I need to get these feelings out of me before I internally combust.

I storm up the stairs, across the landing, and into my bedroom. The first thing I see is his hoodie, scrunched up in a ball on the bed.

And it's like I've been punched in the gut, because the way I felt an hour ago when I placed this hoodie on the bed, the warm feeling that comes when you have a crush on someone, comes rushing back to me. And my anger begins to transform into sadness.

I wonder if he would have ever told me, if I hadn't figured it out myself.

I pick up the hoodie, and even though I know I absolutely shouldn't, I bury my face in it. And right away I feel this dry lump in my throat. It's like he's died or something. That's how it feels. Or like he was never real.

He was never Beau Greene.

He was only ever Big Red.

FORTY-SIX

I call an emergency Ballerz meeting that Saturday night to tell Adam and Solange about Beau.

'So he's gay?' asks Adam, once I've finished.

'Why is that the first place your mind goes?' I ask.

'Because it's always the most interesting part,' he says.

'I've literally just told you that Beau Greene is St Anselm's answer to Banksy. *Beau Greene!* And that he beat the crap out of JJ on Halloween, and you think him being gay is the most interesting part?'

He shrugs. 'JJ deserved it, to be fair.'

'Ignore him,' says Solange. 'What are you going to do?'

'I'm not going to *do* anything. Obviously I'm never speaking to Beau ever again.'

'Really?' she says.

'Yeah.'

She presses her lips together and nods, really slowly. 'Poor Beau.'

'What do you mean, "poor Beau"?' I say. 'Poor me!'

Her eyebrows raise into two perfect arches and she looks at Adam, who gives her the internationally recognised *well, this is awkward* face (motionless face, crazy wide eyes looking to the left).

'What?' I say.

'Nothing,' she says.

'You clearly have an opinion.'

'I don't.'

'Then what's with the judgemental face?'

'I'm not judging,' she says.

'Said none of us, ever . . .' whispers Adam.

I've spent the best part of an afternoon going over everything that's happened over the last term, slotting Beau Greene into all of the Big-Red-shaped gaps, while kicking myself for being so dumb. I've also spent the best part of an afternoon ignoring his messages and calls, as there's nothing he could possibly say that would make this situation any better (other than if he told me he was only joking and he wasn't really Big Red and it was all a misunderstanding, but then, I think that would piss me off so dramatically we still couldn't be friends anyway. Either way, we're done. Totally. Completely. Done). I called my Ballerz over because I need them to diffuse my feelings of rage. I need them to be completely on my side on this one, because what Beau did was so wrong. I *don't* need them to be in any way understanding or mindful of him.

'Look, I just feel bad for him,' says Solange. 'That's all.'

'Why would anybody feel bad for him?' I scoff.

'Don't you think having to deal with a homophobic parent who attacked him is pretty heavy?' she asks. 'He opened up to you, Roman. He trusted you, and now you're just going to pretend he doesn't even exist? I know he made a mistake, but that's totally harsh.'

'He *lied* to me.'

'He kept the truth from you.'

'There's a very small difference,' says Adam. 'Tiny. Microscopic—'

'He's ruined my life!' I say. 'He could have stopped all the crap I've had to deal with this term—'

'No, he couldn't,' she says calmly. 'The stuff you've been dealing with wasn't Big Red's fault. You've been dealing with crap since well before Big Red was around. We all have. Beau couldn't have magically erased every homophobic idiot at school.'

I know she thinks she's helping, but I really don't need to think about what Beau is going through right now. I'm the one who's been made an absolute fool of here. Not him. She should be supporting me, and agreeing with everything I say like a best friend should. Not talking about Beau like he's been grievously wronged. He hasn't. *I* have. I'm the one who's been grievously wronged.

'Well, he definitely didn't make it any easier for me,' I say.

'But don't you think he sort of tried?' she asks. 'I mean, he got revenge on Tyler for you—'

'Which led to Tyler attacking me again!' I protest.

'He didn't know that would happen,' Solange says calmly. 'Plus, he got JJ back for you and didn't you say that JJ finally apologised for how he treated—'

'He physically attacked JJ!' I say. 'That's not OK, Solange!'

'Roman has a point there,' says Adam. 'I mean, we all wanted to punch JJ for what he did last term, but none of us actually did it.'

This is another thing that's been playing on my mind all day, in addition to the lies. Violence. I hate violence. It's a language I don't understand at all. Attacking JJ makes Beau no better than the lowliest of troglodytes, no better than Tyler Hudson.

'Look – I'm no psychiatrist,' says Solange, 'but you can't put all the blame on Beau. His dad had done the same thing to him. *His dad*. It doesn't make attacking JJ right . . . but having that going on at home must have messed him up pretty badly. I can't imagine what it must be like to go home and not feel safe. Even if his dad hasn't been around recently, you don't heal from something like that right away.'

'His dad has been around recently,' I say, almost unwillingly. 'He came back.'

'Seriously?' says Solange. 'Does the school know?'

'Yeah. I think so. His dad rang Duncan and she told him that we're friends, and Beau freaked out—'

'Because he was scared,' says Solange.

'I dunno,' I say.

'Oh for God's sake, Roman.'

'What?'

'The more you tell me, the worse I feel for him.'

'Why?'

'Yeah – why are you all of a sudden Team Beau?' says Adam. 'You don't even know him that well.'

'I'm not on team anyone. I just feel bad for him,' she says. 'It sounds like he's going through a lot. It sounds like he needs friends.'

She looks at me when she says the last part, like this is somehow my fault, and I should be a better friend. Which is totally annoying. I mean, what does she want me to do – just pretend the last few months didn't happen? This Big Red stuff has been major; it has totally shaped my life this term. I can't just let that go. I can't just move on as if it was nothing, because it really wasn't.

'You just don't get it,' I say.

She takes a deep breath, sitting up taller, before she says, 'No, I think it's you who doesn't get it, Roman.'

'Are you sure you want to do this?' Adam asks Solange, because he sees she's gearing up for a speech and knows that this could potentially lead to another argument of epic proportions.

'I'm sorry,' begins Solange, 'but I have to say it. Look, Roman, I've sat here and listened to you talk about a guy who was so into you he worked out a plan to humiliate the guy who was bullying you. I've listened to you talk about a guy who literally kicked the crap out of the guy who'd been messing you around. I've listened to you talk about a guy who left you a load of, frankly, pretty *amazing* art around the school, risking a lot to do so, just to get your attention. And yeah, the secret got so big that it ended up turning into a lie, but that doesn't change the intention behind it. We've all seen how he looks at you. Beau's clearly crazy about you. Why can't you cut him some slack, and just talk to him? We all make mistakes.'

'Because I can't,' I say sharply, feeling I really shouldn't have to be defending myself to my friends like this.

She presses her lips together as if she's about to say something to argue this point, but her mouth falls open pretty quickly, because there's really nothing left to say.

FORTY-SEVEN

I'm standing in the kitchen as Mam unpacks a load of bags for life.

'Everything's gone up again,' she says. 'Two twenty-nine for a pack of bacon. I nearly choked in the aisle but I didn't want to give them the satisfaction.'

'Can I talk to you?' I ask.

She pokes her head around the fridge door. 'What is it, lover?'

I shrug. I don't know where to start. I spent last night hovering somewhere between wanting to smash up every ornament in my bedroom and wanting to lie down on the carpet and sleep for a hundred years. I'm emotionally drained. And I've tried so hard to not burden Mam with all my stuff this term, but now I need her. I need my mam to make all of the bad things go away, like she did when I was a kid.

She stops unpacking and comes over, throwing her arms around me without needing to be asked, because she's my mam and she knows exactly what I need. Right away I bury my head in her shoulder, pressing my eyes against her so no light can get in and all I am is wrapped up in her for a moment.

'What's happened?' she asks, stroking my hair.

'Beau Greene happened,' I say.

'Is he OK?'

'Other than being the worst human being on the entire planet, he's fine.'

'Oh dear,' she says.

'Yup. He was the bad guy all along, and I'm such an idiot for not seeing it.'

She pulls out a chair at the table and walks over to the kettle, quickly flicking the on button down. 'I think you need to tell me what's happened,' she says, returning and taking a seat opposite me.

I hesitate for a moment, because I feel bad. I really should have told her everything sooner. Maybe then my life wouldn't be such a tragedy. But there's no time like the present, so after a deep breath, I dive into everything that's happened this term, right from the first postcard. I go as slowly as I can, leaving no detail unexplained, because I want to make sure she knows everything before she gives me the world-changing piece of advice that will fix my entire life. Because that's exactly what I need her to do – I've reached the point where world-changing advice is what it's going to take.

I talk about Big Red circles, and Yves Klein blue squares, and as I do I think of Beau's synaesthesia, and I recognise even more of him in the clues he left. I talk about exploding bottles of Coke, and graffiti. I talk about JJ, and everything that *really* happened last term – not the sugar-coated version I sold her so she wouldn't worry. I tell her how horrible it was, how horrible it's been, because I don't have any room inside of me for lies any more. I crave the truth. Maybe if I had just told the truth to begin with, I wouldn't be here now. I talk about Halloween, and JJ and Wynter's kiss, and what Beau did to JJ afterwards. I talk about how everybody at school, even Mrs Duncan, accused me of attacking JJ. I talk about Beau's dad, and the scar at the back of his head, and the night I thought I'd lost him to the sea, and how I can't sleep without wearing his hoodie, even now. I talk about everything, even the stuff I'm embarrassed about, because I need her to know and mainly because I can't carry all of this around by myself any more.

And she listens. She nods and frowns and smiles in all of the right places, like the perfect audience, until I'm completely empty of words and the kitchen is silent.

'You've been through a lot this term, Roman,' she says.

'And the worst part is – he knew everything,' I say. 'I told him stuff I didn't even tell Adam and Solange. I trusted him above my oldest friends, and all the while he was behind it. He's a wolf dressed in a skater boy's clothing.'

Mam stands and opens the cupboard above the kettle, taking out two city mugs (Venice and Cambridge, I think). 'Hot chocolate?' she says.

I nod. 'I just wish he'd told me.'

She scoops some low-calorie chocolate-flavoured powder into the mugs and adds hot water. She stirs them up, the teaspoon clanging as it circles the mug. Then she plonks one down on a floral coaster in front of me.

'Give it a minute,' she says. 'It'll be hot.'

'Solange hates me too,' I say.

'I'm sure that's not true.'

'She thinks I'm being too harsh by ignoring him. But she doesn't know what she's talking about – she hasn't had to live

292

this! This JJ Dixon stuff has been my life for months. And Beau made it ten times worse—'

'He wouldn't have known that, though, my love,' she says.

'Oh, don't you start.'

'I'm not starting anything,' she says, holding both hands up.

'I really thought I could survive anything after Year Ten. Alas, I didn't prepare myself for complete and utter betrayal.'

I pick up the steaming Venice mug and take a sip. Considering it's low calorie, the hot chocolate tastes surprisingly good.

'I wish you'd told me about JJ,' she says.

'It was my problem to fix,' I say.

'Roman, I'm your mother. Your problems are my problems.'

'I think part of me didn't want to admit what had happened. I think I was still holding out for some sort of reconciliation this term – so much so that I convinced myself he was painting murals and leaving postcards for me. *God.* I'm tragic.'

'You're not tragic at all.'

'I feel like I am. I feel so embarrassed about everything, and it's all Beau's fault.'

She takes a deep breath. 'OK, what do you want me to do?'

'There's nothing you can do.'

'I mean now. When I'm with the girls, we have two different approaches for when someone is having a rant – we either listen, or we give advice. Sometimes a good old rant will do it and adding another opinion to the mix isn't helpful, but other times someone needs advice. So . . . is this one of those times you want me to listen, or is this one of those times you want advice?'

I shrug. 'I want to know what you think.'

'So, advice it is,' she says. 'Good – I was hoping you were going to say that. I think, firstly, you have to figure out what you want.'

'Is that it? Is that your big piece of world-changing advice?'

'It sounds simple, I know, but think about it – what do you really want to happen now? Because, look, you can't change the past, but you can choose how you move on from it.'

I take another sip, allowing the hot chocolate to do whatever hot chocolate does in situations like these. I haven't really given much thought to what I want to happen next; I've been too busy thinking about right now.

'I guess I want things to go back to how they were before,' I say. 'Before Beau Greene.' But even as I say it, the image of his empty seat in English class jumps into my head, and I realise I can't just go back. I can't pretend he never existed. 'But I can't really picture it. When I thought about what the rest of the year would look like, he was always in those pictures . . .'

This is enough for Mam to place her hot chocolate back down on the coaster and reach forward for my hand.

'Then there's your answer, my love,' she says.

'What's my answer?'

'If a future without him seems impossible, then you have to find a way to make a future with him.'

'That's impossible.'

'Why?'

'Um . . . haven't you listened to everything I've just said?'

'I've listened to every last bit, and I'm so sorry this has happened to you, Roman. But if you want a future with Beau in it, then you're going to have to find a way to move on from everything.'

'But I can't just forget about all the things he's done and pretend everything is fine. He's done really bad stuff – he beat up JJ!'

'I'm not saying it's going to be easy,' she says. 'You'll have to find ways to forgive things you might have thought were unforgivable before. But the real world isn't black and white. And if you want Beau in your life, then you have to put the work in.' She takes a gulp of hot chocolate. 'I'm just going to say one more thing now, something that Grandma says to me when I think I can't move on from something. Forgiveness is just giving up hope that the past could be any different.'

I've been waiting for that word to crop up. *Forgiveness*. Even though Beau did all the bad stuff, it's like I'm the one who's responsible; I'm the one who has to forgive.

And I don't think that's fair at all. I'm not going to take responsibility for him ruining our friendship. I'm absolutely not there yet. No way.

After hearing Mam's advice, I take the rest of my hot chocolate to bed.

As soon as I get into my bedroom, I notice something lying on the carpet right by the bed.

It's one of Big Red's old postcards.

I turn it over and read the message on the back.

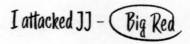

I attacked JJ – Big Red

Urgh!

Before I know it, I'm tearing it up, into smaller and smaller pieces, until it's no longer a postcard but a load of torn edges, lying like rubbish on the bedroom floor.

FORTY-EIGHT

The conversation with Mam plays on my mind for a good few days. I can't stop thinking about what I said out loud without meaning to: that a future without Beau was impossible.

I walk through the days with this empty space in my chest, which I need to fill but don't know how. My favourite foods don't do the trick. No matter how many of my favourite things I try (painting my nails, shopping for vintage bargains at Tynemouth Market, watching classic queer culture films), the only thing that helps is wearing his hoodie to bed; the only thing that makes me feel any sort of truth is being wrapped up in him. In the blink of an eye we've gone from crushing to crashing, and I still can't seem to let him go. I mean, *WTF*?

I don't see him at school all week. It's like he's disappeared. He doesn't come to English class. I don't see him in the corridors or main hall at lunch. At the end of the day he isn't waiting for me at the gates. The sound of skateboard wheels on pavement doesn't follow me home. It's like Beau Greene never was.

And it feels thunderously shit.

FORTY-NINE

Every winter, Mam, Mikey and me head into the village to watch the Christmas lights get switched on. It's one of our many Christmas traditions. There's really nothing more fabulous than seeing the village bedecked in sparkly fairy lights. (I really can't understand why the lights can't stay up all year round; it would make the place look so much better.)

We bundle Mikey up in his chair, tuck some extra blankets around him, and make the short journey through the snow-covered streets to our favourite spot at the end of the high street, near where a doughnut vendor sets up every year. This is no coincidence. Everyone in my family is a huge fan of doughnuts.

As we turn the corner into the village, I see that apparently the entire world has turned out to watch Tynemouth turn into a magical grotto. Seriously. I didn't even know there were this many people living here. The high street has been cordoned off, so no cars can drive down it. Where there is usually a row of parked cars, there are loads of stalls – most of them selling mulled wine, and hot food, and baked treats. The air smells of cinnamon and sugar. Divine.

At the far end of the high street, by the ruins of the old priory, a stage has been set up. Someone from the local radio station is doing some sort of show; behind them there's a massive clock counting down the seconds until, I'm guessing, the lights are switched on. We have twenty-eight minutes to go.

I wheel Mikey towards our favourite doughnut van and join the queue.

'Isn't this just fab?' says Mam.

'Why is it so busy this year?' I ask.

'I suppose they're making more of a thing of it,' she says. 'The stage is new, isn't it?'

We order a box of warm, cinnamon-sugar-covered doughnuts and two hot chocolates, then set up camp right in the middle of the high street so we can see both the giant Christmas tree by homophobic old Queen Victoria at one end, and the stage at the other. (The countdown clock now says nineteen minutes.)

The song 'Merry Xmas Everybody' comes on, and everybody starts singing along, grabbing friends or loved ones and holding them close, or just jumping around like nutters. I place my hot chocolate on the pavement and grab Mikey's hands. Then I start dancing with him, swaying him from side to side, which he absolutely loves. The huge smile he gives me is enough to melt even the iciest of hearts. I sing and sway, pulling silly faces and wobbling my head, and he laps it up, giggling louder than I've ever heard him giggle before.

'Ro Ro,' he says, shaking his head.

Instantly I stop. 'Mam, did you hear that?'

'What?' she says.

'Mikey just said my name.'

'Ro Ro,' he says again.

'Omigod! He just did it again!'

Mam strokes his cheek. 'He's started to say little things here and there,' she says, beaming. 'He knows I'm Ma Ma; he knows you're Ro Ro.'

'This is amazing!' I say, throwing my arms around him. 'You clever, clever person.'

Mam breaks a tiny bit off her doughnut and rubs it against his smiling mouth. Mikey is fed through a syringe, which is attached to a peg in his stomach because he can't swallow, but Mam likes to give him a taste of food. I think she does this in the hopes that one day he might be able to swallow. And she might be right. I mean, we were told he'd never talk.

'He knows my name is Roman,' I say, resting my ear on his head.

'Of course he knows your name is Roman,' says Mam. 'What else would it be?'

I shrug as if to say *I don't know*, because I suppose she's right; my name is Roman, and if my baby brother can get to grips with this, I see no reason why everybody else can't.

The Christmas music ends and the presenter introduces a troupe of dancers from the local pantomime. It's *Cinderella* this year. In a flurry of bare legs and scraped-back ponytails, the stage is suddenly filled. Twenty kids in leotards and not much else freeze their arses off as they sing along to a version of 'Uptown Funk' by Bruno Mars.

I grab a doughnut and dunk it in my hot chocolate. The taste that fills my mouth is pure heaven. As I chew I'm reminded of how much I love this time of year, and all the food and music and joy. I've been so preoccupied with misery lately, I'd forgotten about joy. But with the taste of chocolate cinnamon heaven in my mouth, surrounded by music and cheer and lights, and my little family, I start to feel a little part of myself returning.

The pantomime performance finishes, the dancers running off the stage as quickly as they can, presumably to wrap themselves in seventeen layers of woolly scarves, and the final countdown to the lights being switched on begins.

'*Ten, nine, eight . . .*'

I grab Mikey's hands again. 'Are you ready, my little munchkin?'

'*Seven, six . . .*'

Everyone shouts together as one huge Christmas mob: '*Five, four, three, two . . . one!*'

Suddenly the high street ignites in a flurry of fairy lights (very dramatic). There are bells and stars and snowflakes, reindeer and sleighs, going all the way from Queen Victoria to the sea. It really is quite fabulous. The Mariah Carey Christmas song 'All I Want for Christmas Is You' begins to play, and I grab Mikey's hands again and begin to dance like an idiot.

I sing and sway, living my 90s diva fantasy.

And just as I'm about to reach the chorus, just as I'm about to sing the words that mean it's officially Christmas, I lock eyes with someone, someone I haven't seen for ages.

'Hello, Beau,' says Mam.

'Hey,' he says.

I stop dancing, stop moving, and possibly stop breathing all at the same time.

I didn't think he'd be here. He's new to the village; he wouldn't know about such traditions as attending the Christmas lights switch-on. But then, I guess everyone else is here, so why not him? I should have thought about this, because now I'm standing here feeling like I want to drown myself in a vat of mulled wine.

'This is my little sister, Cindy,' he says to Mam.

'Hello, Cindy,' says Mam, bending down. 'That's a very pretty dress.'

She's wearing a full Anna from *Frozen* dress, complete with cape and boots. (She's so extra.)

'It is,' she says, giving us a twirl.

Beau looks my way, and his mouth twists into a sort of smile. 'Hey,' he says.

'Hi,' I say, turning my face away, and therefore hiding my Christmas joy from him so he can't confuse it with forgiveness, because I don't know if I'm ready for that.

'Isn't this fab?' asks Mam, trying to break away the tension. 'They don't usually make this much of an effort.'

'It's really nice,' says Beau to her, though I can still feel him staring at me. 'The last place we lived didn't do anything like this.'

'It really gets everyone in the festive mood,' says Mam.

'Yeah,' says Beau, still standing there, still staring.

'Is your mam with you?' Mam asks.

'No, she's had to work,' he says. 'Cindy has been looking forward to seeing the lights for weeks, so I'm on big brother duties tonight.' He reaches forward and rubs his finger against Mikey's cheek. 'Hi, Mikey, are you enjoying the lights?'

Mikey smiles, his eyes lighting up at Beau's touch.

'He's had a lovely time,' says Mam. 'He always loves the lights switch-on – loves the colours and everything, don't you, my gorgeous one?'

'Hello, Mikey,' says Cindy. 'Do you like my dress? It's purple and green and blue.' She spins and Mikey laughs.

'It looks like he likes it very much,' says Mam.

'He does,' says Cindy.

Beau keeps staring and my eyes begin to sting. I really don't know what to do. I don't know how to be around him. I don't know what to say to him. Part of me wants to run away and hide, because part of me always wants to run away and hide. The other part wants to fall into him, stop this iciness between us, and hug it out until my insides feel warm as fresh doughnuts.

'We'd better be going,' he says finally. 'I promised Cindy one of those snowflake iced biscuit things.'

'How canny,' says Mam. 'Goodbye, Cindy, it was lovely to meet you.'

'Nice to meet you,' she says. 'Goodbye, Mikey. Goodbye, Roman.'

'Bye, Cindy,' I say.

'I suppose I'll see you around,' says Beau, looking at me.

I don't respond.

'*Roman,*' says Mam, once she's sure they're out of earshot.

'Don't start,' I say.

'I'm not saying anything – but you didn't have to be rude.'

'How was I rude?'

'You didn't say goodbye to him.'

'He doesn't deserve my goodbyes.'

'Oh, stop it. He's such a lovely boy, bringing his sister to the lights switch-on.'

'Don't be fooled,' I say, rolling my eyes. 'He's a villain in chunky-knitted headwear.'

FIFTY

When we get home, we pile into the warmth of the living room, where Mam unwraps Mikey's layers, and I flick on Disney+. Another tradition we have after the lights switch-on is watching *The Nightmare Before Christmas* ('Taking over Christmas is no way to fill the gaping hole you feel inside'). It's probably my favourite Christmas film of all time.

'Can I get you anything?' asks Mam, as she heads for the kitchen.

'I'm fine,' I say.

I get the film ready while Mam pours herself a cup of something hot, entering the living room already in her slippers.

'I feel like my toes have frozen,' she says, snuggling into her usual corner spot.

I grab a blanket from the arm of the sofa and wrap it round myself.

Then I ready myself to get lost in Tim Burton's dark Halloween/Christmassy world.

The opening credits play – that weird bit with all the doors on the trees, each representing a different holiday – and then comes the opening number, 'This is Halloween'.

It's strange, it's been weeks since Halloween, but as I think about it, I still get this tightening feeling in my stomach, like the knot that's in there has somehow been pulled. Halloween has clearly been tainted for me thanks to the megabitch that is Wynter Brown. (Thanks, Wynter!) Although, it's not only her I'm thinking about tonight. Tonight, I'm reminded of Beau too: how he came with me when my other friends wouldn't, how he let me dress him as the Joker, how he stood by my side when Wynter threw me out on the street like I was a bag of rubbish.

He stayed with me.

He stood by me.

And I know violence is wrong, but when he lashed out at JJ that night, he was scared and probably still traumatised by what his dad had done to him. I don't know if it's down to all the Christmas spirit warming up my icy insides right now, but seeing him tonight was sort of nice. Just being that close to him again, just talking to him again, reminded me of how we used to be. (I knew this would happen. My guard never stays up for long.)

'What are you thinking about, lover?' says Mam.

I didn't even realise she was staring at me.

'Nothing at all,' I say.

'I know that look.'

'Just watch the film.'

She leans across to me and grabs the remote. Then she presses the pause button. 'The film can wait.'

'What are you doing?' I protest. 'You're breaking a Christmas tradition.'

'We can play it again in a minute,' she says. 'I just want you to talk to me.'

'I think I'm all talked out.'

'Then I'll do the talking,' she says, leaning forward. 'You're thinking about Beau. You're thinking about how you should have talked to him tonight.'

'Wrong. I'm not thinking about that.'

She raises her eyebrows.

'OK,' I say. 'I'm thinking about him, but I'm not thinking about what just happened. I'm thinking about Halloween.'

'And?'

'And how fabulous I looked.'

Another eyebrow raise.

'OK, enough with the eyebrow acting – this isn't *Hollyoaks*.'

'Roman, tell me the truth.'

The truth. I should have learnt by now. The truth is always the best way. But it isn't always the easiest.

I take a deep breath before I answer. 'I'm thinking about Beau coming with me to Wynter's party,' I say. 'I'm thinking about how he stood up for me when nobody else did.'

'Why don't you talk to him about how you're feeling?' Mam asks.

'Because I'm embarrassed. This whole thing is so awkward.'

'Come on, Roman. I can see it in your face how much you're missing him. And I think he feels the same way too.'

'You do?'

'Oh yeah,' she says, dramatically nodding her head. 'He was giving me *major* still-into-you vibes.'

'Stop talking like that – it's weirding me out.'

She points the remote at the TV. 'Just find a way. Don't let this turn into one of your life's regrets.'

Then she hits the play button.

FIFTY-ONE

Over the next few days, I change my mind a lot. Round and round I go, convinced talking to Beau is a good idea one minute, and then backtracking the next. It's exhausting, and confusing to the point of delirium. By the end of the week all I want to do is dig a hole and jump in. I really have no idea how to manoeuvre my way around this situation, or my feelings. I sometimes wonder if I hadn't been through what I had with JJ – my first betrayal – I would have forgiven Beau by now. Is it a case of once bitten, twice shy? Am I being too stubborn? Am I throwing away a friendship and the potential of something more, for an issue that could be resolved? I really don't know. There's no clear route out of this, and I'm starting to think I'm running out of time. I mean, Christmas holidays are around the corner, and then it'll be a new calendar year, and then it'll be Easter break, and prom time, and exam time, and then I'll never see him again. Basically, Year 11 is over, and I'm starting to think that this means Beau and me are over too.

And I'm still not sure how I feel about this.

'I saw him in French this morning,' says Adam as we walk to science class together. 'I must say – he looked *très fatigué*.'

'I haven't seen him since the lights switch-on,' I say.

'I love that you still go to that,' he says. 'Did you talk to him?'

'No. Mam did most of the talking; I remained aloof, as always, which is becoming soooo draining by the way.'

'It is?'

'Yeah. I thought I could keep it up, but I'm starting to think this whole ignoring him thing is actually making things worse, and it would be better if I just had it out with him.'

'Hallelujah,' he says, raising his hands to the ceiling.

I look at him as if to say, *What the hell was that?*

'You do know the Ballerz are Team Beau now, right?'

'There are no teams!' I say. 'Wait. You're *both* Team Beau? What about me – what about Team Roman?'

'I thought there were no teams.'

'You're supposed to be *my* friends, not his.'

'Wow,' he says, stopping.

'What?'

'You don't own us, you know. We're free to have other friends.'

'I know, but not . . . *him*.'

'I don't see why not. Solange thinks everything he did was for a good reason. And now I do too.'

'Judas,' I say.

'Oh, come off it, sis. We'll always be your Ballerz. It's just – sometimes friends can see your stuff clearer than you can. If we were talking about JJ Dixon right now, I would be Team Roman all the way. But Beau is one of the good guys, and you're so obviously still into him. Plus, most of the stuff he did was pretty badass.'

'Never say "badass" to me again . . . so what are we saying, that he's just forgiven?'

He shrugs, and then sashays away ahead of me.

'Hey!' I say. 'Don't just walk away.'

'We're going to be late,' he says.

'I need your help.'

'You don't need my help, Roman. There's nothing I, or Solange, or anyone else can do to help. This is all on you now.'

God. I mean, what the hell is the point of friends if they're not going to help you out at a time like this? I really don't know what I'm supposed to do. Talking to Beau would mean complete abandonment of my (very high) standards, but then carrying on ignoring him like this means that pretty soon I'll be nothing but an emotionally exhausted husk in a rabbit-skin cape. Surely there has to be another way.

Above the door to the science lab there hangs a crucifix (because the school is riddled with them). As we approach it, I smack my hands together as if praying and say, 'Why is my life so hard?'

This makes Adam stop in his tracks. He turns around, folding his arms across his leather jacket so tightly I can hear the fabric squeaking. (I'm guessing it might not be genuine leather.)

'Oh, come down off the cross, sis,' he says. 'We need the wood.'

FIFTY-TWO

The path to Christmas break is paved with rituals befitting a Catholic high school. Every year we have to sit through carol concerts, advent assemblies and a questionable nativity play put on by Years 7 and 8. It's like a rite of passage; we aren't allowed to celebrate until we've endured every verse of 'Silent Night' about fifty times.

St Anselm's doesn't have a drama department (don't even get me started), so every year the nativity is directed by Ms Mead. I always thought this was a terrible travesty due to her general lack of energy and ideas, but since finding out about her thespian roots I may have changed my mind on this. This year the play isn't so bad, if you can get over the Geordie accents. (I mean, Mary *could* have come from North Shields.) It's billed as an original musical, all based around a camel called Meredith (played by a puppet) who wants to visit the baby Jesus but has reservations because he's a camel (as in, Meredith is a camel – not Jesus. I'm fairly certain Jesus Christ wasn't a camel). Make of that what you will. It's billed as a journey of perseverance in the face of adversity, which is sort of cute. Anyway, in the end he gets there, and they all live happily ever after.

I actually never took part in the production when I was in

Year 7 or 8 because I was way too busy figuring myself out. And I'm so glad I didn't put myself forward. I mean, I know Ryan Albright would have been an absolute mess. (If the chance came my way now, it would be a very different story. Roman Bright would have stolen the show, with or without the camel puppet.)

Before I know it, all Christmas rituals are done and dusted, and it's the last day of what has been the most eventful term of my life. I don't think I've needed a break more. I'm looking forward to a couple of weeks of eating chocolate and watching Christmas films with Mam. Christmas holidays are all about family, and I intend to spend a whole lot of time with mine.

(That is, until that weird period after the big day when nobody really knows what to do other than eat themselves into early-onset diabetes. This is usually the time Adam and me hang out, so I imagine a few girly sleepovers will be in order. I've already started making a list of all of my Bette Midler favourites, because he needs to be educated in the wonder that is the Divine Miss M. Solange won't be there. She's heading to the airport right after the bell rings. Her Christmas break will be spent in France with her dad. She'll be seeing Noelle again too, for the first time since summer, which is pretty major. She'll be spending the holidays falling in love all over again. And, although I've turned into somewhat of a cynic these past few weeks, I can't think of anybody who deserves love more than she does.)

There's only one more lesson until Christmas can officially begin. Of course, that lesson has to be English, the lesson I share with Beau Greene, because why wouldn't it be? Why would the last day of term be an easy one? It would be totally off-brand if it were.

For obvious reasons, we no longer sit together in class. But Beau couldn't have just kept skipping English all term; there's no way Duncan would have allowed it. There's a spare table on the opposite side at the back of the classroom. *The Quiet Table*. It has various uses – mainly it's used as a detention table. It's basically the teenage equivalent of the Naughty Step. Well. This is where he's been sitting recently, and it's here I see him as I walk into the classroom. I must say it feels totally appropriate.

I hurry to my table and slide into my seat. There's a sheet of plain A4 paper waiting for me on top, along with two biro pens. And right away I know what this means.

We're doing an end-of-term quiz.

Oh, cheese and crust.

Ms Mead enters the room wearing a pair of sparkly Christmas pudding earrings and a jumper than has *HOE, HOE, HOE* written on it. Which I think is both hilarious and highly inappropriate in equal measure. Although, something tells me she isn't entirely sure of the meaning of the word *hoe*.

'Settle down, Year Eleven,' she says, because it's last lesson on the last day of term, which means we've turned into a bunch of savages, standing on chairs and tables, tinsel wrapped around random body parts. There's even music playing – Elton John, I think. 'Now. Since you've all worked so hard this term, today, as a treat, we're doing a festive quiz!'

Her face lights up like an advent candle, while the mood in the classroom drops, because we all know that Ms Mead's 'festive quizzes' are always coursework-related. Basically it's an exam. We're doing an exam, disguised as a quiz. She did the same thing last year. The Christmas Quiz was based around Shakespeare's *Macbeth*. I mean – WTF? What's festive about paranoia and murder?

'You'll be working in teams of two,' she says. 'So decide a team name between your tables and write it at the top of the sheet.' She looks at the back of the class. 'Beau, you can sit with Ryan.'

My hand goes up quicker than a pre-lit Christmas tree.

'Yes, Ryan?'

'I'd like to work alone,' I say.

'Ryan, Beau needs a partner, and so do you. Remember, two heads are always better than one.'

'Not always,' I say. 'Sometimes too many cooks spoil the broth.'

I hear Beau's chair scrape against the floor. I hear his heavy footsteps coming towards me. Then, his familiar smell. The smell of outside, of fresh bedding dried in the sun, and newly cut grass. It comes rolling over me as he pulls out his old chair and takes a seat.

'Hey,' he says.

'Hi,' I say.

'You OK?'

I nod. 'Mmm hmm.'

He slides the sheet of paper across the table. 'We need to think of a festive team name.'

How about Big Red Ruined My Christmas or Lonely This Christmas or It's a Not So Wonderful Life, I think.

'What about Jingle Ballerz?' he says.

I sharply turn my head to him. 'I don't think so.'

'OK. Um . . . how about, like, something with 'quizmas' in the title, like Merry Quizmas or Quizmas Crackers?'

'Sure.' I take one of the pens and write *QUIZMAS CRACKERS* at the top in capital letters.

'Great. Quizmas Crackers. This should be fun.'

'It won't be,' I say. 'This will neither be fun, nor, in fact, a quiz. This will be coursework dressed in a quiz's clothing. Just so you know.'

'OK?' he says, scrunching up his nose as if he's about to sneeze.

'Quieten down now,' says Ms Mead, banging her stapler (which now has a piece of green tinsel wrapped around it) on the desk. 'Eyes down – first question.'

As predicted, the quiz is all about the stuff we've studied this term. Considering he looked half asleep most of the time, I'm surprised to realise Beau actually has been paying attention. He whizzes through questions about *Jekyll and Hyde* and literary non-fiction and narrative writing, so quickly that all I have to do is sit back and observe. As I watch him chewing the end of the pen, scribbling out his thoughts on the page, asking questions out loud before quickly answering them himself, I get the grey area feeling in my stomach. The wings down there flap so ferociously I start to feel sick. I'm reminded of things I don't want to be reminded of, like how Beau is the sweet guy who wears silly hats, how he let me dress him up for Halloween, how he took his sister to the Christmas lights switch-on in the village. Sitting next to him again like this makes me feel like we're back in the time before everything happened. It's sort of messing with my head. Actually, it's sort of messing with my everything, because every part of me is aching to have those times back. I try not to, but every now and again I allow myself to really look at him; to admire his long eyelashes, his smooth skin, the way the tiny hairs run down the back of his neck. This is the closest I've been to him in ages, and it's making me want things that I know I can't have. (Damn these grey area feelings. They seem intent on making a fool out of me.)

I spend most of the class in silence, biting the end of my thumbnail until it's practically all gone.

When the bell goes to mark the end of term, there's an almighty cheer – show's over, kids. We're no longer St Anselm's students. We are now free beings, able to express ourselves however we like. For two whole weeks, at least.

I pick up Marlene, throwing her over my shoulders, as Beau moves awkwardly beside me, rearranging his winter coat, zipping and unzipping himself, taking a sharp breath in as if he's about to speak, but then saying nothing at all. This goes on for a solid minute as I pack my bag, carefully tuck my chair back under the table, and then walk down the aisle towards the door, giving Ms Mead a quick 'Merry Christmas, miss,' before heading out into the cold.

As I make my way towards the gates, I hear a familiar sound rolling up behind me, the sound of wheels on pavement.

'Roman,' says Beau. 'Can we talk?'

I turn my head to one side, but I don't stop walking. 'Yeah,' I say. 'We can talk.'

'I just wanted to say . . . I'm so sorry about everything I did.'

'OK.' I shrug. 'Is that it?'

'I just wanted you to know because . . . I wish we could be friends again. I've missed you. Sitting next to you in class right now just reminded me how much.'

Me too.

I feel the same.

'OK,' I say, again.

'And if there's anything I can do, or anything that I can say, that will make you change your mind about me, then I'll do it.'

I keep walking, across the zebra crossing, into the village, and he keeps rolling behind me. And I don't say anything, even though I have so much to say. Actually, I think I have too much to say, which is why I can't say anything. The way I feel right now is so overwhelming, like running into the North Sea in winter.

It isn't until we turn on to the high street, on to magical sparkling lights, that I feel part of the ice inside melt away. I've always been a sucker for anything sparkly. (I'm basically a magpie.) The lights twinkle, and I'm reminded of cinnamon doughnuts dunked in hot chocolate, and Mikey's smiling face, and before I know it, I'm talking to him.

'I just wish you'd told me the truth,' I hear myself say, though my voice sounds different; it's sort of higher and softer and crackling a little around the edges. 'As you, not Big Red.'

'If I could go back and change things, I would,' he says.

'But you can't,' I say. 'You can't change the past. All you can do is decide how you want it to affect your future. Mam told me that.'

'That's pretty deep.'

'She has her moments.'

'I'm sorry,' he says. 'I can't say it enough. I'd write it in letters six feet high on every building in school if it meant you'd believe me.'

He wheels his skateboard in front of me so I have to stop. Then he pulls back his hood and looks right at me, his eyes searching the depths of me for what I'm really feeling, because he knows I'm being guarded right now. We've known each other long enough to tell.

'I got it wrong,' he says. 'I never meant to make things harder for you.'

I would give my entire nail varnish collection, and even half (not all) of my wardrobe for us to go back to the way we were, to go back to that uncomplicated time when we could laugh and have fun and I could rely on him. These past few weeks have been so crappy without that. I didn't realise how close we'd become until we weren't close any more. And I miss him. I do. I know we can't go back to how it was before, but the truth is, I can't keep going round and round in circles either; it's driving me mad. I have to either accept what he's saying and find a way to move on with him, or I have to move schools. These are my options. (To be clear – there are no other schools in the village.)

'OK,' I say.

'OK?' he asks.

'Yeah. OK. I can't do this any more – I can't keep pretending that you don't exist. It's draining the life out of me.'

'That's . . . that's amazing,' he says.

'It's not going to be easy,' I say. 'You hurt me, Beau. And some days I feel so mad at you I want to bite my own hand off. But then, other days I miss you so much I want to bite my other hand off. And I want to keep my hands. So, yeah – I accept your apology.'

'That's so awesome,' he says, gripping his hands into fists.

'Can we make a promise to each other right now, though?' I ask, because I still have something really important to say, something I need him to understand. 'Can we just promise to always tell each other the truth – no matter how gristly and tough it is? There are lots of grey areas in life, but if we're going to move on from this, I can't have any grey areas with you. I just can't.'

'I promise,' he says, really quickly.

'No more secrets?'

'No more secrets.'

He holds out his pinkie finger and I interlock it with mine. Then, before I know it, he's pulled me in for a hug. And it feels so nice to be this close to him again. We stay like this for I don't know how long, without talking or overthinking or doing anything other than just being together, just standing in the middle of the high street, under magical sparkling Christmas lights, hugging away all the crappy feelings of the past few weeks.

FIFTY-THREE

I head straight up to my room after dinner, not so I can paint my nails, or overthink everything, but so I can wear his hoodie.

As soon as I'm in it I can feel the warmth of his body pressing against me. I can smell him. I take in a deep breath, rubbing my face in his hood. And I feel so chilled and happy. It's like there are no more grey area feelings. I'm starting to feel in Technicolor again.

I jump on to the bed and starfish the duvet, taking in all of this moment: two whole weeks off school, Christmas, Beau Greene (the sigh that I let out feels like it goes on for a month). I'm just about to bury myself under a pile of scatter cushions when I hear a tapping sound off the window. Right away I sit forward, diving at the curtains, as excited as if it's already Christmas morning.

I move the curtains to one side and I see him, his frostbitten face smiling back at me from underneath his chunky-knit hat.

'We have to stop meeting like this,' I say, as I push the window open.

He laughs, a swirl of hot breath framing his face. 'Is that mine?' he says, pointing at the hoodie.

'Um . . . is it?' I say nonchalantly (and also instantly embarrassed that he's caught me in the middle of one of my nightly rituals). 'I can't remember, really.'

'I've been looking for that. I thought I'd lost it.'

'You definitely gave it to me. I've got receipts.'

'Receipts?'

'Beau, we've only just made up – don't start an argument now.'

I push the window up further so he can climb in. 'What are you doing here?' I ask.

'I wanted to see you,' he says. 'Is that OK?'

'Yeah. Course it is. Come in. It's freezing out there.'

He slides one leg through the window and ducks under on to my bed.

'I think it's cute that you're wearing my hoodie,' he says.

'I was just cold. Don't read anything into it.'

He crawls to the top of the bed, and then makes himself comfortable amongst the very many scatter cushions.

'You do know you're allowed to come in through the front door, right?' I say. 'Mam is like your biggest fan.'

'Oh, she is?' he says. 'I wasn't sure after everything . . .'

'Don't worry. Everybody's been on Team Beau pretty much the whole time. Annoyingly.'

He looks away from me, his mouth twisting into a smile. 'Well, tell everybody *thanks* from me.'

'I'm sure you'll get the chance to tell them yourself,' I say. 'Unless you'd rather spray-paint it on the kitchen wall, or something.'

His mouth drops open.

'Too soon?' I ask.

'Maybe,' he says. Though his smile tells me he knows that I'm totally joking.

'You're really good, by the way,' I say. 'At painting, I mean. How come you didn't take art?'

'Dad.'

'Oh.'

'Yep. He didn't want a son who took art, so I went with geography instead. I'm terrible at geography.'

'Who isn't?' I say, rolling my eyes. 'How are things going with your dad, anyway?'

He shrugs. 'I haven't seen him since the night he left. I know he calls to speak to Cindy sometimes.'

'I'm sorry,' I say.

'What for?'

'That you're going through this. And that you haven't had anyone to talk to about it. I think I could have been a better friend to you.'

He begins to shake his head. 'I love that you still don't know.'

'Know what?'

'Roman – you've done so much for me. You changed my life in ways I didn't think were possible.'

'I did?'

'Yeah. From the first moment I saw you being so open and confident and proud of who you are I felt differently about myself. It's thanks to you that Mum now knows about Dad, and about me being gay – two things that I thought would never happen. So you don't have to apologise for anything, Roman Bright.'

I splay a hand across my shoulder, throwing my head back when he says this, because the mention of my full chosen name always deserves some sort of dramatic performance.

'I've wanted to tell you that for ages,' he says. 'But I wasn't brave enough.'

'You're brave enough to paint the entire art block wall, but not brave enough to speak?'

He shrugs. 'I think I get the point across better when I paint. Will you be taking art next year?'

'Oh please, let me make it to the end of Year Elven in one piece before I start thinking about what happens after.'

He shuffles closer to me again, and then rests his head on the cushion nearest to me. From this angle his eyelashes look immense. 'I know one thing that will be happening next year,' he says.

'What's that?' I say, my hand automatically playing with his curls.

'We'll still be friends. Now I know what it's like to be without you, I don't want to go through that again.'

I can't stop the crazy-wide smile from spreading across my face when he says this, because I feel exactly the same way.

I lean forward and twist myself around until I'm lying right beside him. He puts one arm over me, and then the other, and before I know it I'm resting my head on his chest, listening to the fluttering of his heart inside it.

We stay like that for most of the weekend.

After

FIFTY-FOUR

Beau asked me to meet him at the school gates today. I'm wearing a new shirt. Miranda Priestly. She's vintage Christian Dior. I got her from Tynemouth Market. You have to be prepared to rummage, but you can find some real gems – it's where I found Marlene. I always feel sad when summer term begins and I have to hang Marlene up again. Miranda Priestly is helping to soften the blow. She's named after the character in *The Devil Wears Prada* ('That's all'), because she's fierce and fabulous and totally ruthless. And, yes, I'm still talking about the shirt. She's far too fabulous for a school shirt, and the troglodytes of St Anselm's don't deserve her at all, but if I have to stand here at the gates with the entire school watching me, I need to be sure I look amazing.

Today, I am definitely sure of this.

Roman-before would have died inside at the thought of standing at the gates, because Roman-before didn't want to give anyone the opportunity to be cruel. Well, I can safely say that Roman-after cares a lot less about what other people think. And, weirdly, they seem to care a lot less about me too. They totally leave me alone these days. Who knew it would be so easy? All I had to do was pretend they didn't matter and *poof*, just like that, they didn't.

The school buses pull up and hundreds of grey blazers spill out on to the pavement and shuffle through the gates. Wynter Brown's daddy's Range Rover, which is about the size of my bedroom, drives up on to the kerb too. The back door opens, and she gracefully steps out, swinging her hair over one shoulder. I smile at her as she struts past – not a wide smile, nothing meaningful – but enough for her to know that I'm way too fabulous to hold a grudge.

She doesn't return it.

She never does.

I've started to wonder if her high school experience really is as wonderful as I always thought. The girl never smiles. She's totally drop-dead gorgeous, and totally drop-dead miserable. Which is crazy, because I always thought being gorgeous was the key to happiness. Apparently I was wrong, and the Wynter Browns of the world are having just as crappy a high school experience as the rest of us.

The stragglers approach the gate from all sides of the village, and there's still no sign of Beau. I'm just about to join them, heading for registration, when I notice this guy looking at me from across the street. He has this cool haircut, curly on top and shaved at the sides. He's tall, with a totally cute smile; he flashes his teeth at me as he crosses the zebra crossing, and it's then that I recognise Beau Greene.

'Wow,' I say, clicking my fingers up and down, 'all the snaps for you. You look great.'

'The barber said I could have filled a pillow with the amount of hair he cut off,' he says.

I grab his shoulders and spin him round, inspecting

every last part of him. Now the curls have been cut away, the scar on his head is easily visible. I get the feeling this might be intentional.

'What made you want to change?' I ask.

'I don't think of it as changing,' he says, very matter-of-factly.

'No?'

'No. I finally watched *Grease* last night.'

'You did?' I ask, confused by the apparent change of subject.

He knows I haven't watched *Grease* for months. There are a lot of triggering storylines in that film that I don't think I'm ready to revisit. Turns out, it's not just about A-line skirts and teenage pregnancy. It's about me not fitting in.

'I can see why you loved it so much,' he says. 'It's all about accepting yourself – owning it, sort of thing.'

'You think so?'

'Definitely! That ending! It's genius – how the sweet girl decides to show up dressed as a T-Bird, how she transforms into one of the guys. It's all about being yourself, no matter what – ground-breaking stuff if you consider when it was made. It's so you.'

I don't want to burst his bubble right now, but, as far as I'm concerned, *Grease* is all about society's need to exclude non-gender-conforming kids from the party. Cynical, I know. I guess Roman-after is a little world-wearier.

'Don't you think she's just changing for the hot guy?' I ask.

'No, that's the beauty of it. She wasn't prim and proper Sandra Dee because she wanted to be – she was trapped in this generic good girl image, which had probably been forced on her by her parents, by the way.'

'Interesting theory.'

'All the way through she's an outsider, looking in. The ending is about her stepping into her sexuality and being proud of who she's really been all along. That's such a *you* thing to do. Don't you agree?'

Here's the thing I've come to learn about Beau Greene over this past year – the guy is smart, smarter than smart; he doesn't say much, but when he does, it's so mind-blowing I feel like I need to sit down.

'Yeah,' I say. 'Yeah, I guess I do.'

'I don't think I'm Patty Simcox, though.'

'Did I say you were?'

'You did.'

'Oh. Wow. Sorry. That really wasn't a compliment coming from me.'

'I guessed it might not have been. So I decided to do a Sandy, and cut my hair.'

'And in the process you shook off your good girl image?'

'Exactly.'

'*Doing a Sandy*. Maybe we make that a thing?'

'We could totally make that a thing.'

'OK – it's a thing!'

We walk towards the gates, me in my new shirt, and him with his new haircut, and I feel sort of unstoppable.

'You're going to be the talk of the yard today, you know,' I say.

'Then tomorrow it will be right back to you.'

'I suppose I can give you a day.'

It's like the sky is a different colour today, or something. The world feels brighter. The air is clearer, filled with the smell of warmed cobblestones and sea salt. The colours are more intense: the red of the rooftops; the pastel blue of the sky; even old homophobic Queen Victoria looks fresher, her bronze-turned-greenness shimmering in the sunlight. Summer has arrived in the village, and it feels wonderfully familiar. I'm starting to remember how much I enjoy summers here. I'm starting to remember what it feels like to go paddle-boarding on Longsands beach, or swimming in King Eddy's Bay. I'm starting to remember all the summers that came *before* the train wreck of the last one.

'I've got something for you,' I say, passing him a flyer for Turner's Funfair. 'Here.'

'What time does it start?' he asks, taking it.

'Don't you ever read the Ballerz group?'

'Sometimes. There are too many messages.'

'I fought long and hard to get you added to that group. I expect a little more enthusiasm. We're meeting there at eight p.m.'

He nods, giving me this weird half smile, which suddenly makes me feel totally self-conscious.

'What?' I ask.

'Nothing. Nothing at all.'

FIFTY-FIVE

The doorbell sounds at seven thirty.

'That'll be Beau,' I say, descending the staircase.

'Wow,' says Mam.

'I know.'

She cracks open the front door and a column of sunlight beams into the house. Through it, Beau Greene appears in his tux, clutching a bouquet of three pink hydrangeas.

'Hey,' he says.

'Hi.'

'That dress looks even better the second time around.'

She's been hanging on the back of my wardrobe door for what feels like for ever. And at one point I so very nearly stuffed her back in, burying her for all eternity. But I had a feeling she would get her moment.

I can't think of a better look for our Ballerz non-prom than Cruella, because Cruella is a total punk, and she'd never attend a prom, only ever a non-prom.

(We first had the idea after the Christmas break. When the new term started, we all agreed we were dreading prom and decided we wouldn't go. But this didn't satisfy me. I wanted to have my ballgown moment. The non-prom idea came to me one morning when I was brushing my teeth.

And I must say, it's one of my finest.)

'These are for you,' he says, handing me the hydrangeas. 'I picked them from our garden.'

'Thanks. They're fabulous.'

I bury my nose inside them, looking at him through my eyelashes. I've never felt more beautiful.

'Enjoy yourselves,' says Mam, wheeling Mikey to the door. He's dressed for non-prom too, wearing a shirt under his dungarees with a cute silver bow tie.

'You look like a superstar,' I say, bending down to smooth his hair.

'Ro Ro,' he says, giggling.

Mam steps towards me with her phone held out. 'You look gorgeous,' she says. 'Give me a pose.'

I place my hands on my hips and push my shoulders forward, giving her my best impression of a British *Vogue* cover star.

'Fabulous!' she says.

I walk out the door, joining Beau. He's wearing Converse trainers instead of smart shoes, which is totally suitable for our non-prom.

'How are we getting there?' I ask.

'Your carriage awaits, m'lady,' he says, presenting his skateboard like it's a Rolls-Royce.

'I can't get on that.'

'Of course you can.'

'I'll fall off.'

'No, you won't.'

'Look, not to be a total diva or anything, but I can't have an arse-over-tit situation whilst wearing Cruella.'

'Do you trust me?'

'Yes.'

'Then don't worry about it. Just hold on.'

I walk down the garden path, slowly, elegantly, the early evening sun pressing warm hands against my bare shoulders. I climb on to Beau's skateboard, wrapping my hands around his back. He smells like him, like sheets dried outside in the summer sun.

'Are you ready?' he asks.

'Do you know what – I think I am,' I say. '*Drive, Thelma, drive!*'

He looks over his shoulder at me. 'Huh?'

'*Thelma and Louise?*' I say. 'Oh come on, how can you not know that one?'

'Another one for the list?' he says, chuckling to himself, before pushing off against the pavement.

I rest my cheek against his back as we roll along the seafront, the sun throwing diamonds right across the water as far as I can see. The fairground is on the field just above the sand dunes. As we roll across the promenade, I can see a Waltzer, and a Ferris wheel, and that boat thing where you go forward and back really quickly until you feel like you're about to throw up. (I won't be trying this one tonight – Cruella deserves more than being covered in those chicken nuggets I just ate.)

Pretty soon we come to a stop, halfway towards the fair.

'Why are we stopping here?' I ask.

He does the strange smile thing again as he offers me his hand to help me off the skateboard. 'I wanted to have a moment alone with you before we met the others.' He pulls me over to the railing and puts his arms around my waist. 'I think you might be the most interesting, funny and brilliant person I've ever met, Roman.'

He smiles his beautiful smile, dimples poking holes in his cheeks, then places his hand on the back of my neck and pulls me in for the most insane kiss. I literally feel like I'm floating above the sea, flying on blue spray-painted wings as his soft lips press firmly against mine. I never get tired of feeling this way; this is the way romance is supposed to feel, without mixed signals, or sleepless nights, or confusion.

'I was thinking,' he begins, 'we've been seeing each other for a while now.'

'We have,' I say.

'And it's been really nice.'

'It has.'

'And so . . . I wondered if you fancied becoming my *theyfriend*.'

The smile comes from somewhere on my insides. 'Yes,' I say, nodding like crazy. 'I would definitely love that.'

He pulls me in for another insane kiss, our first as an official couple.

'Wait,' I say, 'does this make you my boyfriend?'

'Um . . . yeah,' he says.

'Just checking. I don't think gender-defining titles should be assumed,' I say, smiling.

When we arrive at the funfair, Adam and Solange are waiting at the entrance.

Adam is wearing a navy blue suit, with the jacket thrown over his shoulders like a cape. He's wearing smoky eye make-up too. Very Adam Lambert. Solange is draped in this totally gorgeous bright orange maxi dress, her hair twisted on top of her head and decorated with an orange orchid. Stunning. Under the dress she's wearing oxblood Doc Martens, because she's Solange and she's a queer icon.

'That dress is everything,' says Adam, as I saunter towards them, hand in hand with Beau.

'You like?' I ask.

'Wow,' says Solange, staring at my dress.

'I know,' I say.

'So, how did it go?' she says, looking at both of us with wide eyes.

'They said yes,' says Beau. 'We're official!'

'Woohoo!' she says, throwing her arms around both of us.

'Congrats, sis,' says Adam, joining in the hug too. 'I'm happy for you.'

'This is the best news ever,' says Solange, holding me by the shoulders. '*God*. This dress really is everything. Now we know why Wynter threw you out of her party. She was clearly jealous.'

'Clearly,' says Beau.

'Speaking of Wynter,' says Adam, 'something has happened.'

'Something bad?'

'Not exactly,' says Solange. 'I guess it depends how you look at it.'

'OK,' I say. 'Tell me.'

'She's here,' says Adam.

'WHAT?'

'They're all here,' says Solange.

I look over her shoulder into the fairground and see so many faces I recognise from Year 11. There's Charlene Franklin, looking all sorts of glamorous with Hollywood waves in her hair. Jonny Dale and Norman Stokes have come dressed as Marvel characters (Dr Strange and Loki, I think? I totally knew they were cosplayers). Gemma Crow, Sheryl Higgin and Natalie Elliott – the harem of broken dolls – all look totally individual for once, dressed differently to Wynter (who's come as a Playboy bunny, which I sort of love). I see some tuxes and gowns, but I also see hot pants, leather jackets and T-shirts held together by safety pins. Everyone is wearing their own version of non-prom attire, all of them completely owning their identities.

'Is this real?' I ask.

'Apparently so,' says Solange. 'I got a DM from JJ earlier today.'

'JJ's here?'

'Everybody is here!' says Adam. 'Well, almost.'

'No Tyler Hudson?'

'Of course not.'

'Thank God.'

'The whole year wanted to show their support for our non-prom,' says Solange. 'It's because they're all invested in their prom king and queen campaigns, and don't want to appear homophobic, but whatever. They're here. JJ asked if it would be OK. I guess he thinks he owes you.'

'I thought it was a good idea,' says Adam, sounding hesitant.

'It really was!' I say.

I used to stand outside school on prom night just to get a

glimpse of the Year 11 girls and their ballgowns. Ever since Year 7, I've dreamt of being just like them and having my moment in a totally stunning gown for the whole year to see. I'd sort of let go of that dream. But now, here, with my best friends and our non-prom, it looks like that dream wasn't quite ready to let go of me.

I guess Year 11 has changed me a lot, in ways that I didn't think it was possible for me to change. I think this year has sort of been about learning life stuff way more than it has been about learning school stuff. Above everything else, I've realised that being a queer kid is hard. Society constantly tells us we're wrong – we look wrong, we talk wrong, and we love in the wrong way. Society was not built for non-binary queer kids. But what I've realised is: there is safety and love and all the things you want out there; there are good people too, even if it sometimes feels like the majority of them are bad. The majority of society might never accept people like me, but I'm no longer concerned with people who can't see how brilliant I am. Being a one-off masterpiece is way better than being an imitation. And if you're lucky enough to even have one person around you who sees you for who you really are, then you're one of the really lucky ones.

I now know that I definitely am.

'Shall we go in?' asks Beau.

'Yeah,' I say. 'Come on, guys, let's do this.'

I throw my arm around Solange, who throws her arm around Adam.

And then all four of us walk, arm in arm, into our very own fairground happy ending.

ACKNOWLEDGEMENTS

Let me start by saying this book very nearly didn't happen. It is down to the support and encouragement of so many people that it did, and I'm so grateful to everyone who listened, encouraged, questioned, pushed and held my hand until I felt brave enough to take this leap of faith. Firstly, I would like to thank my parents. Without their constant love and support I never would have been able to follow my dreams for as long as I had to for them to come true. It's been a long road, and they've been invested in this journey as much as I have, at times probably more so. Mam and Dad, from the bottom of my heart, thank you. I would like to thank my family for believing in me, especially Granma – Jean Frances Glen, the writer of the family – who knew about Roman, but never got to meet them; my sister, Charlotte; my nephew, Finn; and my cousin, Oscar, for inspiring a very special character in this book. To the rest of my cousins, aunties and uncles (who are too many to mention) – thank you for being my constant support network. I would also like to thank my friends Tricia, Lizzie, Michael, Victoria, Stella, Roxanne (Sheila), Kieran, Charlie, Anna, Jess and Steven for lifting me up when I needed it, and in particular my OGs from the school days: Aynsley, Sian and Sarah, who stood by my side through my 'Roman Years'. This book wouldn't exist without each and every one of you.

I'd like to say a huge thank you to Becky Bagnell, my incredible agent at Lindsay Literary Agency; you gave me the final push I needed to trust myself and for this I will be eternally grateful. Thank you to Lena McCauley, my superstar commissioning editor at Hachette Children's Group; you have been at the very centre of this project, liaising with everyone involved so brilliantly and with such kindness it's been truly inspiring. I really don't know how you do the job you do! Becky and Lena – I can't thank both of you enough for changing my life at a time when my life needed to change. I'd like to thank my desk editor Laura Pritchard, and copy editor Becca Allen, for bringing this story to life on the page. I'd like to thank Lucie Corbasson-Guévenoux for the incredible cover illustration, and Michelle Brackenborough for the brilliant cover design. I'd also like to give a massive shout-out to Emily Finn, Dominic Kingston and Jasmin Kauldhar at HCG and Hope Publicity for your unbelievable enthusiasm for this project.

Finally, I would like to thank you, the reader, for choosing this book. When I started writing stories there was no space on bookshelves for characters like Roman and Beau. This story and so many other brilliant queer stories now have a place in the world thanks to you, and I think that's pretty arse-clenchingly fabulous actually!

Photo © Ben Wulf Photography

Daniel Tawse is from Newcastle. They spent their childhood going on adventures in the wilds of Northumberland, and teenage years writing diaries about how much they didn't fit in. Nowadays, Daniel spends their time turning those diaries into stories for a wider audience, and is an advocate for queer representation and visibility in the arts. Through their work, Daniel aims to provide authentic queer characters to demonstrate positive and relatable queer voices for all readers. Elsewhere, Daniel has studied theatre at the Arts Educational Schools, London, and holds a master's degree in British History from the University of Northumbria.

 @DanielTawse

Also available as an audiobook

DANIEL TAWSE

ALL ABOUT ROMANCE

Want to be the first to hear about the
best new teen and YA reads?

nt exclusive content, offers and competitions?

Want to chat about books with people who
love them as much as you do?

Look no further...

bkmrk

Find your place

🐦 📷 f @teambkmrk

SNEAK
PEAKS

BONUS
CONTENT

OFFERS
AND
GIVEAWAYS

See you there!

bkmrk.co.uk